I0628855

ANTHONY TRENT, MASTER CRIMINAL

ANTHONY TRENT, MASTER CRIMINAL

WYNDHAM MARTYN

A WYNDHAM MARTYN BOOK

A WYNDHAM MARTYN BOOK

Published by Wildside Press LLC.
www. wildsidebooks. com

CHAPTER I

THE FIRST STEP

Austin the butler gave his evidence in a straightforward fashion. He was a man slightly below middle height, inclined to portliness, but bore himself with the dignity of one who had been likened to an archbishop.

Although he had been examined by a number of minor officials, hectored by them, threatened or cajoled as they interpreted their duty, his testimony remained the same. And when he hoped this tedious business was all over, he was brought before Inspector McWalsh and compelled to begin all over again. It was McWalsh's theory that a man may be startled into telling the truth that will convict him. He had a habit of leaning forward, chin thrust out, great fists clenched, and hurling accusations at suspects.

He disliked Austin at sight. The feeling was not wholly of national origin. McWalsh liked witnesses, no less than criminals, to exhibit some indications of the terrors his name had inspired to the guilty. Austin gazed about him as though the surroundings were not to his taste. His attitude was one of deferential boredom. He recognized the inspector as one representing justly constituted authority to be accepted with respect in everything but a social sense.

Inspector McWalsh permitted himself to make jocose remarks as to Austin's personal appearance. McWalsh passed for a wit among his inferiors.

"At half past twelve on Tuesday I came into the library," the butler repeated patiently, "and asked Mr. Warren if he wanted anything before I went to bed."

"What did he say?" demanded the inspector.

"That he did not want anything and that I could go to bed."

"And you did?"

"Naturally," the butler returned.

"What duties have you the last thing before retiring?"

"I see that the doors and windows are fastened."

The inspector sneered. The small black eyes set in his heavy red face regarded the smaller man malevolently.

"And you did it so damn well that within an hour or so, ten thousand dollars' worth of valuables was walked off with by a crook! How do you account for that?"

"I don't try to," the butler answered suavely, "that's for you gentlemen of the police. I have my duties and I attend to them as my testimonials show. I don't presume to give you advice but I should say it was because the crook was cleverer than your men."

"Don't get funny," snapped McWalsh. He had on the table before him Austin's modest life history which consisted mainly in terms of service to wealthy families in England and the United States. These proved him to be efficient and trustworthy. "I want answers to my questions and not comments from you."

Austin's manner nettled him. It was that slightly superior air, the servants' mark of contempt. And never before had the inspector been referred to as "a gentleman of the police;" he suspected a slight.

"Let's get this thing straight," he went on. "You went to bed when your services were no longer required. Your employer said to you, 'You can go to bed, Austin, I don't want anything, ' so you locked up and retired. You didn't know anything about the burglary until half past six o'clock on Wednesday morning—this morning—— You aroused your employer who sent for the police. That's correct?"

"Absolutely," Austin returned. He was, plainly, not much interested.

"And you still stick to it that Mr. Warren made that remark?"

Austin looked at the inspector quickly. His bored manner was gone.

"Yes," he said deliberately. "To the best of my knowledge those were his words. I may have made a mistake in the phrasing but that is what he meant."

"What's the good of your coming here and lying to me?" The inspector spoke in an aggrieved tone.

"I was brought here against my will," Austin reminded him, "and I have not lied, although your manner has been most offensive. You see, sir, I'm accustomed to gentlefolk."

McWalsh motioned him to be silent.

"That'll do," he commanded, "I'm not interested in what you think. Now answer this carefully. What clothes was Mr. Warren wearing?"

"Evening dress," said the butler, "but a claret-colored velvet smoking jacket instead of a black coat."

"How was he looking?"

"Do you mean in what direction?"

"You know I don't. I mean was he looking as usual? Was there anything unusual in his look?"

"Nothing that I noticed," Austin told him, "but then his back was to me so I am not competent to judge."

"When you speak to any one don't you go up and look 'em in the face like a man same as I'm talking and looking at you?"

Austin permitted himself to smile.

"Do you suggest I should look at Mr. Warren as you are looking at me? Pardon me, sir, but I should lose my place if I did."

McWalsh flushed a darker red.

"Why didn't you look at him in your own way then?"

"It's very clear," Austin answered with dignity, "that you know very little of the ways of an establishment like ours. I stood at the door as I usually do, asked a question I have done hundreds of times and received the same answer I do as a rule. If I'd known I was to have to answer all these questions I might have recollected more about it."

"What was Mr. Warren doing?"

"Reading a paper and smoking."

"He was alone?"

"Yes."

"And all the other servants had gone to bed?"

"Yes."

"You heard no unusual sounds that night?"

"If I had I should have investigated them."

"No doubt," sneered the other, "you look like a man who would enjoy running into a crook with a gun."

"I should not enjoy it," Austin returned seriously.

Inspector McWalsh beckoned to one of his inferiors.

"Keep this man outside till I send for him and see he don't speak to his boss who's waiting. Send Mr. Warren right in."

Conington Warren, one of the most popular men in society, member of the desirable clubs, millionaire owner of thoroughbreds, came briskly in. He was now about fifty, handsome still, but his florid face was marked by the convivial years. Inspector McWalsh had long followed the Warren colors famous on the big race courses. His manner showed his respect for the owner of his favorite stable.

"I asked you to come here," he began, "because you told my secretary over the phone that you had some new light on this burglary. So far it seems just an ordinary case without any unusual angles."

"It's not as ordinary as you think," said Conington Warren. He offered McWalsh one of his famous cigars. "Incidentally it does not show me up very favorably as I'm bound to admit."

McWalsh regarded his cigar reverently. Warren smoked nothing but these superb things. What a man! What a man!

"I can't believe that, Mr. Warren," he returned.

"Are you interested in the thoroughbreds, McWalsh?"

"Am I?" cried the other enthusiastically. "Why when I couldn't spend a few hours at old Sheepshead Bay I nearly resigned. Why, Mr. Warren, I made enough on Conington when he won the Brooklyn Handicap to pay the mortgage off on my home!"

"Then you'll understand," the sportsman said graciously. "It's like this. Last year I bought a number of yearlings at the Newmarket sales in England. There's one of them—a chestnut colt named Saint Beau—who did a most remarkable trial a day or two since. In confidence, inspector, it was better than Conington's best. Make a note of that but keep it under your hat."

"I surely will, sir," cried the ecstatic McWalsh.

"When I heard the time of the trial I gave a little dinner to a number of good pals at Voisin's."

The names he mentioned were all of them prominently known in the fashionable world of sport.

"We had more champagne than was good for us and when the dinner was over we all went to Reggie Camplyn's rooms where he invented the Saint Beau cocktail. I give you my word, inspector, the thing has a thoro'bred kick to it. It's one of those damned insidious cocktails wrapped up in cream to make you think it's innocent. After I'd had a few I said to Camplyn, 'You've made me what I am to-night; I insist on sleeping here."

"But you didn't!" cried McWalsh.

"Until four in the morning. The Saint Beau cocktail made me so ill at four that I got up and walked down to my house."

"What time did you get there?"

"Exactly at five. I felt the need of the cool air, so I took a long walk first."

"Then at half past twelve you were at——"

"Voisin's as a score of people can prove. I had a table in the balcony and saw all the people I ever knew it seemed to me."

"But this morning you told the officers who made an investigation of the robbery a totally different story. You corroborated your butler's evidence that you were at home at half past twelve and told him to go to bed because you didn't want anything else. How do you account for that?"

The inspector was troubled. His only consolation was that he would have another session soon with the supercilious Austin. He licked his lips at the thought. But he did not wish to involve the horseman in any difficulties if he could avoid it.

Conington Warren laughed easily.

"You know how it is, inspector. You can understand that sometimes a man suddenly waked out of heavy sleep can forget what happened the night before for the time being. That's what happened with me. I clean forgot the dinner, Camplyn's Saint Beau cocktail, everything. I only knew I had the devil of a head. I always rely on Austin."

"When did you remember?" McWalsh demanded.

"When Camplyn came in to see me and ask for the ingredients of the cocktail which he claims I invented. Then I recollected everything and telephoned to you."

"I knew that damned fellow was lying," McWalsh cried. "He thought he was clever. He'll find out just how smart he is! Tell me, Mr. Warren, what did he want to put up that fiction for?"

Warren put a hot hand to a head which still ached.

"I can't imagine," he answered. "I've never found him out in a lie yet. He's too damn conceited to descend to one. I don't think you should suspect Austin."

"I'm sorry, Mr. Warren, but I've got to. He lied to you and he lied to me and—ten thousand dollars' worth of stuff was stolen. He's in the outer room now. I'll have him brought in."

Austin entered with his precise and measured tread and bowed with respectful affection to his employer. He liked Conington Warren better than any American with whom he had taken service. The hearty, horse-loving type was one which appealed to Austin. He had several times been obliged to throw up lucrative jobs because employers persisted in treating him as an equal.

"This is a bad mix-up," his master began. "The inspector seems to think you have been deceiving him."

"He has and he knows it," cried McWalsh.

"He's inclined to be hasty, sir," said Austin tolerantly.

"See here," snapped the inspector, "you say you found Mr. Warren in his library at half past twelve. Did you hear him enter the house?"

"No," the butler returned, "he has his key."

"The thing we want to clear up," interrupted Mr. Warren in a kindly tone, "is simply this. What did I say to you when you spoke to me?"

Austin looked uncomfortable.

"It was a gesture, sir, rather than a word. You waved your arm and I knew what you meant."

"You are one prize liar!" roared the inspector. "You said something quite different when I asked you."

"I don't see that it matters much," Austin returned acidly. "On Monday night Mr. Warren may have said for me to go to bed. On Tuesday he may have waved his hand impatient like. On Wednesday he may have asked for cigars or the evening papers. I remember only that on this occasion I was not asked for anything." He turned to his employer, "I should like to remind you, sir, that we are giving a dinner party to-night and I ought to be seeing after it now. Can I go, sir?"

"You cannot," cried Inspector McWalsh, "you're under arrest!"

"I told you he was hasty, sir," said Austin without emotion. "What for may I ask?"

"Let me answer him please, inspector," begged Conington Warren. "You told the police that you saw me sitting in my library. Are you prepared to swear to that, Austin?"

"Certainly, sir," said the man. "You were in the big turkish rocker, smoking one of the cigars you are smoking now and reading the Sporting Times."

"I'd give a thousand dollars to know who that was!" Warren commented. "It wasn't I at all. I was dining at Voisin's at that hour."

For the first time Austin was acutely disturbed.

"I don't understand," he stammered. "It looked like you, sir, it did indeed."

"And if you'd only gone up like a man and looked in his face you'd have seen the burglar," McWalsh said scowling.

Austin looked at the speaker coldly.

"It is not my business to suspect my employer of being a crook. If it's crime to be deceived then I'm guilty. I admit I didn't look very closely. I was sleepy and wanting to get to bed, but I did notice that whoever it was wore a claret colored velvet smoking jacket."

"I've a list here," said McWalsh, "given my men by the footman of the people who called at Mr. Warren's house yesterday. Look it over and see if you can supplement it."

"There was one other visitor," Austin said slowly, "an intimate friend of Mr. Warren's, but I don't know his name. I didn't admit him."

"That's curious," said his employer. "I thought you knew every one who was intimate enough to come to my home. What was he like?"

"I didn't see him full face," the other admitted, "but he was tall, about your height, but dark in coloring with a rather large nose. It struck me he was a trifle in liquor if I may say so."

"I don't remember any one like that," Warren asserted.

"The gentleman," said Austin anxious to establish his point, "who bet you ten thousand dollars that his filly could beat your Saint Beau at five furlongs."

"This is all damned nonsense," returned Conington Warren a little crossly, "I'm in possession of my full senses now at all events. I made no such wager."

"I told you he was a crook, Mr. Warren," cried McWalsh gleefully. "See what he's trying to put over on you now!"

"Surely, sir," said the butler anxiously, "you remember asking a gentleman to come into your dressing room?"

"You're crazy," his master declared, "I asked nobody. Why should I?"

"He was standing just inside the room as I passed by. He was very merry. He was calling you 'Connie' like only your very intimate friends do."

"And what was I saying?" Warren returned, impressed with the earnestness of one in whom he believed.

"I didn't listen, sir," the butler answered. "I was just passing along the hall."

"Did you hear Mr. Warren's voice?" McWalsh demanded suddenly.

Austin reflected.

"I wouldn't swear to it," he decided.

"What time was it?" Warren asked.

"A little after ten," said Austin.

"I left the house at eight, so you are not likely to have heard me. I was at Voisin's from half past eight until nearly one. When did you first see this supposed friend?"

"I was going up the main stairway as he was about to come down toward me. Almost directly I saw him—and I didn't at the time think he saw me—he turned back as if you had called him from your room. He said, 'What is it, Connie?' then he walked down the corridor and stood half way in your room talking to you as I supposed. He looked like a gentleman who might belong to your clubs, sir, and spoke like one. What was I to think?"

"I'm not blaming you," said Conington Warren. "I'm as puzzled as you are. Didn't Yogotama see him when he went to my room to get my smoking jacket which you say he wore? What was Yogotama doing to allow that sort of thing?"

"You forget, sir," explained Austin, "that Yogotama wasn't there."

"Why wasn't he?"

"Directly he got your note he went off to the camp."

"This gets worse and worse," Warren asserted. "I sent him no note."

"He got one in your writing apparently written on the stationery of the Knickerbocker Club. I saw it. You told him to go instantly to your camp and prepare it for immediate occupancy. He was to take Evans and one of the touring cars. He got the note about half past eight."

"Just after you'd left the house," McWalsh commented.

"It didn't take Yogotama a half hour to prepare," added Austin.

"What do you make of it, inspector?" Warren demanded.

"A clever crook, that's all," said the other, "but he can't pull anything like that in this town and get away with it."

Austin made a polite gesture implying doubt. It incensed the official.

"You don't think so, eh?"

"Not from what I've seen of your methods. I've no doubt you can deal with the common ruck of criminals, but this man is different. It may be easy enough for a man to deceive you people by pretending to be a gentleman but we can see through them. Frankly," said Austin growing bolder, "I don't think you gentlemen of the police have the native wit for the higher kind of work."

Warren looked from one to the other of them. This was a new and rebellious Austin, a man chafing under a personal grievance, a belligerent butler.

"You mustn't speak like that to Inspector McWalsh," he commanded. "He is doing his duty."

"That may be sir," Austin remarked, "but how would you like to be called 'Little Lancelot from Lunnon'?"

"You look it," McWalsh said roughly. "Anyway I've no time to argue with house servants. What you've got to do is to look through our collection of pictures and see if you can identify any of 'em with the man you say you saw."

Austin surveyed the faces with open aversion.

"He's not here," said Austin decisively. "He was not this criminal type at all. I tell you I mistook him for a member of Mr. Warren's clubs, the kind of gentleman who dines at the house. These," and he pointed derisively to the pillories of crime. "You wouldn't be likely to see any of these at our house. They are just common."

McWalsh sneered.

"I see. Look more like policemen I suppose?"

Austin smiled blandly.

"The very thing that was in my mind."

CHAPTER II

ANTHONY TRENT TALKS ON CRIME

Anthony Trent was working his typewriter at top speed when there came a sudden, peremptory knocking at his door.

"Lord!" he grumbled, rising, "it must be old Lund to say I'm keeping him awake."

He threw open his door to find a small, choleric and elderly man clad in a faded dressing gown. It was a man with a just grievance and a desire to express it.

"This is no time to hammer on your typewriter," said Mr. Lund fiercely. "This is a boarding house and not a private residence. Do you realize that you generally begin work at midnight?"

"Come in," said Anthony Trent genially. With friendly force he dragged the smaller man along and placed him in a morris chair. "Come in and give me your opinion of the kind of cigar smoked by the president of the publishing house for whose magazines I work noisily at midnight."

Mr. Lund found himself a few seconds later sitting by an open window, an excellent cigar between his teeth, and the lights of New York spread before him. And he found his petulance vanishing. He wondered why it was that although he had before this come raging to Anthony Trent's door, he always suffered himself to be talked out of his ill humors. It was something magnetic and engaging that surrounded this young writer of short stories.

"I can't smoke a cigar when I'm working," said Trent, lighting a pipe.

"Surely," said Mr. Lund, not willing so soon to be robbed of his grievance, "you choose the wrong hours to work. Mrs. Clarke says you hardly ever touch your typewriter till late."

"That's because you don't appreciate the kind of story I write," Anthony Trent told him. "If I wrote the conventional story of love or matrimony I could work so many hours a day and begin at nine like any business man. But I don't. I begin to write just when the world I write of begins to live. My men and women are waking into life now, just when the other folks are climbing into their suburban beds."

"I understood you wrote detective stories," Mr. Lund remarked. His grievances were vanishing. His opinion of the president of Trent's magazine was a high one.

"Crook stories," Anthony Trent confided. "Not the professional doings of thoughtless thugs. They don't interest me a tinker's curse. I like subtlety in crime. I could take you now into the great restaurants on Broadway or Fifth Avenue and point out to you some of the kings of crime—men who are clever enough to protect themselves from the police. Men who play the game as a good chess player does against a poorer one, with the certainty of being a move ahead."

Mr. Lund conjured up a vision of such a restaurant peopled by such a festive crowd. He felt in that moment that an early manhood spent in Somerville had perhaps robbed him of a chance to live.

"They all get caught sooner or later," asserted the little man in the morris chair.

"Because they get careless or because they trust another. If you want to be a successful crook, Mr. Lund, you'll have to map out your plan of life as carefully as an athlete trains for a specific event. Now if you went in for crime you'd have to examine your weaknesses."

"Thank you," said Mr. Lund a little huffily, "I am not going in for a life of crime. I am perfectly content with my own line." This, with unconscious sarcasm for Mr. Lund, pursued what he always told the borders was "the advertising."

"There are degrees in crime I admit," said Anthony Trent, "but I am perfectly serious in what I say. The ordinary crook has a low mental capacity. He generally gets caught in the end as all such clumsy asses should. The really big man in crime often gets caught because he is not aware of his weaknesses. Drink often brings out an incautious boasting side of a man. If you are going in for crime, Mr. Lund, cut out drink I beg of you."

"I do not need your advice," Mr. Lund returned with some dignity. "I have tasted rum once only in my life."

Trent looked at him interested.

"It would probably make you want to fight," he said.

"I don't care to think of it," said Mr. Lund.

"And the curious part of it is," mused Trent, "that in the sort of crowd these high class crooks mix with it is most unusual not to drink, and the man who doesn't is almost always under suspicion. The great thing is to be able to take your share and stop before the danger mark is reached. Did you ever hear of Captain Despard?"

"I think not," Lund answered.

"A boyhood idol of mine," Anthony Trent admitted. "One of the few gentleman crooks. Most of the so-called gentlemen criminals have been anything but gentlemen born. Despard was. I was in Devonshire on my last trip to the other side and I made a pilgrimage to the place where he was born. Funny to think that a man brought up in one of the 'stately homes of England, how beautiful they stand, ' should come to what he was."

"Woman, I suppose," said Lund, as one man of the world to another.

"Not in the beginning," Anthony Trent answered. "He was a cavalry officer in India—Kipling type you know—and had a craze for precious stones. Began to collect them honestly enough and found his pay and private fortune insufficient. He got kicked out of his regiment anyway and went to Cape Town. One night a very large diamond was stolen from a bedroom of the Mount Nelson hotel and he was suspected. They couldn't prove anything, but came over here to New York and sold it, under another name, and with a different history, to one of the Pierpoints. The trouble with Captain Despard was that he used to drink heavily when he had pulled a big thing off. While he was planning a *coup* he was temperate and he never touched a drop while he was working."

"Started to boast, I suppose?" Lund suggested.

"No," said Anthony Trent. "Not that sort at all. He lived at a pretty fair sort of club here in the forties and was well enough liked until the drink was in him. It was then that he began to think of his former mode of life and the kind he was now living. He used to think the other members were trying to slight him or avoid him. He laboriously picked quarrels with some of them. He beat up one of them in a fist fight in the club billiard room. This fellow brooded over his licking for a long time and then with another man, also inflamed with cocktails, went up to Despard's room to beat him up. Despard was out, so they broke his furniture. They found that the legs of chairs and tables had been hollowed so as to conceal what Despard stole. It was in one of the chairs that they found the Crediton pearls which had been missing for a year. They waited for him and he was sent to Sing Sing but escaped. He shot a man later in Denver and was executed. He might have been living comfortably but for getting suspicious when he had been drinking."

"You must have studied this thing deeply," Lund commented.

"I have," Anthony Trent admitted; "I know the histories of most of the great criminals and their crimes. The police do too, but I know more than they. I make a study of the man as well as his crime. I find vanity at the root of many failures."

"*Cherchez la femme*," Mr. Lund insisted.

"Not that sort of vanity," Anthony Trent corrected. "I mean the sheer love to boast about one's abilities when other men are boasting of theirs. There was a man called Paul Vierick, by profession a second story man. He was short, stout and a great consumer of beer and in his idle hours fond of bowling. He was staying in Stony Creek, Connecticut, one summer, when a tennis ball was hit up high and lodged in a gutter pipe on the roof. Vierick told the young man who had hit it there how to get it. It was so dangerous looking a climb that the lad refused. Some of the guests suggested in fun that Vierick should try. They made him mad. He thought they were laughing at his two hundred pound look. They were not to know that a more expert porch climber didn't exist than this man who had been a professional trapeze man in a circus. They say he ran up the side of that house like a monkey. Directly he had done it and people began talking he knew he'd been unwise. He had been posing as a retired dentist and here he was running up walls like the count in Dracula. He moved away and presently denied the story so vehemently that an intelligent young lawyer investigated him and he is now up the river."

"That's an interesting study," Mr. Lund commented. He was thoroughly taken up with the subject. "Do you know any more instances like that?"

"I know hundreds," Anthony Trent returned smiling. "I could keep on all night. Your town of Somerville produced Blodgett the Strangler. You must have heard of him?"

"I was at school with him," Lund said almost excitedly. It was a secret he had buried in his breast for years. Now it seemed to admit him to something of a kinship with Anthony Trent. "He was always chasing after women."

"That wasn't the thing which got him. It was the desire to set right a Harvard professor of anatomy on the subject of strangulation. Blodgett had his own theories. You may remember he strangled his stepfather when he was only fifteen."

"He nearly strangled me once," Mr. Lund exclaimed. "He would have done if I hadn't had sufficient presence of mind to bite him in the thumb."

"Good for you," said the other heartily. "You'll find the history of crime is full of the little mistakes that take the cleverest of them to the chair. And yet," he mused, "it's a great life. One man pitting his courage and knowledge against all the forces organized by society to stamp him out. You've got to be above the average in almost every quality to succeed if you work alone."

Mr. Lund felt a trifle uncomfortable. The bright laughing face that had been Anthony Trent to him had given place to a sterner cast of countenance. The new Trent reminded him of a hawk. There was suddenly brought to the rather timid and elderly man the impression of ruthless strength and tireless energy. He had been a score of times in Anthony Trent's room and had always found him amusing and light hearted. Never until to-night had they touched upon crime. The New York over which Mr. Lund gazed from the seat by the window no longer seemed a friendly city. Crime and violence lurked in its every corner, he reflected.

Mr. Lund was annoyed with himself for feeling nervous. To brace up his courage he reverted to his former grievance. The sustaining cigar had long ceased to give comfort.

"I must protest at being waked up night after night by your typewriting machine. Everybody seems to be in bed and asleep but you. I must have my eight hours, Mr. Trent."

Anthony Trent came to his side.

"Everybody asleep?" he gibed. "Why, man, the shadows are alive if you'll only look into them. And as to the night, it is never quiet. A myriad strange sounds are blended into this stillness you call night." His voice sank to a whisper and he took the discomfited Lund's arm. "Can you see a woman standing there in the shadow of that tree?"

"It might be a woman," Lund admitted guardedly.

"It is," he was told; "she followed not ten yards behind you as you came from the El. She's been waiting for a man and he ought to be by in a few minutes now. She's known in every rogues' gallery in the world. Scotland Yard knows her as Gypsy Lee, and if ever a woman deserved the chair she does."

"Not murder?" Lund hazarded timidly. He shivered. "It's a little cold by the window."

"Don't move," Anthony commanded. "You may see a tragedy unroll itself before your eyes in a little while. She's waiting for a banker named Pereira who looted Costa Rica. He's a big, heavy man."

"He's coming now," Lund whispered. "I don't like this at all, Mr. Trent."

"He won't either," muttered the other.

Unable to move Mr. Lund watched a tall man come toward the shadows which hid Gypsy Lee.

"We ought to warn him," Mr. Lund protested.

"Not on your life," he was told. "This time it is punishment, not murder. She saved his life and he deserted her. Pereira's pretending to be drunk. I wonder why. He dare not touch a drop because he has Bright's disease in the last stages."

A minute later Mr. Lund, indignant and commanding as his inches permitted, was shaking an angry finger at his host.

"You've no right to frighten me," he exclaimed, "with your Gypsy Lee and Pereira when it was only poor Mrs. Clarke waiting for that drunken scamp of a husband who spends all he earns at the corner saloon."

Heavy steps passed along the passage. It was Clarke making his bedward way to his wife's verbal accompaniment.

"You ought to be pleased to get a thrill like that for nothing," said Anthony Trent laughing. "I'd pay good money for it."

"I don't like it," Mr. Lund insisted. "I thought you meant it."

"I did," the other asserted, "for the moment. New York is full of such stories and if they don't happen in this street they happen in another. They always happen after midnight and I've got to put them down on the old machine. Somewhere a Gypsy Lee is waiting for a defaulting South American banker or a Captain Despard is planning to get a priceless stone, or a humbler Vierick plotting to climb into an inviting window, or some one like your boyhood chum Blodgett planning to get his hands around some one's throat."

Anthony Trent leaned from the window and breathed in the soft night air.

"It's a great old city," he said, half affectionately, "and I make my living by letting my hook down into the night and drawing up a mystery. You mustn't mind if I sometimes rattle the old Royal when better folks are asleep."

"If you'll take the advice of an older man," said Mr. Lund with an air of firmness, "you'll let crook stories alone and choose something a little healthier. Your mind is full of them."

Still a little outraged Mr. Lund bowed himself from the room. Anthony Trent fed his ancient briar and took the seat by the window.

"I wonder if he's right," mused Anthony Trent.

CHAPTER III

THE DAY OF TEMPTATION

The dawn had long passed and the milkmen had awakened their unwilling clients two hours agone before Anthony Trent finished his story. He was not a quick worker. His was a mind that labored heavily unless the details of his work were accurate. This time he was satisfied. It was a good story and the editor for whom he was doing a series would be pleased. He might even increase his rates.

Crosbeigh, the editor of the magazine which sought Anthony Trent's crook stories, was an amiable being who had won a reputation for profundity by reason of eloquent silences. He would have done well in any line of work where originality was not desired. He knew, from what his circulation manager told him, that Trent's stories made circulation and he liked the writer apart from his work. Perhaps because he was not a disappointed author he was free from certain editorial prejudices.

"Sit down," he cried cordially, when Anthony Trent was shown in. "Take a cigarette and I'll read this right away." Crosbeigh was a nervous man who battled daily with subway crowds and was apt to be irritable.

"It's great," he said when he had finished it, "Great! Doyle, Hornung, well—there you are!" It was one of his moments of silent eloquence. The listener might have inferred anything.

"But they are paid real money," replied Anthony Trent gloomily.

"You get two cents a word," Crosbeigh reminded him, "you haven't a wife and children to support."

"I'd be a gay little adventurer to try it on what I make at writing," Trent told him. "It takes me almost a month to write one of those yarns and I get a hundred and fifty each."

"You are a slow worker," his editor declared.

"I have to be," he retorted. "If I were writing love slush and pretty heroine stuff it would be different. Do you know, Crosbeigh, there isn't a thing in these stories of mine that is impossible? I take the most particular care that my details are correct. When I began I didn't know anything about burglar alarms. What did I do? I got a job in the shop that makes the best known one. I'm worth more than two cents a word!"

"That's our maximum," Crosbeigh asserted. "These are not good days for the magazine business. Shot to pieces. If I said what I knew. If you knew what *I* got and how much I had to do with it!"

Anthony Trent looked at him critically. He saw a very carefully dressed Crosbeigh to-day, a man whose trousers were pressed, whose shoes were shined, who exuded prosperity. Never had he seen him so apparently affluent.

"Come into money?" he enquired. "Whence the prosperity? Whose wardrobe have you robbed?"

"These are my own clothes," returned Crosbeigh with dignity, "at least leave me my clothes."

"Sure," said Trent amiably, "if I took 'em you'd be arrested. But tell me why this sartorial display. Are you going to be photographed for the 'great editors' series?"

"I'm lunching with an old friend," Crosbeigh answered, "a man of affairs, a man of millions, a man about whom I could say many things."

"Say them," his contributor demanded, "let me in on a man for whom you have arrayed yourself in all your glory. Who is your friend? Is she pretty? I don't believe it's a man at all."

"It's a man I know and respect," he said, a trifle nettled at the comments his apparel had drawn. "It's the man who takes me every year to the Yale-Harvard boat race."

"Your annual jag party? He's no fit company for a respectable editor."

"It is college spirit," Crosbeigh explained.

"You can call it by any name but it's too strong for you. What is the name of your honored friend?"

"Conington Warren," Crosbeigh said proudly.

"That's the millionaire sportsman with the stable of steeple-chasers, isn't it?" Trent demanded.

"He wins all the big races," Crosbeigh elaborated.

"He's enormously rich, splendidly generous, has everything. Only one thing—drink." Crosbeigh fell into silence.

"You've led him astray you mean?" The spectacle of the sober editor consorting with reckless bloods of the Conington Warren type amused Trent.

"Same year at college," Crosbeigh explained, "and he has always been friendly. God knows why," the editor said gloomily. The difference in their lot seemed suddenly to appall him.

"There must be something unsuspectedly bad in your make-up," Trent declared, "which attracts him to you. It can't be he wants to sell you a story."

"There are all sorts of rumors about him," Crosbeigh went on meditatively, "started by his wife's people, I believe. He was wild. Sometimes he has hinted at it. I know him well enough to call him 'Connie' and go up to his dressing-room sometimes. That's a mark of intimacy. My Lord, Trent, but it makes me envious to see with what luxury the rich can live. He has a Japanese valet and masseur, Togoyama, and an imported butler who looks like a bishop. They know him at his worst and worship him. He's magnetic, that's what Connie is, magnetic. Have you ever thought what having a million a year means?"

"Ye Gods," groaned Trent, "don't you read my lamentations in every story you buy from me at bargain rates?"

"And a shooting box in Scotland which he uses two weeks a year in the grouse season. A great Tudor residence in Devonshire overlooking Exmoor, a town house in Park Lane which is London's Fifth Avenue! And you know what he's got here in his own country. Can you imagine it?"

"Not on forty dollars a week," said Anthony Trent gloomily.

"You'd make more if you were the hero of your own stories," Crosbeigh told him.

Anthony Trent turned on him quickly, "What do you mean?"

"Why this crook you are making famous gets away with enough plunder to live as well as Conington Warren."

"Ah, but that's in a story," returned the author.

"Then you mean they aren't as exact and possible as you've been telling me?"

"They are what I said they were," their author declared. "They could be worked out, with ordinary luck, by any man with an active body, good education and address. The typical thick-witted criminal wouldn't have a chance."

It was a curious thing, thought Anthony Trent, that Crosbeigh should mention the very thing that had been running in his mind for weeks. To live in such an elaborate manner as Conington Warren was not his ambition. The squandering of large sums of money on stage favorites of the moment was not to his taste; but he wanted certainly more than he was earning. Trent had a passion for fishing, golf and music. Not the fishing that may be indulged in on Sunday and week-day on fishing steamers, making excursions to the banks where one may lose an ear on another angler's far flung hook, but the fly fishing where the gallant trout has a chance to escape, the highest type of fishing that may appeal to man.

And his ambitions to lower his golf handicap until it should be scratch could not well be accomplished by his weekly visit to Van Cortlandt Park. He wished to be able to join Garden City or Baltusrol and play a round a day in fast company. And this could not be accomplished on what he was making.

And as to music, he longed to compose an opera. It was a laudable ambition and would commence, he told himself, with a grand piano. He had only a hard-mouthed hired upright so far. Sometimes he had seen himself in the rôle of his hero amply able to indulge himself in his moderate ambitions. It was of this he had been thinking when Mr. Lund came to his room. And now the very editor for whom he had created his characters was making the suggestion.

"I was only joking," Crosbeigh assured him.

"It is not a good thing to joke about," Anthony Trent answered, "and an honest man at forty a week is better than an outlaw with four hundred."

He made this remark to set his thoughts in less dangerous channels, but it sounded dreadfully hollow and false. He half expected that Crosbeigh would laugh aloud at such a hackneyed sentiment, but Crosbeigh looked grave and earnest. "Very true," he answered. "A man couldn't think of it."

"And why not?" Anthony Trent demanded; "would the fictional character I created do as much harm to humanity as some cotton mill owner who enslaved little children and gave millions to charity?"

A telephone call relieved Crosbeigh of the need to answer. Trent swept into his brief case the carbon copy of his story which he had brought by mistake.

"Where are you going?" the editor demanded.

"Van Cortlandt," the contributor answered; "I'm going to try and get my drive back. I've been slicing for a month."

"Conington Warren has a private eighteen-hole course on his Long Island place," Crosbeigh said with pride. "I've been invited to play."

"You're bent on driving me to a life of crime," Trent exclaimed frowning. "An eighteen-hole private course while I struggle to get a permit for a public one!"

But Anthony Trent did not play golf that afternoon at Van Cortlandt Park. As a matter of fact he never again invaded that popular field of play.

Outside Crosbeigh's office he was hailed by an old Dartmouth chum, one Horace Weems.

"Just in time for lunch," said Weems wringing his hand. Weems had always admired Anthony Trent and had it been possible would have remodeled himself physically and mentally in the form of another Trent. Weems was short, blond and perspired profusely.

"Hello, Tubby," said Trent without much cordiality, "you look as though the world had been treating you right."

"It has," said Weems happily. "Steel went to a hundred and twelve last week and it carried me up with it."

Weems had been, as Trent remembered, a bond salesman. Weems could sell anything. He had an ingratiating manner and a disability to perceive snubs or insults when intent on making sales. He had paid his way through college by selling books. Trent had been a frequent victim.

"What do you want to sell me this time?" he demanded.

"Nothing," Weems retorted, "I'm going to buy you the best little lunch that Manhattan has to offer. Anywhere you say and anything you like to eat and drink." Weems stopped a cruising taxi. "Hop in, old scout, and tell the pirate where to go."

Trent directed the man to one of the three famous and more or less exclusive restaurants New York possesses.

"I hope you have the price," he commented, "otherwise I shall have to cash a check I've just received for a story."

"Keep your old check," jeered Weems, "I'm full of money. Why, boy, I own an estate and have a twelve-cylinder car of my own."

Over the luncheon Horace Weems babbled cheerfully. He had made over three hundred thousand dollars and was on his way to millionaire-dom.

"You ought to see my place up in Maine," he said presently.

"Maine?" queried his guest. It was in Maine that Anthony Trent, were he fortunate enough, would one day erect a camp. "Where?"

"On Kennebago lake," Weems told him and stopped when an expression of pain crossed the other's face. "What's the matter? That sauce wrong?"

"Just sheer envy," Trent admitted, "you've got what I want. I know every camp on the Lake. Which is it?"

"The Stanley place," said Weems. "The finest camp on the whole Lake. I bought it furnished and it's some furniture believe me. There's a grand piano—that would please you—and pictures that are worth thousands, one of 'em by some one named Constable. Ever hear of him?"

"Yes," Trent grunted, "I have. Fancy you with a Constable and a grand piano when you don't know one school of painting from another and think the phonograph the only instrument worth listening to!"

"I earned it," Weems said, a little huffily. "Why don't you make money instead of getting mad because I do?"

"Because I haven't your ability, I suppose," Trent admitted. "It's a gift and the gods forgot me."

"Some of the boys used to look down on me," said Weems, "but all I ask is 'where is little Horace to-day?' This money making game is the only thing that counts, believe me. Up in Hanover I wasn't one, two, three, compared with you. Your father was well off and mine hadn't a nickel. You graduated *magna cum laude* and I had to work like a horse to slide by. You were popular because you made the football team and could sing and play." Weems paused reflectively, "I never did hear any one who could mimic like you. You should have taken it up and gone into vaudeville. How much do you make a week?"

"Forty—with luck."

"I give that to my chauffeur and I'm not rich yet. But I shall be. I'm out to be as rich as that fellow over there."

He pointed to a rather high colored extremely well dressed man about town to whom the waiters were paying extreme deference.

"That's Conington Warren," Weems said with admiration in his voice, "he's worth a million per annum."

Anthony Trent turned to look at him. There was no doubt that Conington Warren was a personage. Just now he was engaged in an argument with the head waiter concerning *Château Y'Quem*. Trent noticed his gesture of dismissal when he had finished. It was an imperious wave of his hand. It was his final remark as it were.

"Some spender," Weems commented. "Who's the funny old dodger with him? Some other millionaire I suppose."

"I'll tell him that next time I see him," laughed Trent beholding Crosbeigh, Crosbeigh who looked wise where vintages were discussed and knew not one from another. A well-dressed man paused at Warren's side and Weems, always anxious to acquire information, begged his guest to be silent.

"Did you get that?" he asked when the man had moved away.

"I don't make it a habit to listen to private conversations," Trent returned stiffly.

"Well I do," said Weems unabashed. "If I hadn't I shouldn't have got in on this Steel stuff. I'm a great little listener. That fellow who spoke is Reginald Camplyn, the man who drives a coach and four and wins blue ribbons at the horse show. Warren asked him to a dinner here to-morrow night at half past eight in honor of some horse who's done a fast trial." Weems made an entry in his engagement book.

"Are you going, too?" Trent demanded.

"I'm putting down the plug's name," said Weems, "Sambo," he said. "That's no name for a thoroughbred. Say couldn't you introduce me?"

"I don't know him," Trent asserted.

"You know the man with him. That's enough for me. If you do it right the other fellow's bound to introduce you. Then you beckon me over and we'll all sit down together."

"That isn't my way of doing things," replied Trent with a frown.

Weems made a gesture of despair and resignation.

"That's why you'll always be poor. That's why you'll never have a grand piano and a Constable and a swell place up in Maine."

Anthony Trent looked at him and smiled.

"There may be other ways," he said slowly.

"You try 'em," Weems retorted crossly. "Here you are almost thirty years old, highly educated, prep school and college and you make a week what I give my chauffeur."

"I think I will," Trent answered.

Weems attacked his salad angrily. If only Trent had been what he termed aggressive, an introduction could easily have been effected. Then Weems would have seen to it that he and Warren left the restaurant together. Some one would be bound to see them. Then, for Weems had an expansive fancy, it would be rumored that he, Horace Weems, who cleaned up on Steel, was friendly with the great Conington Warren. It might lead to anything!

"Well," he commented, "I'd rather be little Horace Weems, who can't tell a phonograph from a grand piano than Mr. Anthony Trent, who makes with luck two thousand a year."

"I'm in bad company to-day," replied Trent. "First Crosbeigh and now you tempting me. You know very well I haven't that magic money making ability you have. My father hadn't it or he would have left money when he died and not debts."

"Magic!" Weems snorted. "Common sense, that's what it is."

"It's magic," the other insisted, "as a boy you exchanged a jack knife for a fishing pole and the fishing pole for a camera and the camera for a phonograph and the phonograph for a canoe and the canoe for a sailing boat and so on till you've got your place in Maine and a chauffeur who makes more than I do! Magic's the only name for it."

"You must come up and see me in Maine," Weems said, later.

"Make your mind easy," Trent assured him, "I will."

CHAPTER IV

BEGINNING THE GAME

When he left Weems, it was too late to start a round of golf so Trent took his homeward way intent on starting another story. Crosbeigh was always urging him to turn out more of them.

His boarding house room seemed shabbier than ever. The rug, which had never been a good one, showed its age. The steel engravings on the wall were offensive. "And Weems," he thought, "owns a Constable!"

His upright piano sounded thinner to his touch. "And Weems," he sighed, "has been able to buy a grand."

Up from the kitchen the triumphant smell of a "boiled New England dinner" sought out every corner of the house. High above all the varied odors, cabbage was king. The prospect of the dinner table was appalling, with Mr. Lund, distant and ready to quarrel over any infringement of his rights or curtailment of his portion. Mrs. Clarke ready to resent any jest as to her lord's habits. The landlady eager to give battle to such as sniffed at what her kitchen had to offer. Wearisome banter between brainless boarders tending mainly to criticism of moving picture productions and speculations as to the salaries of the stars. Not a soul there who had ever heard of William Blake or Ravel! Overdressed girls who were permanently annoyed with Anthony Trent because he would never take them to ice-cream parlors. Each new boarder as she came set her cap for him and he remained courteous but disinterested.

One of the epics of Mrs. Sauer's boarding house was that night when Miss Margaret Rafferty, incensed at the coldness with which her advances were received and the jeers of her girl friends, brought as a dinner guest a former sweetheart, now enthusiastically patrolling city sidewalks as a guardian of the peace. It was not difficult to inflame McGuire. He disliked Anthony Trent on sight and exercised an untrammeled wit during the dinner at his expense. It was afterwards in the little garden where the men went to smoke an after dinner cigar that the unforgivable phrase was passed.

McGuire was just able to walk home. He had met an antagonist who was a lightning hitter, whose footwork was quick and who boxed admirably and kept his head.

After this a greater meed of courtesy was accorded the writer of stories. But the bibulous Clarke alone amused him, Clarke who had been city editor of a great daily when Trent was a police reporter on it, and was now a Park Row derelict supported by the generosity of his old friends and acquaintances. Only Mrs. Clarke knew that Anthony Trent on numerous occasions gave her a little money each week until that day in the Greek kalends when her husband would find another position.

Anthony Trent settled himself at his typewriter and began looking over the carbon copy of the story he had just sold to Crosbeigh. He wished to assure himself of certain details in it. Among the pages was an envelope with the name of a celebrated Fifth Avenue club embossed upon it. Written on it in pencil was Crosbeigh's name. Unquestionably he had swept it from the editorial desk when he had taken up the carbon copy of his story.

Opening it he found a note written in a rather cramped and angular hand. The stationery was of the Fifth Avenue club. The signature was unmistakable, "Conington Warren." Trent read:

> "My dear Crosbeigh:
>   "I am sending this note by Togoyama because I want to be sure that you will lunch with me at Voisin's to-morrow at one o'clock. I wish affairs permitted me to see more of my old Yale comrades but I am enormously busy. By the way, a little friend of mine thinks she can write. I don't suppose she can, but I promised to show her efforts to you. I'm no judge but it seems to me her work is very much the kind you publish in your magazine. We will talk it over to-morrow. Of course she cares nothing about what you would pay her. She wants to see her name in print.
>   "Yours ever,
>   "CONINGTON WARREN."

Trent picked up an eraser and passed it over the name on the envelope. It had been written with a soft pencil and was easily swept away.

Over the body of the letter he spent a long time. He copied it exactly. A stranger would have sworn that the copy had been written by the same hand which indited the original. And when this copy had been made to Trent's satisfaction, he carefully erased everything in the original but the signature. Then remembering Weems' description of the Conington Warren camp in the Adirondacks, he wrote a little note to one Togoyama.

It was five when he had finished. There was no indecision about him. Twenty minutes later he was at the Public Library consulting a large volume in which were a hundred of the best known residences in New York. So conscientious was the writer that there were plans of every floor and in many instances descriptions of their interior decoration. Anthony Trent chuckled to think of the difficulties with which the unlettered crook has to contend. "Chicago Ed. Binner," for example, had married half a hundred servant maids to obtain information as to the disposition of rooms that he could have obtained by the mere consultation of such a book as this.

It was while Mrs. Sauer's wards were finishing their boiled dinner that some of them had a glimpse of Anthony Trent in evening dress descending the stairs.

"Dinner not good enough for his nibs," commented one boarder seeking to curry the Sauer favor.

"I'd rather have my boarders pay and not eat than eat and not pay," said Mrs. Sauer grimly. It was three weeks since she had received a dollar from the speaker.

"Drink," exclaimed Mr. Clarke, suddenly roused from meditation of a day now dead when a highball could be purchased for fifteen cents. "This food shortage now. That could be settled easily. Take the tax off liquor and people wouldn't want to eat so much. It's the high cost of drinking that's the trouble. What's the use of calling ourselves a free people? I tell you it was keeping vodka from the Russians that caused the whole trouble. Don't argue with me. I know."

Mr. Clarke went from the dinner table to his bed and awoke around midnight possessed with the seven demons of unsatiated thirst. He determined to go down and call upon Anthony Trent. He would plead for enough money to go to the druggist and get his wife's prescription filled. Trent, good lad that he was, always fell for it. And, he argued, it was a friendly act to do, this midnight call on a hard working young writer who had once been at his command.

For the first time Anthony Trent's door was locked. And the voice that snapped out an interrogation was different from the leisurely and amiable invitation to enter which was usual. The door was suddenly flung open, so sudden that poor Clarke was startled. And facing him, his fists clenched and a certain tensity of attitude that was a strange one to the visitor, was Anthony Trent still in evening dress. Clarke construed it into an expression of resentment at his intrusion. He could not understand the sudden affability that took possession of his former reporter.

"Come in, Mr. Clarke," said Trent cordially. "I am sorry your wife's heart is troubling her but I agree with you that you should rush with all haste to the nearby druggist and have that prescription filled. And as the man who owes you money did not pay you to-day as he promised, but will without fail to-morrow at midday, take this five dollar bill with my blessing."

"How did you know?" gasped Clarke.

"I am a mind reader," Trent retorted. "It saves time." He led Mr. Clarke gently to the door. "Now I'm tired and want to go to sleep so don't call in on your way back with the change. Just trot up to bed as quietly as you can."

When the door was locked and a chair-back wedged against the handle, Trent lowered the shades. Then he cleared his table of the litter of paper. A half dozen pages of the first draft of his new story held his attention for a few seconds. Then he deliberately tore the pages into little fragments, threw them into the waster paper basket. And to this cenotaph he added the contents of the table drawer, made up of notes for future stories, the results of weeks of labor.

"Dust to dust," he murmured, "ashes to ashes!"

It was the end of the career of Anthony Trent, writer.

And on the table which had formerly held only writing paper a quaint miscellany was placed. Eight scarf pins, each holding in golden claws stones of price. Apparently Conington Warren had about him only what was good. And there was a heavy platinum ring with a ruby of not less than four carats, a lady's ring. It would not be difficult for a man so clever with his hands and apt mechanically to remove these jewels from their setting. Nor was there any difficulty in melting the precious metals.

It seemed to Trent that he had gloated over these glistening stones for hours before he put them away.

Then he took out a roll of bills and counted them. Conington Warren, it seemed, must have had considerable faith in the excellent Togoyama now hurrying to the Adirondack camp, for he had left three thousand dollars in the upper left hand drawer of a Sheraton desk.

Morning was coming down the skies when Trent, now in dressing gown, lighted his pipe and sat down by the window.

"Well," he muttered softly, "I've done it and there's no going back. Yesterday I was what people call an honest man. Now——?"

He shrugged his shoulders and puffed quickly. Out of the window grey clouds of smoke rose as fragrant incense.

He had never meant to take up a career of crime. Looking back he could see how little things coming together had provoked in him an insatiable desire for an easier life. In all his personal dealings heretofore, he had been scrupulously honest, and there had never been any reflection on his honor as a sportsman. He had played games for their own sake. He had won without bragging and lost with excuses. Up in Hanover there were still left those who chanted his praise. What would people think of him if he were placed in the dock as a criminal?

His own people were dead. There were distant cousins in Cleveland, whom he hardly remembered. There was no family honor to trail in the dust, no mother or sweetheart to blame him for a broken heart.

He stirred uneasily as he thought of the possibility of capture. Even now those might be on his trail who would arrest him. It would be ironical if, before he tasted the fruits of leisure, he were taken to prison—perhaps by Officer McGuire! It had all been so absurdly easy. Within a few minutes of receiving the forged note the Japanese was on his way to the mountains.

The bishop-like butler who adored his master according to Crosbeigh, had seemed utterly without suspicion when he passed Trent engaged in animated converse with his supposed employer. The bad moment was when the man had come into the library where the intruder was hiding himself and stood there waiting for an answer to his question. Trent had seen to it that the light was low. It was a moment of inspiration when he called to mind Conington Warren's imperious gesture as he waved away Voisin's head waiter, and another which had made him put on the velvet smoking jacket. And it had all come out without a hitch. But he was playing a game now when he could never be certain he was not outguessed. It might be the suave butler was outside in the shadows guiding police to the capture.

He looked out of the window and down the silent street. There was indeed a man outside and looking up at him. But it was only poor Clarke whose own prescription had been too well filled. He had captured, so he fancied, an errant lamppost wantonly disporting itself.

Anthony Trent looked at him with a relief in which disgust had its part. He swore, by all the high gods, never to sink to that level. A curious turn of mind, perhaps, for a burglar to take. But so far the sporting simile presented itself to him. It was a game, a big game in which he took bigger risks than any one else. He was going to pit his wit, strength and knowledge against society as it was organized.

"I don't see why I can't play it decently," he said to himself as he climbed into bed.

CHAPTER V

ANTHONY PULLS UP STAKES

When those two great Australians, Norman Brooks and Anthony Wilding, had played their brilliant tennis in America, Trent had been a close follower of their play. He had interviewed them for his paper. In those days he himself was a respectable performer at the game. Brooks had given him one of his own rackets which was no longer in first class condition. It was especially made for the Australian by a firm in Melbourne. So pleased was Trent with it that he, later, sent to Australia for two more. It happened that the manager of the sporting goods store in Melbourne was a young American who believed in the efficacy of "follow up" letters. It was a large and prosperous firm and it followed up Anthony Trent with thoroughness. He received square envelopes addressed by hand by every third Australian mail.

Mrs. Sauer's boarders, being of that kind which interests itself in others' affairs and discusses them, were intrigued at these frequent missives from the Antipodes.

Finally Trent invented an Uncle Samuel who had, so he affirmed, left his native land when an adventurous child of nine and made a great fortune among the Calgoorlie gold fields. Possessing a nimble wit he related to his fellow boarders amazing accounts of his uncle's activities. The boarders often discussed this uncle, his strange dislike of women, the beard which fell to his knees, the team of racing kangaroos which drew his buggy, and so forth.

At the breakfast table on the morning when Anthony Trent faced his world no longer an honest man, it was observed that he was disinclined to talk. As a matter of fact he wanted a reasonable excuse for leaving the Sauer establishment. The woman had been kind and considerate to him and he had few grievances.

The mail brought him an enticing letter from Melbourne offering him all that the tennis player needs, at special prices.

"I trust your uncle is well," Mrs. Clarke observed.

It was in that moment Trent got his inspiration.

"I'm afraid he is very ill," he said sadly, "at his age—he must be almost ninety——"

"Only eighty-four," Mrs. Clarke reminded him. She remembered the year of his emigration.

"Eighty-four is a great age to attain," he declared, "and he has lived not wisely but well. I feel I should go out and see if there's anything I can do."

"You are going to leave us?" gasped Mrs. Sauer. His going would deprive her of a most satisfactory lodger.

"I'm afraid my duty is plain," he returned gravely.

Thus he left Mrs. Sauer's establishment. Years later he wondered whether if he had enjoyed better cooking he would have fallen from grace, and if he could not with justice blame a New England boiled dinner for his lapse.

For a few days he stayed at a quiet hotel. He wanted a small apartment on Central Park. There were reasons for this. First, he must live alone in a house where no officious elevator boys observed his going and his coming. Central Park West offered many such houses. And if it should happen that he ever had to flee from the pursuit of those who guarded the mansions that faced him on the park's eastern side, there was no safer way home than across the silent grass. He was one of those New Yorkers who know their Central Park. There had been a season when a friend gave him the use of a saddle horse and there was no bridle path that he did not know.

He was fortunate in finding rooms at the top of a fine old brownstone house in the eighties. There were four large rooms all overlooking the Park. That he was compelled to climb five flights of stairs was no objection in his eyes. A little door to the left of his own entrance gave admission to a ladder leading to the roof. None of the other tenants, so the agent informed him, ever used it. Anthony Trent was relieved to hear it.

"I sleep badly," he said, "possibly because I read a great deal and am anxious to try open air sleeping. If I might have the right to use the roof for that I should be very willing to pay extra."

"Glad to have you there," said the agent heartily, "you'll be a sort of night watchman for the property." He laughed at his jest. "Insomnia is plain hell, ain't it? I used to suffer that way. I walk a great deal now and that cures me. Do you take drugs?"

"I'm afraid of them," Anthony Trent declared. "I walk a good deal at night when the streets are quiet."

The agent reported to his office that Trent was a studious man who slept badly and wanted to sleep on the roof; also that he took long tramps at night. A good tenant, in fine. Thus he spread abroad the report which Trent desired.

The selection of a housekeeper was of extreme importance. She must be an elderly, quiet body without callers or city relatives. Her references must be examined thoroughly. He interviewed a score of women before he found what he wanted. She was a Mrs. Phoebe Kinney from Agawam, a village overlooking Buzzard's Bay. A widow, childless and friendless, she had occupied similar positions in Massachusetts but this would be the first one in New York. He observed in his talk with her that she conceived the metropolis to be the world center of wickedness. She assured her future employer that she kept herself to herself because she could never be certain that the man or woman who addressed a friendly remark to her might not be a criminal.

"Keep that attitude and we two shall agree splendidly," he said. "I have few friends and no callers. I am of a studious disposition and cannot bear interruptions. If you had friends in New York I should not hire you. I sometimes keep irregular hours but I shall expect to find you there all the time. You can have two weeks in the summer if you want them."

Next day Mrs. Kinney was inducted to her new home. It was a happy choice for she cooked well and had the New England passion for cleanliness. Trent noticed with pleasure that she was even suspicious of the tradespeople who sent their wares up the dumb waiter. And she discouraged their gossip who sold meat and bread to her. The many papers he took were searched for their crimes by Mrs. Kinney. Discovery of such records affirmed her in her belief of the city's depravity.

In his examination of her former positions Trent discovered that she had been housekeeper to the Clent Bulstrodes. He knew they were a fine, old Boston family of Back Bay, with a mansion on Beacon street. When he questioned her about it she told him it was as housekeeper of their summer home on Buzzards' Bay. Young Graham Bulstrode had been a tennis player of note years before. Many a time Anthony Trent had seen him at Longwood. He had dropped out because he drank too much to keep fit. The two were of an age. Mrs. Kinney related the history of the Bulstrode family at length and concluded by remarking that when she first saw her employer at the agency she was reminded of Mr. Graham. "But he looks terrible now," she added, "they say he drinks brandy before breakfast!"

The next day the society columns of the *Herald* informed him that the Clent Bulstrodes had bought a New York residence in East 73d street, just off the Avenue. This information was of peculiar interest to Trent. Now he was definitely engaged in a precarious profession he was determined to make a success of it. He had smoked innumerable pipes in tabulating those accidents which brought most criminals to sentence. He believed in the majority of cases they had not the address to get away with plausible excuses. It was an ancient and frayed excuse, that of pretending to be sent to read the water or electric meter. And besides, it was not Trent's intention to take to disguises of this sort.

He was now engaged in working out the solution of his second adventure. He was to make an attempt upon the house of William Drummond, banker, who lived in 93rd street and in the same number as did the Clent Bulstrodes, twenty blocks to the south. He had learned a great deal about Drummond from Clarke, his one-time city editor. Clarke remembered most of the interesting things about the big men of his day. He told Trent that Drummond invariably carried a great deal of money on his person. He expatiated on the Drummond history. This William Drummond had begun life on an Iowa farm. He had gradually saved a little money and then lent it at extravagant interest. Later he specialized on mortgages, foreclosing directly he knew his client unable to meet his notes. His type was a familiar one and had founded many fortunes. Clarke painted him as a singularly detestable creature.

"But why," demanded Anthony Trent, "does a man like that risk his money if he's so keen on conserving it? One would think he wouldn't take out more than his car fare for fearing either of being robbed or borrowed from."

"As for robbing," Clarke returned, "he's a great husky beast although he's nearly sixty. And as to being borrowed from, that's why he takes it out. He belongs to a lot of clubs—not the Knickerbocker type—but the sort of clubs where rich young fellows go to play poker. They know old Drummond can lend 'em the ready cash without any formalities any time they wish it. Ever sit in a poker game, son, and get a hunch that if you were able to buy just one more pile of chips you'd clean up?"

"I have," said the other smiling, "but my hunch has generally been wrong."

"Most hunches are," Clarke commented. "Theirs are, too, but that old scoundrel makes thousands out of just such hunches. He puts it up to the borrower that it's between club members and so forth, not a money lending transaction. Tells 'em he doesn't lend money as a rule, and so forth and so on. I know he was asked to resign from one club for it. He's a bloodsucker and if I had an automobile I'd watch for him to cross the street and then run him down."

"Has he ever stung you?" Trent asked.

"Me? Not on your life. He specializes in rich men's sons. He wouldn't lend you or me a nickel if we were starving. You remember young Hodgson Grant who committed suicide last year. They said it was the heat that got him. It was William Drummond."

"Why does he keep up a house on such a street as he does? I should think he'd live cheaper."

"A young second wife. Threw the old one away, so to speak, and got a high stepper that makes him speed up. She thinks she will get into society. Not a chance, son, not a chance. I know."

It was on some of William Drummond's money that Anthony Trent had set his heart. It salved what was still a conscience to know that he was taking back profits unlawfully made, bleeding a blood sucker.

Owing to the second Mrs. Drummond's desire to storm society she cultivated publicity. There were pictures of herself and her prize winning Red Chows in dog papers. In other magazines she was seen driving her two high stepping hackneys, Lord Ping and Lady Pong, at the Mineola Horse Show. Also, there was an article on her home in a magazine devoted to interior decoration. A careful study of it answered every question concerning its lay-out that the most careful cracksman needed to know. Trent spent a week in learning how Drummond occupied his time. The banker invariably left his most profitable club at midnight, never earlier. By half past twelve he was in his library smoking one of the cigars that had been given him that night. Then a drink of gin and water. Afterwards, bed. The house was protected by the Sherlock system of burglar alarm, a tiresome invention to those who were ignorant of it. Anthony Trent regarded it as an enemy and had mastered it successfully for there were tricks of lock opening not hard to one as mechanically able as he and many a criminal had talked to him openly when he had covered police headquarters years before.

Drummond drank very little. When asked he invariably took a cigar. He was possessed of great strength and still patronized the club gymnasium. For two hours one night Drummond sat near him at a certain famous athletic club. On that night there were certain changes to be observed in the appearance of Anthony Trent. He seemed to have put on twenty pounds in weight and ten years in age. The art of make-up which had been forced upon him in college theatricals had recently engaged his attention. It was an art of which he had thought little until for his paper he had once interviewed Beerbohm Tree and had seen the amazing changes skilful make-up may create.

Ordinarily he slipped in and out silently, not encouraging Mrs. Kinney to talk. On this particular night he asked her a question concerning a missing letter and she came out into the lighted hall.

"You gave me quite a shock," she said. "You look as like Mr. Graham Bulstrode as one pea is like another, although I've never seen him in full evening dress."

She was plainly impressed by her employer's magnificence although she feared this unusual flush on his ordinarily pale face meant that he had been having more to drink than was good for him.

It was the tribute for which Trent had waited. If Mrs. Kinney had never seen the son of her former master in the garb of fashion, her present employer had, and that within the week. And he had observed him carefully. He had seen that Bulstrode was wearing during the nights of late Autumn an Inverness cape of light-weight black cloth, lined with white silk. To Trent it seemed rather stagey but that did not prevent him from ordering its duplicate from Bulstrode's tailor. Bulstrode clung to the opera hat rather than to the silk hat which has almost superseded it. To-night Trent wore an opera hat.

Bulstrode came into the athletic club at half past eleven. He was slightly under the influence of liquor and his face no redder than that of Trent who waited across the street in the shadow of the Park wall. No sooner had Bulstrode been whirled off in a taxi than Anthony Trent went into the club. To the attendants it seemed that he had returned for something forgotten. With his Inverness still on and his hat folded he lost himself in the crowded rooms and found at last William Drummond. The banker nodded cordially. It was evident to the impostor that the banker wished to ingratiate himself with the new member. The Bulstrodes had enormous wealth and a name that was recognized. To his greeting Anthony Trent returned a solemn owl-like stare. "Shylock!" he hiccoughed insolently.

Drummond flushed but said nothing. Indeed he looked about him to see if the insult had been overheard by any other member. Inwardly Trent chuckled. He had now no fear of being discovered. Bulstrode probably knew few men at the club. He had not been in town as a resident for a month yet. He sank into a chair and read an evening paper watching in reality the man Drummond.

CHAPTER VI

FOOLING SHYLOCK DRUMMOND

The night that he entered Drummond's house was slightly foggy and visibility was low. He was dressed as he had been when he encountered Drummond at the club. He had seen the banker climb the five steps to his front door at half past twelve. At half past one the lights were switched off in the bedroom on the second floor. At two the door gently opened and admitted Anthony Trent. He left it unlocked and ready for flight. And he memorized the position of the furniture so that hasty flight would be possible.

It was not a big house. The articles of furniture, the pictures, rugs and hangings were splendid. The interior decorators had taken care of that. But he had seen them all in the magazine. Trent knew very well that to obtain such prizes as he sought could not be a matter of certainty. Somewhere in this house was a lot of currency. And it might be in a safe. Old fashioned safes presented few difficulties, but your modern strong box is a different matter. Criminal investigator as he was, he knew one man seldom attempted to dynamite a safe. It was a matter for several men. In itself the technique was not difficult but he had no accomplices and at best it is a matter better fitted for offices in the night silences than a private residence.

He had been told by criminals that it was astonishing how careless rich men were with their money. Anthony Trent proposed to test this. He had made only a noiseless progress on a half dozen stairs on his upward flight when a door suddenly opened, flooding the stairway with light. It was from a room above him. And there were steps coming along a corridor toward him. Feeling certain that the reception rooms leading off the entrance hall were empty, he swiftly opened a door and stepped backward into the room, watching intently to see that he had escaped the observation of some one descending the staircase.

From the frying pan's discomfort to the greater dangers of the fire was what he had done for himself. He found himself in a long room at one end of which he stood, swearing under breath at what he saw. At the other Mr. William Drummond was seated at a table. And Mr. Drummond held in his hand an ugly automatic of .38 calibre. Covering him with the weapon the banker came swiftly toward him. It was the unexpected moment for which Anthony Trent was prepared. Assuming the demeanor of the drunken man he peered into the elder man's face. He betrayed no fear of the pistol. His speech was thickened, but he was reasonably coherent.

"It is old Drummond, isn't it?" he demanded.

"What are you doing here?" the other snapped, and then gave a start when he saw to whom he spoke. "Mr. Bulstrode!"

"I've come," said the other swaying slightly, "to tell you I'm sorry. I don't know why I said it but the other fellers said it wasn't right. I've come to shake your hand." He caught sight of the weapon. "Put that damn thing down, Drummond."

Obediently the banker slipped it into the pocket of his dressing gown. He followed the swaying man as he walked toward the lighted part of the room. He was frankly amazed. Wild as he was, and drunken as was his evening custom, why had this heir to the Bulstrode millions entered his house like a thief in the night? And for what was he sorry?

In a chair by the side of the desk Anthony Trent flung himself. He wanted particularly to see what the banker had hidden with a swift motion as he had risen. The yellow end of some notes of high denomination caught his eye. Right on the table was what he sought. The only method of getting it would be to overpower Drummond. There were objections to this. The banker was armed and would certainly shoot. Or there might be a terrific physical encounter in which the younger man might kill unintentionally. And an end in the electric chair was no part of Trent's scheme of things. Also, there was some one else awake in the house.

Drummond resumed his seat and the watcher saw him with elaborate unconcern slide an evening paper over the partially concealed notes.

"Just what is on your mind, Mr. Bulstrode?" he began.

"I called you 'Shylock, '" Trent returned. "No right to have said it. What I should have said was, 'Come and have a drink. ' Been ashamed of myself ever since."

Drummond looked at him fixedly. It was a calculating glance and a cold one. And there was the contempt in it that a sober man has for one far gone in drink.

"And do you usually break into a man's house when you want to apologize?" There was almost a sneer in his voice.

"Break in?" retorted the other, apparently slow at comprehending him, "the damn door wasn't locked. Any one could get in. Burglars could break through and steal. Most foolish. I lock my door every night. All sensible people do. Surprised at you."

"We'll see about that," said Drummond. He took a grip on his visitor's arm and led him through the hall to the door. It was unlocked and the burglar alarm system disconnected. It was not the first time that Drummond's man had forgotten it. In the morning he would be dismissed. Apparently this irresponsible young ass had got the idea in his stupid head that he had acted offensively and had calmly walked in. It was the opportunity for the banker to cultivate him.

"As I came in," Trent told him, "some one was coming down the stairs. Better see who it was."

Drummond looked at him suspiciously. Trent knew that he was not yet satisfied that his visitor's story was worthy of belief. Then he spoke as one who humors a child.

"We'll go and find out."

Outside the door they came upon an elderly woman servant with a silver tray in her hands.

"Madame," she explained, "was not able to eat any luncheon or dinner and has waked up hungry."

Drummond raised the cover of a porcelain dish.

"Caviar sandwiches," he grunted, "bad things to sleep on."

He led the way back to the room. In his scheming mind was a vague scheme to use this bêtise of Graham Bulstrode as a means to win his wife social advancement. Mrs. Clent Bulstrode could do it. Money would not buy recognition from her. Perhaps fear of exposure might. He glanced with contempt at the huddled figure of the heir to Bulstrode millions. The young man was too much intoxicated to offer any resistance.

Tall, huge and menacing he stood over Anthony Trent. There was a look in his eye that caused a certain uneasiness in the impostor's mind. In another age and under different conditions Drummond would have been a pirate.

"If it had been any other house than mine," he began, "and you had not been a fellow clubman an unexpected call like this might look a little difficult of explanation."

Anthony Trent acted his part superbly. Drunkenness in others had always interested him. Drummond watching his vacuous face saw the inebriated man's groping for a meaning admirably portrayed.

"What do yer mean?"

"Simply this," said Drummond distinctly. "At a time when I am supposed to be in bed you creep into my house without knocking or ringing. You come straight into a room where very valuable property is. While I personally believe your story I doubt whether the police would. They are taught to be suspicious. There would be a lot of scandal. Your mother, for instance, would be upset. New York papers revel in that sort of thing. You have suppressed news in Boston papers but that doesn't go here." He nodded his head impressively. "I wouldn't like to wager that the police would be convinced. In fact it might take a lot of publicity before you satisfied the New York police."

The idea seemed to amuse the younger man.

"Let's call 'em up and see," he suggested and made a lurching step toward the phone.

"No, no," the other exclaimed hastily, "I wouldn't have that happen for the world."

Over his visitor's face Drummond could see a look of laboring comprehension gradually stealing. It was succeeded by a frown. An idea had been born which was soon to flower in high and righteous anger.

"You're a damned old blackmailer!" cried Anthony Trent, struggling to his feet. "When a gentleman comes to apologize you call him a robber. I'm going home."

Drummond stood over him threatening and powerful.

"I don't know that I shall let you," he said unpleasantly. "Why should I? You are so drunk that in the morning you won't remember a word I've said to you. I'm going to make use of you, you young whelp. You've delivered yourself into my hands. If I were to shoot you for a burglar I should only get commended for it."

"Like hell you would," Trent chuckled, "that old girl with the caviar sandwiches would tell the jury we were conversing amiably. You'd swing for it, Drummond, old dear, and I'd come to see your melancholy end."

"And there's another thing," Drummond reminded him, "you've got a bad record. Your father didn't give up the Somerset Club because he liked the New York ones any better. They wanted to get you away from certain influences there. I've got your whole history."

"Haven't you anything to drink?" Anthony Trent demanded.

From a cupboard in his black walnut desk Drummond took a large silver flask. He did not want his guest to become too sober. Since it was the first drink that Anthony Trent had taken that night he gulped eagerly.

"Good old Henessey!" he murmured. "Henessey's a gentleman," he added pointedly.

"Look here," said Drummond presently after deep thought. "You've got to go home. I'm told there's a butler who fetches you from any low dive you may happen to be."

"He hates it," Trent chuckled. "He's a prohibitionist. I made him one."

Drummond came over to him and looked him clear in the eye.

"What's your telephone number?" he snapped.

Trent was too careful a craftsman to be caught like that. He flung the Bulstrode number back in a flash. "Ring him up," he commanded, "there's a direct wire to his room after twelve."

"What's his name?" Drummond asked.

"Old Man Afraid of His Wife," he was told. Mrs. Kinney had told him of the nickname young Bulstrode had given the butler.

Drummond flushed angrily. "His real name? I'm not joking."

"Nor am I," Trent observed, "I always call him that." He put on an expression of obstinacy. "That's all I'll tell you. Give me the phone and let me talk."

It was a bad moment for Anthony Trent. It was probable that William Drummond was going to call up the Bulstrode residence to make certain that his visitor was indeed Graham Bulstrode. And if the butler were to inform him that the heir already snored in his own bed there must come the sudden physical struggle. And Drummond was armed. He had not failed to observe that the door to the entrance hall was locked. When Drummond had spoken to the servant outside he had taken this precaution. For a moment Trent entertained the idea of springing at the banker as he stood irresolutely with the telephone in his hand. But he abandoned it. That would be to bring things to a head. And to wait might bring safety.

But he was sufficiently sure of himself to be amused when he heard Drummond hesitatingly ask if he were speaking to Old Man Afraid of His Wife. The banker hastily disclaimed any intention of being offensive.

"Mr. Graham Bulstrode is with me," he informed the listener, "and that is the only name he would give. I am particularly anxious that you inform his father I am bringing him home. Also," his voice sank to a whisper, "I must speak to Mr. Bulstrode when I come. I shall be there within half an hour. He will be sorry all his days if he refuses to see me." As he hung up the instrument he noted with pleasure that young Bulstrode was conversing amicably with his old friend Henessey, whose brandy is famous.

Drummond had mapped it all out. He would not stay to dress. Over his dressing gown he would pull an automobile duster as though he had been suddenly disturbed. He would accuse Graham of breaking in to steal. He would remind the chastened father of several Boston scandals. He could see the Back Bay blue blood beg for mercy. And the end of it would be that in the society columns of the New York dailies it would be announced that Mr. and Mrs. William Drummond had dined with Mr. and Mrs. Clent Bulstrode.

No taxi was in sight when they came down the steps to the silent street. Drummond was in an amazing good humor. His captor was now reduced through his friendship with Henessey to a silent phase of his failing. He clung tightly to the banker's stalwart arm and only twice attempted to break into song. Since the distance was not great the two walked. Trent looked anxiously at every man they met when they neared the Bulstrode mansion. He feared to meet a man of his own build wearing a silk lined Inverness cape. It may be wondered why Anthony Trent, fleet of foot and in the shadow of the park across which his modest apartment lay, did not trip up the banker and make his easy escape. The answer lies in the fact that Trent was not an ordinary breaker of the law. And also that he had conceived a very real dislike to William Drummond, his person, his character and his aspirations. He was determined that Drummond should ride for a fall.

A tired looking man yawning from lack of sleep let them into the house. It was a residence twice the size of Drummond's. The banker peered about the vast hall, gloomy in the darkness. In fancy he could see Mrs. Drummond sweeping through it on her way to dinner.

"Mr. Bulstrode is in the library," he said acidly. That another should dare to use a nickname that fitted him so aptly filled him with indignation. He barely glanced at the man noisily climbing the stairs to his bedroom, the man who had coined the opprobrious phrase. Drummond was ushered into the presence of Clent Bulstrode.

The Bostonian was a tall man with a cold face and a great opinion of his social responsibilities. The only New Yorkers he cared to know were those after whose families downtown streets had been named.

"I am not in the habit, sir," he began icily, "of being summoned from my bed at this time of night to talk to a stranger. I don't like it, Mr. Dummles——"

"Drummond," his visitor corrected.

"The same thing," cried Bulstrode. "I know no one bearing either name. I can only hope your errand is justified. I am informed it has to do with my son."

"You know it has," Drummond retorted. "He broke into my house tonight. And he came, curiously enough, at a time when there was a deal of loose cash in my room. Mr. Bulstrode, has he done that before? If he has I'm afraid he could get into trouble if I informed the police."

It was a triumphant moment when he saw a look of fear pass over Bulstrode's contemptuous countenance. It was a notable hit.

"You wouldn't do that?" he cried.

"That depends," Drummond answered.

Upon what it depended Clent Bulstrode never knew for there came the noise of an automobile stopping outside the door. There was a honking of the horn and the confused sound of many voices talking at once.

Drummond followed the Bostonian through the great hall to the open door. They could see Old Man Afraid of His Wife assisting a young inebriate in evening dress. And his Inverness cape was lined with white silk and over his eyes an opera hat was pulled.

The chauffeur alone was sober. He touched his hat when he saw Mr. Bulstrode.

"Where have you come from?" he demanded.

"I took the gentlemen to New Haven," he said.

"Has my son been with you all the evening?"

"Yes, sir," the chauffeur returned.

Drummond, his hopes dashed, followed Bulstrode to the library. "Now," said the clubman sneering, "I shall be glad to hear your explanation of your slander of my son. In the morning I can promise you my lawyers will attend to it in detail."

"I was deceived," the wretched Drummond sought to explain. "A man dressed like your son whom I know by sight came in and——"

He went through the whole business. By this time the butler was standing at the open door listening.

"I can only say," Mr. Bulstrode remarked, "that these excuses you offer so glibly will be investigated."

"Excuses!" cried the other goaded to anger. "Excuses! I'll have you know that a father with a son like yours is more in need of excuses than I am."

He turned his head to see the butler entering the room. There was an unpleasant expression on the man's face which left him vaguely uneasy.

"Show this person out," said Bulstrode in his most forbidding manner.

"Wait a minute," Drummond commanded, "you owe it to me to have this house searched. We all saw that impostor go upstairs. For all we know he's in hiding this very minute."

"You needn't worry," Old Man Afraid of His Wife observed. "He went out just before Mr. Graham came back in the motor. I was going to see what it was when the car came between us." The man turned to Clent Bulstrode. "It's my belief, sir, they're accomplices."

"What makes you say that?" demanded his master. He could see an unusual expression of triumph in the butler's eye.

"The black pearl stick pin that Mr. Graham values so much has been stolen from his room."

"What have I to do with that?" Drummond shouted.

"Simply this," the other returned, "that you introduced this criminal to my house and I shall expect you to make good what your friend took."

"Friend!" repeated the outraged Drummond. "My friend!"

"It is a matter for the police," Bulstrode yawned.

Drummond watched his tall, thin figure ascending the stairs. Plainly there was nothing left but to go. Never in his full life had things broken so badly for William Drummond. He could feel the butler's baleful stare as he slowly crossed the great hall. He felt he hated the man who had witnessed his defeat and laughed at his humiliation. And Drummond was not used to the contempt of underlings.

Yet the butler had the last word. As he closed the door he flung a contemptuous good-night after the banker.

"Good-night," he said, "Old Man Afraid of the Police."

A broken and dispirited man William Drummond, banker, came to his own house. The pockets in which he had placed his keys were empty. There was no hole by which they might have been lost and he had not removed the long duster. Only one man could have taken them. He called to mind how the staggering creature who claimed to be Graham Bulstrode had again and again clutched at him for support. And if he had taken them, to what use had they been put?

It seemed he must have waited half an hour before a sleepy servant let him in. Drummond pushed by him with an oath and went hastily to the black walnut desk. There, seemingly unmoved, was the paper that he had pulled over the notes when the unknown came into the room. It was when he raised it to see what lay beneath that he understood to the full what a costly night it had been for him. Across one of his own envelopes was scrawled the single word—Shylock.

CHAPTER VII

THE DANGER OF SENTIMENT

After leaving Drummond's house Anthony Trent started without intemperate haste for his comfortable apartment. In accordance with his instructions, Mrs. Kinney retired not later than ten. There might come a night when he needed to prove the alibi that she could unconsciously nullify if she waited up for him.

In these early days of his career he was not much in fear of detection and approached his door with little of the trepidation he was to experience later when his name was unknown still but his reputation exceedingly high with the police. Later he knew he must arrange his mode of life with greater care.

New York, for example, is not an easy city for a man fleeing from police pursuit. Its brilliant lighting, its sleeplessness, the rectangular blocks and absence of helpful back alleys, all these were aids to the law abiding.

He had not chosen his location heedlessly. From the roof on which he often slept he could see five feet distant from its boundary, the wall that circumscribed the top of another house such as his but having its entrance on a side street. It would not be hard to get a key to fit the front door; and since he would make use of it infrequently and then only late at night there was little risk of detection.

Thinking several moves ahead of his game was one of Trent's means to insure success. He must have some plausible excuse in case he were caught upon the roof. The excuse that suggested itself instantly was a cat. He bought a large and frolicsome cat, tiger-striped and a stealthy hunter by night, and introduced him to Mrs. Kinney. That excellent woman was not pleased. A cat, she asserted, needed a garden. "Exactly," agreed her employer, "a roof garden." So it was that Agrippa joined the household and sought to prey upon twittering sparrows. And since Agrippa looking seventy feet below was not in fear of falling, he leaped the intermediate distance between the roofs and was rewarded with a sparrow. Thereafter he used what roof offered the best hunting.

Two maiden ladies occupied the topmost flat, the Misses Sawyer, and were startled one evening at a knock upon their door. An affable young gentleman begged permission to retrieve his cat from their roof. The hunting Agrippa had sprung the dreadful space and feared, he asserted plausibly, to get back.

The Misses Sawyer loved cats, it seemed, but had none now, fearing to seem disloyal to the memory of a peerless beast about whom they could not talk without tear-flooded eyes. They told their neighbor cordially that whenever Agrippa strayed again he was to make free of the roof.

"Ring our bell," said one of them, "and we'll let you in."

"But how did you get in?" the other sister demanded, suddenly.

"The door was open," he said blandly.

"That's that dreadful Mr. Dietz again," they cried in unison. "He drinks, and when he goes out to the saloon, he puts the catch back so there won't be the bother of a key. I have complained but the janitor takes no notice. I suppose we don't offer him cigars and tips, so he takes the part of Dietz."

By this simple maneuver Anthony Trent established his right to use the roof without incurring suspicion.

The Drummond loot proved not to be despised by one anxious to put a hundred thousand dollars to his credit. The actual amount was three thousand, eight hundred dollars. Furthermore, there was some of the Drummond stationery, a bundle of letters and the two or three things he had taken hastily from young Bulstrode's room. He regretted there had been so small an opportunity to investigate the Bulstrode mansion but time had too great a value for him. The black pearl had flung itself at him, and some yale keys and assorted club stationery—these were all he could take. The stationery might prove useful. He had discovered that fact in the Conington Warren affair. If it had not been that the butler crept out of the dark hall to watch him as he left the Bulstrode house, he would have tried the keys on the hall door. That could be done later. It is not every rich house which is guarded by burglar resisting devices.

It was the bundle of letters and I. O. U. 's that he examined with peculiar care. They were enclosed in a long, blue envelope on which was written "Private and Personal."

When Trent had read them all he whistled.

"These will be worth ten times his measly thirty-eight hundred," he said softly.

But there was no thought of blackmail in his mind. That was a crime at which he still wholesomely rebelled. It occurred to him sometimes that a life such as his tended to lead to progressive deterioration. That there might come a time when he would no longer feel bitterly toward blackmailers. It was part of his punishment, this dismal thought of what might be unless he reverted to the ways of honest men. Inasmuch as a man may play a crooked game decently, so Anthony Trent determined to play it.

Many of the letters in the blue envelope were from women whose names were easily within the ken of one who studied the society columns of the metropolitan dailies. Most of them seemed to have been the victims of misplaced bets at Belmont Park or rash bidding at Auction. There was one letter from the wife of a high official at Washington begging him on no account to let her husband know she had borrowed money from him. A prominent society golfing girl whose play Trent had a score of times admired for its pluck and skill had borrowed a thousand dollars from Drummond. There was her I. O. U. on the table. Scrawling a line on Drummond stationery in what seemed to be Drummond handwriting, Anthony Trent sent it back to her. There were acknowledgments of borrowings from the same kind of rich waster that Graham Bulstrode represented. A score of prominent persons would have slept the better for knowing that their I. O. U. 's had passed from Drummond's keeping. The man was more of a usurer than banker.

What interested Anthony Trent most of all was a collection of letters signed "N. G." and written on the stationery of a very exclusive club. It was a club to which Drummond did not belong.

The first letter was merely a request that Drummond meet the writer in the library of the athletic club where Anthony Trent had seen him.

The second was longer and spelled a deeper distress.

"It's impossible in a case like this," wrote "N. G.," "to get any man I know well to endorse my note. If I could afford to let all the world into my secret, I should not have come to you. You know very well that as I am the only son your money is safe enough. I must pay this girl fifty thousand dollars or let my father know all about it. He would be angry enough to send me to some god-forsaken ranch to cut wild oats."

The third letter was still more insistent. The writer was obviously afraid that he would have to beg the money from his father.

"I have always understood," he wrote, "that you would lend any amount on reasonable security. I want only fifty thousand dollars but I've got to have it at once. It's quite beyond my mother's power to get it for me this time. I've been to that source too often and the old man is on to it. E. G. insists that the money in cash must be paid to her on the morning of the 18th when she will call at the house with her lawyer. I am to receive my letters back and she will leave New York. Let me know instantly."

The next letter indicated that William Drummond had decided to lend "N. G." the amount but that his offer came too late.

"I wish you had made up your mind sooner," said "N. G." "It would have saved me the devil of a lot of worry and you could have made money out of it. As it is my father learned of it somehow. He talked about the family honor as usual. But the result is that when she and her lawyer call at ten on Thursday morning the money will be there. No check for her; she's far too clever, but fifty thousand in crisp new notes. As for me,

I'm to reform. That means I have to go down town every morning at nine and work in my father's brokerage business. Can you imagine me doing that? I blame you for it, Drummond. You are too cautious by a damn sight to please me."

Anthony Trent was thus put into possession of the following facts. That a rich man's son, initials only known, had got into some sort of a scrape with a girl, initials were E. G., who demanded fifty thousand dollars in cash which was to be paid at the residence of the young man's father. The date set was Thursday the eighteenth. It was now the early morning of Tuesday the sixteenth.

Trent had lists of the members of all the best clubs. He went through the one on whose paper N. G. had written. There were several members with those initials. Careful elimination left him with only one likely name, that of Norton Guestwick. Norton Guestwick was the only son and heir of a very rich broker. The elder Guestwick posed as a musical critic, had a box in the Golden Horseshoe and patronized such opera singers as permitted it. Many a time Anthony Trent had gazed on the Guestwick family seated in their compelling box from the modest seat that was his. Guestwick had even written a book, "Operas I Have Seen," which might be found in most public libraries. It was an elaborately illustrated tome which reflected his shortcomings as a critic no less than his vanity as an author. A collector of musical books, Trent remembered buying it with high hopes and being disgusted at its smug ineffectiveness.

He had seldom seen Norton in the family box but the girls were seldom absent. They, too, upheld the Arts. Long ago he had conceived a dislike for Guestwick. He hated men who beat what they thought was time to music whose composers had other ideas of it.

Turning up a recent file of *Gotham Gossip* he came upon a reference to the Guestwick heir. "We understand," said this waspish, but usually veracious weekly, "that Norton Guestwick's attention to pretty Estelle Grandcourt (née Sadie Cort) has much perturbed his aristocratic parents who wish him to marry a snug fortune and a girl suited to be their daughter-in-law. It is not violating a confidence to say that the lady in question occupies a mansion on Commonwealth avenue and is one of the most popular girls in Boston's smart set."

While many commentators will puzzle themselves over the identity of the dark lady of the immortal sonnets, few could have failed to perceive that E. G. was almost certain to be Estelle Grandcourt. Sundry tests of a confirmatory nature proved it without doubt. He had thus two days in which to make his preparations to annex the fifty thousand dollars. There were difficulties. In these early days of his adventuring Anthony Trent made no use of disguises. He had so far been but himself. Vaguely he admitted that he must sooner or later come to veiling his identity. For the present exploit it was necessary that he should find out the name of the Guestwick butler.

He might have to get particulars from Clarke. But even Clarke's help could not now be called in and it was upon this seemingly unimportant thing that his plan hinged. In a disguise such as many celebrated cracksmen had used, he might have gained a kitchen door and learned by what name Guestwick's man called himself. Or he might have found it out from a tradesman's lad. But to ask, as Anthony Trent, what might link him with a robbery was too risky.

Unfortunately for Charles Newman Guestwick his book, which had cost Trent two dollars and was thrown aside as worthless, supplied the key to what was needed.

It was the wordy, garrulous book that only a multi-millionaire author might write and have published. The first chapter, "My Childhood," was succeeded by a lofty disquisition on music. Later there came revelations of the Guestwick family life with portraits of their various homes. The music room had a chapter to itself. Reading on, Anthony Trent came to the chapter headed, rather cryptically, "After the Opera."

"It is my custom," wrote the excellent Guestwick, "to hold in my box an informal reception after the performance is ended. My wide knowledge of music, of singers and their several abilities lends me, I venture to say, a unique position among amateurs.

"We rarely sup at hotel or restaurant after the performance. In my library where there is also a grand piano—we have three such instruments in our New York home and two more at Lenox—Mrs. Guestwick and my daughters talk over what we have heard, criticizing here, lauding there, until a simple repast is served by the butler who always waits up for us. The rest of the servants have long since retired. My library consists of perhaps the most valuable collection of musical literature in the world.

"I have mentioned in another chapter the refining influence of music on persons of little education. John Briggs, my butler, is a case in point. He came to me from Lord Fitzhosken's place in Northamptonshire, England. The Fitzhoskens are immemoriably associated with fox-hunting and the steeple-chase and all Briggs heard there in the way of music were the cheerful rollicking songs of the hunt breakfast. I sent him to see Götterdämmerung. He told me simply that it was a revelation to him. He doubted in his uneducated way whether Wagner himself comprehended what he had written."

There were thirty other chapters in Mr. Guestwick's book. In all he revealed himself as a pompous ass assured only of tolerance among a people where money consciousness had succeeded that of caste. But

Anthony Trent felt kindly toward him and the money he had spent was likely to earn him big dividends if things went well.

Caruso sang on the night preceding the morning on which Estelle Grandcourt was to appear and claim her heart balm. This meant a large attendance; for tenors may come and go, press agents may announce other golden voiced singers, but Caruso holds his pride of place honestly won and generously maintained. It had been Trent's experience that the Guestwicks rarely missed a big night.

It was at half past nine Anthony Trent groaned that a professional engagement compelled him to leave the Metropolitan. He had spent money on a seat not this time for an evening of enjoyment, but to make certain that the Guestwicks were in their box.

There was Charles Newman Guestwick beating false time with a pudgy hand. His lady, weighted with Guestwick jewels, tried to create the impression that, after all, Caruso owed much of his success to her amiable patronage. The two daughters upheld the Guestwick tradition by being exceedingly affable to those greater than they and using lorgnettes to those who strove to know the Guestwicks.

Mr. John Briggs, drinking a mug of ale and wondering who was winning a light weight contest at the National Sporting Club, was resting in his sitting-room. He liked these long opera evenings, which gave him the opportunity to rest, as much as he despised his employer for his inordinate attendance at these meaningless entertainments. He shuddered as he remembered "The Twilight of the Gods."

At ten o'clock when Mr. Briggs was nodding in his chair the telephone bell rang. Over the wire came his employer's voice. It was not without purpose that Anthony Trent's unusual skill in mimicry had been employed. As a youth he had acquired a reputation in his home town for imitations of Henry Irving, Bryan, Otis Skinner and their like.

"Is this you, Briggs?" demanded the supposed Mr. Guestwick.

"Yes, sir," returned Briggs.

"I wish you to listen carefully to my instructions," he was commanded. "They are very important."

"Certainly, sir," the man returned. He sensed a something, almost agitation in the usually placid voice. "I hope there's nothing serious, sir."

"There may be," the other said, "that I can't say yet. See that every one goes to bed but you. Send them off at once. You must remain up until a man in evening dress comes to the front door and demands admittance. It will be a detective. Show him at once to the library and leave him absolutely undisturbed. Absolutely undisturbed, Briggs, do you understand?"

"I'll do as you say, sir," Briggs answered, troubled. He was sure now that serious sinister things were afoot and wished the Guestwicks had been as well disposed to dogs in the house as had been that hard drinking, reckless Lord Fitzhosken. Suddenly an important thought came to him. "Is there any way of making sure that the man who comes is the detective?"

"I am glad you are so shrewd, Briggs," said the millionaire. "It had not occurred to me that an impostor might come. Say to the man, 'What is your errand?' I shall instruct him to answer, 'I have come to look at Mr. Guestwick's rare editions.'"

"Very good, sir," said Briggs.

"Unless he answers that, do not admit him. You understand?"

"Perfectly," the butler made answer.

At half past ten a man in evening dress rang the door of the Guestwick mansion. He was a tall man with a hard look and a biting, gruff voice.

Briggs interposed his sturdy body between the stranger and the entrance.

"What is your errand?" said Briggs suavely.

"I have come to look at Mr. Guestwick's rare editions," he was told.

"Step inside," urged Briggs with cordiality.

"Everybody in bed?" the man snapped.

"Except me," said the butler.

"Any one here except the servants?"

"We have no house guests," said Briggs. "We don't keep a deal of company."

"Show me to the library," the stranger commanded.

Briggs, now stately and offended, led the way. Briggs resented the tone the detective used. In his youth the butler had been handy with the gloves. It was for this reason he was taken into service by the fox-hunting nobleman so that he might box with his lordship every day before breakfast. Briggs would have liked the opportunity to put on the gloves with this frowning, overbearing, hawk-nosed detective.

"You've got your orders?" cried the stranger.

"I have," Briggs answered, a trace of insolence perceptible.

"Then get out and don't worry me. Remember this, answer no phone messages or door bells. My men outside will attend to the people who want to get into this house."

Briggs tried new tactics. He was feverishly anxious to find out what was suspected.

"As man to man," Briggs began with a fine affability.

Imperiously he was ordered from the room.

Anthony Trent sank into a chair and laughed gently. It had all been so absurdly easy. Two good hours were before him. None would interrupt. It was known that young Norton had been bundled out of town until his charmer had disappeared. *Gotham Gossip* had told him so much. It was almost certain that the Guestwicks would not return to their home until half past twelve. That would give him a sufficient time to examine every likely looking place in the house. The old time crook would no doubt have hit Mr. Briggs over the head with a black jack and run a risk in the doing of it. The representative of the newer school had simply sent all the servants to bed.

Looking quickly about the great apartment, book-lined and imposing, Trent's eyes fell on an edition in twenty fat volumes of *Penroy's Encyclopædia of Music and Art*. Scrutiny told the observer that behind these steel-bound fake books there was a safe. It was an old dodge, this. If the money for Miss Grandcourt was not here there were, no doubt, negotiable papers and jewels. This was just the sort of sacrosanct spot where valuables might be laid away.

To pry open the glass door of the book case, roll back the works of the unknown Penroy and come face to face with the old fashioned safe took less than two minutes. It was amazing that so shrewd a man as Guestwick must be in business matters should rely on this. It was rather that he relied on the integrity of his servants and an efficient system of burglar alarm.

From the cane that Anthony Trent had carelessly thrown on a chair, he took some finely tempered steel drills and presently assembled the tools necessary to his task. As a boy he had been the rare kind who could take a watch apart and put it together again and have no parts left over. It was largely owing to an inborn mechanical skill that he had persuaded himself he could make good at his calling.

It was striking eleven by the ship's clock—six bells—when he rolled the doors open. He rose to his feet and stretched. Kneeling before the safe had cramped his muscles. Sinking into a big black leathern chair he contemplated the strong box that was now at his mercy. He allowed himself the luxury of a cigarette. There passed before his mind's eye a vista of pleasant shaded pools wherein big trout were lying. Weems did not own the only desirable camp on Kennebago.

He was suddenly called back from this dreaming, this castle-building, to a realization that such prospects might never be his. It was the low, pleasant, tones of a cultivated woman's voice which wrought the amazing change.

"I suppose you're a burglar," the voice said. There was no trace of nervousness in her tone.

He sprang to his feet and looked around. Not twenty feet distant he saw her. She was a tall, graceful girl about twenty-two or three, clad in a charming evening gown. Over her white arm trailed a fur cloak costly and elegant. And, although the moment was hardly one for thinking of female charms, he was struck by her unusual beauty. She possessed an air of extreme sophistication and stood looking at him as if the man before her were some unusual and bizarre specimen of his kind.

CHAPTER VIII

WHEN A WOMAN SMILED

Anthony Trent apparently was in no way confused at this interruption. The woman was not to guess that his *nonchalant* manner and the careless lighting of a cigarette, cloaked in reality a feeling of despair at the untoward ending of his adventure. Calmly she walked past him and looked at the assemblage of finely tempered steel instruments of his profession.

"So you're a burglar!" she said with an air of decision.

"That is a term I dislike," said Anthony Trent genially. "Call me rather a professional collector, an abstractor, a connoisseur—anything but that."

"It amounts to the same thing," she returned severely, "you came here to steal my father's money."

"Your father's money," he returned slowly. "Then—then you are Miss Guestwick?"

"Naturally," she retorted eyeing him keenly, "and if you offer any violence I shall have you arrested."

She was amazed to see a pleasant smile break over the intruder's face. He was exceedingly attractive when he smiled.

"What a hard heart you have!"

"You ought to realize this is no time to jest," she said stiffly.

"I am not so sure," he made answer.

She looked at him haughtily. He realized that he had rarely seen so beautiful a girl. There was a look of high courage about her that particularly appealed to him. She had long Oriental eyes of jade green. He amended his guess as to her age. She must be seven and twenty he told himself.

"It is my duty to call the police and have you arrested," she exclaimed.

"That is the usual procedure," he agreed.

She stood there irresolute.

"I wonder what makes you steal!"

"Abstract," he corrected, "collect, borrow, annex—but not steal."

She took no notice of his interruption.

"It isn't as though you were ill or starving—that might be some sort of excuse—but you are well dressed. I've done a great deal of social work among the poor and often I've met the wives of thieves and have actually found myself pitying men who have stolen for bread."

"Jean Valjean stuff," he smiled, "it has elements of pathos. Jean got nineteen years for it if you remember."

She paid no heed to his flippancy.

"You talk like an educated man. Economic determination did not bring you to this. You have absolutely no excuse."

"I have offered none," he said drily.

She spoke with a sudden air of candor.

"Do you know this situation interests me very much. One reads about burglars, of course, but that sort of thing seems rather remote. We've never had any robberies here before, and now to come face to face with a real burglar, cracking—isn't that the word you use?—a safe, is rather disconcerting."

"You bear up remarkably well," he assured her.

It was her turn to smile.

"I'm just wondering," she said slowly. "My father detests notoriety."

The intruder permitted himself to laugh gently. He thought of that pretentious tome "Operas I Have Seen."

"How well Mr. Guestwick conceals it!"

Apparently she had not heard him. It was plain she was in the throes of making up her mind.

"I wonder if I ought to do it," she mused.

"Do what?" he demanded.

"Let you get away. You have so far stolen nothing so I should not be aiding or abetting a crime."

"Indeed you would," he said promptly. "My very presence here is illegal and as you see I have opened that absurd safe."

"What an amazing burglar!" she cried, "he does not want his freedom."

"It is your duty as Mr. Guestwick's daughter to send me to jail and I shan't respect you if you don't."

She was again the haughty young society woman gazing at a curious specimen of man.

"It is very evident," she snapped, "that you don't appreciate your position. Instead of sending you to prison I am willing to give you another chance. Will you promise me never to do this sort of thing again if I let you go?"

Trent looked up.

"I have enjoyed your conversation very much," he observed genially, "but I have work to do. Inside that safe I expect to find fifty thousand dollars and possibly some odd trinkets. I am in particular need of the money and I propose to get it."

Swiftly she crossed the room to a telephone.

"I don't think you'll succeed," she said, her hand on the instrument.

"Put it to the test," he suggested. "The wires are not cut."

"Why aren't you afraid?" she demanded; "don't you realize your position?"

"Fully," he retorted, "but remember you'll have just the same difficulty as I in explaining your presence here. Now go ahead and get the police."

"What do you mean?" she cried. He noticed that she paled at what he said and her hands had been for a moment not quite steady.

"First that you are not a Miss Guestwick. There are only two of them and I have just left them at the Opera. Next you are neither servant nor guest. The servants are all abed and there are no house guests. I am not accustomed to making mistakes in matters of this sort. Now, I'm not inviting confidences and I'm not making threats, but the doors are locked and I intend to get what I came for. Ring all you like and see if a servant answers you. By the way how is it I overlooked you when I came in?"

"I hid behind those portières."

"It was excusable," he commented, "not to have looked there."

She sank into a chair her whole face suffused with gloom. He steeled his heart against feeling sympathy for her. He would liked to have learned all about her but there was not much time. The Guestwicks might return earlier than usual or Briggs might be lurking the other side of the door.

"You've found me out," she said quietly, "I'm not one of the Guestwick girls."

"I told you so," he said a little impatiently.

"Don't you want to know anything about me?" she demanded.

"Some other time," he returned, "I'm busy now."

"But what are you going to do?" she asked.

"I thought I told you. I'm going to see what Mr. Guestwick has which interests me. Then I shall get a bite to eat somewhere and go home to bed."

"Are you going to take that fifty thousand dollars?" she demanded. Her tone was a tragic one.

"That's what I came for," he told her.

"You mustn't, you mustn't," she declared and then fell to weeping bitterly.

Beauty in distress moved Anthony Trent even when his business most engrossed his attention. It was his nature to be considerate of women. When he had garnered enough money to buy himself a home he intended to marry and settle down to domestic joys. As to this weeping woman, there was little doubt in his mind as to the reason she was in the Guestwick home. Perhaps she noticed the harder look that came to his face.

"Whom do you think I am?" she asked.

"I have not forgotten," he answered, "that women also are abstractors at times."

She gazed at him wide open eyes, a look of horror on her face.

"You think I'm here to steal?"

"I wish I didn't," he answered. "It's bad enough for a man, but for a woman like you. What am I to think when I find you hiding in a house where you have no right to be?"

"That's the whole tragedy of it," she exclaimed, "that I've no right to be here. I suppose I shall have to tell you everything. Can't you guess who I am?"

Anthony Trent looked at the clock. Precious seconds were chasing one another into minutes and he had wasted too much time already.

"I don't see that it matters at all to me," he pointed to the safe, "I'm here on business."

It annoyed him to feel he was not quite living up to the debonair heroes he had created once upon a time. They would not have permitted themselves to be so brusque with a lovely girl upon whose exquisite cheeks tears were still wet.

"You must listen to me," she implored, "I'm Estelle Grandcourt. Now do you understand why I've come?"

"For the money that you think is already yours," he said, a trifle sulkily. Matters were becoming complicated.

"Money!" cried the amazing chorus girl, "I hate it!"

His face cleared.

"If that's the case," he said genially, "we shall not quarrel. Frankly, Miss Grandcourt, I love it."

She glanced at him through tear-beaded lashes.

"I suppose you've always thought of a show girl as a scheming adventuress always on the lookout for some foolish, rich old man or else some silly boy with millions to spend."

"Not at all!" he protested.

"But you have," she contradicted, "I can tell by your manner. For my part I have always thought of burglars as brutal, low-browed men without chivalry or courtesy. I've been wrong too. I imagined the gentleman-crook was only a fiction and now I find him a fact. Will you please tell me what you've heard about me. I'm not fishing for compliments. I want, really and truly, to know."

Trent hesitated a moment. He thought, as he looked at her, that never had he seen a sweeter face. She was wholly in earnest.

"Please, please," she entreated.

"It's probably all wrong," he observed, "but the general impression is that Norton Guestwick is a wild, weak lad for whom you set your snares.

And when Mr. Guestwick tried to break it off you asked fifty-thousand dollars in cash as a price."

"Do you believe that?" she asked looking at him almost piteously.

"It was common report," he said, seeking to exonerate himself, "I read some of it in *Gotham Gossip*."

"And just because of what some spiteful writer said you condemn me unheard."

He looked at the inviting safe and fidgeted.

"I'm not condemning," he reminded her. "I don't know anything about the affair. I don't yet see why you are here, Miss Grandcourt."

"Because I have the right to be," she said, looking him full in the face. "I pretended I was a Miss Guestwick. If you wish to know the truth, I am Mrs. Norton Guestwick. I can show you our marriage certificate. This is the first time I have ever been in the house of my father-in-law."

"How did you get in?" he demanded. He felt certain that Briggs the butler had shown him into the library believing it to be unoccupied.

"I bribed a servant who used to be in our employ."

"Your employ?" he queried.

"Why not?" she flung back at him. "Is it also reported that I come from the slums? We were never rich as the Guestwicks are rich, but until my father died we lived in good style as we know it in the South. I am at least as well educated as my sisters-in-law who refuse to recognize that I exist. I was at the Sacred Heart Convent in Paris. I sing and paint and play the piano as well as most girls but do none of these well enough to make a living at it. I came here to New York hoping that through the influence of my father's friends I could get some sort of a position which would give me a living wage." She shrugged her shoulders, "I wonder if you know how differently people look at one when one is well off and when one comes begging favors?"

"None better," he exclaimed bitterly.

"So I had to get in to the chorus because they said my figure would do even if I hadn't a good enough voice. Then I met Norton."

She looked at Anthony Trent with a little friendly smile that stirred him oddly. In that moment he envied Norton Guestwick more than any living creature.

"What do they say about my husband?" she asked.

"You can never believe reports," he said evasively.

"I'll tell you," she returned, "they say he is a waster, a libertine, weak and degenerate. They are wrong. He is full of sweet, generous impulses. His mother has so pampered him that he was almost hopeless till I met him. I expect you think it's conceited of me but I have a great influence on him."

"You would on any man," he said fervently.

She looked at him in a way that suggested a certain subtle tribute to his best qualities.

"Ah, but you are different," she sighed, "you are strong and resolute. You would sway the woman you loved and make her what you wanted her to be. He is clay for my molding and I want him to be a splendid, fine son like my father." She looked at Trent with a tender, proud smile, "If you had ever met my father you would understand."

Anthony Trent shifted uneasily from one foot to the other. He had not dared for months now to think of that kindly country physician who died from the exposure attendant on a trip during a blizzard to aid a penniless patient.

"I know what you mean," he said at length, "and I think it is splendid of you. Good God! why can people like the Guestwicks object to a girl like you?"

"They've never seen me," she explained, "and that's the main trouble. They persist in thinking of me as a champagne-drinking adventuress who wants to blackmail them. That money"—she pointed to the safe, "I didn't ask for it. Mr. Guestwick offered it to me as a bribe to give up my husband and consent to a divorce."

"But I still don't see why you are here," he said.

"Our old servant arranged it. She says they always come up here after the opera, all four of them. If I confront them they must see I'm not the sort of girl they think me. I'm dreading it horribly but it's the only way."

Anthony Trent looked at her with open admiration.

"You'll win," he cried enthusiastically, "I feel it in my bones."

"And when I absolutely refuse to take their money they *must* see I'm not the adventuress they call me."

Anthony Trent had by this time forgotten the money. The mention of it reminded him of his errand and the fleeting minutes.

"If you don't take it, what is going to happen to it?"

"I'm going to tell Mr. Guestwick that he can't buy me."

"But I'm willing to be bought," he said, forcing a smile. "In fact that's what I came for."

She shrunk back as though he had struck her. Her big eyes looked reproach at him. Tremulous eager words seemed forced from her by the agitation into which his words had thrown her.

"You couldn't do that now," she wailed, "not now you know. They'll be in very soon now and what could I say if the money was gone? Don't you see they would send me away in disgrace and Norton would believe that I was just as bad as they said? Then he'd divorce me and I think my heart would break."

"Damn!" muttered Trent. Things were happening in an unexpected fashion. He tried not to look at her piteous face.

"Please be kind to me," she begged, "this is your opportunity to do one great noble thing."

"It really means so much to you?" he asked.

"It means everything," she said simply.

He paced the room for a minute or more. He was fighting a great battle. There remained in him, despite his mode of living, a certain generosity of character, a certain fineness bequeathed him by generations of honorable folk. He saw clearly what the girl meant. She was here to fight for her happiness and the redemption of the man she loved. How small a thing, it seemed to him suddenly, was the necessity he had felt for obtaining the miserable money. What stinging mordant memories would always be his if he refused her!

There was a tenderness, a protective look in his eyes when he glanced down at her. He was his father's son again.

"It means something to me, too," he told her, "to do as you want, and I don't believe there's a person on this green earth I'd do it for but you."

His hand lingered for a moment on her white shoulder.

"Good luck, little girl."

The partly lighted hall full of mysterious shadows awakened no fear in him as he quietly descended the stairs. And when he came to the avenue he did not glance up and down as he usually did to see whether or not he was being followed.

There was a lightness of heart and an exaltation of spirit which he had never experienced. It was that happiness which alone comes to the man who has made a sacrifice. There was never a moment since he had abandoned fiction that he was nearer to returning to its uncertain rewards. Pipe after pipe he smoked when he was once more in his quiet room and asked himself why he had done this thing. There were two reasons hard to dissociate. First, this wonderful girl had reminded him of the man he had passionately admired—his father, the father who had taught him to play fair. And then he was forced to admit he had never been more drawn to any woman than to this girl, who must, before his last pipe was smoked, have won her victory or gone down to defeat. Again and again he told himself that there was no man he envied so much as Norton Guestwick.

CHAPTER IX

"THE COUNTESS"

The next morning Anthony Trent observed that Mrs. Kinney was filled with the excitement that attended the reading of an unusual crime as set forth by the morning papers. It was in those crimes committed in the higher circles of society which intrigued her most, that society which she had served.

As a rule Trent let her wander on feeling that her pleasures were few. Sometimes he thought it a little curious that she should concern herself with affairs in which he was sure, sooner or later, to be involved. It was a relief to know she spoke of them to none but him. He rarely bothered to follow her rambling recitals, contenting himself now and again with exclamations of supposed interest. But this morning he was suddenly roused from his meditations by the mention of the word Guestwick.

"What's that?" he demanded.

"I was telling you about the Guestwick robbery, sir," she said as she filled his cup.

He did not as a rule look at the paper until his breakfast was done. To send her for it now might, later, be used as a chain in the evidence that might even now be forging for him. He affected a luke-warm interest.

"What was it?" he asked.

"Money mad!" returned Mrs. Kinney, shaking her head. "All money mad. The root of all evil."

"A robbery was it?"

"It was like this," Mrs. Kinney responded, strangely gratified that her employer found her recital worth listening to. "There was fifty-thousand dollars in cash in the safe in Mr. Guestwick's library. He's a millionaire and lives on Fifth Avenue. It's a most mysterious case. The butler swears his master rang him up and told him to send all the servants to bed."

At length Mrs. Kinney recited Briggs's evidence before the police captain who was hurriedly summoned to the mansion. "They arrested the butler," said Mrs. Kinney. "Mr. Guestwick says he came from one of those castles in England where dissolute noblemen do nothing but shoot foxes all day and play cards all night. The police theory is that the butler admitted them and then went bed so as to prove an alibi."

"Mr. Guestwick denies sending any such message?"

"Yes. He was at the Opera."

Anthony Trent fought down the desire to rush out into the kitchen and take the paper from before Mrs. Kinney's plate. She had said that Briggs was to have admitted more than one person.

"How many did this suspected butler let in?"

"Only one, the man. He was in evening dress. Briggs suspected him from the first, but daren't go against his master's positive instructions. Briggs, the butler, says the man must have opened the door to his accomplice when he'd been sent off to bed with instructions not to answer any bell or telephone. The other was a beautiful young woman dressed just as she'd come from the Opera herself."

"Who saw her if Briggs did not?" he demanded.

"They caught her," Mrs. Kinney returned triumphantly, "and the arrest of her accomplice is expected any minute. They know who he is."

Anthony Trent put down his untasted coffee.

"That's interesting," he commented. "Do they mention his name?"

"I don't know as they did," she replied. "I'll go fetch the paper."

He read it through with a deeper interest than he had ever taken in printed sheet before. Such was Guestwick's importance that two columns had been devoted to him.

Mr. Guestwick on returning from the Opera was incensed to find none to let him in his own house. He was compelled to use a latchkey. The house was silent and unlighted. Mr. Guestwick, although a man of courage, felt the safety of his women folk would be better guarded if he called in a passing policeman. In the library they came face to face with crime.

There, standing at the closed safe, her skirt caught as the heavy doors had swung to, was a beautiful woman engaged as they came upon her in trying to tear off the imprisoning garments. Five minutes later and she would have escaped said police sapience.

Finger prints revealed her as a very well-known criminal known to the continental police as "The Countess." She was one of a high-class gang which operated as a rule on the French and Italian Riviera, and owed its success to the ease with which it could assume the manners and customs of the aristocracy it planned to steal from. "The Countess," for example, spoke English with a perfection of idiom and inflection that was unequaled by a foreigner. She was believed to come from an old family of Tuscany. Despite a rigid examination by the police she had declined to make any explanation. That, she told them, would be done in court.

Anthony Trent looked at the clock. It was nine and she would be brought before a magistrate at half-past ten.

So he had been fooled! All those high resolves of his had been brought into being by a woman who must have been laughing at him all the while, who must have congratulated herself that her lies had touched a man's heart and left fifty thousand dollars for her.

It was a bitter and harder Anthony Trent that came to the police court; a man who was now almost as ashamed at his determination of last night to abandon his career as he was now anxious to pursue it.

There was possibly some danger in going. Briggs would be there. The woman might point at him in open court. There were a hundred dangers, but they had no power to deter him. He swore to watch her, gain what particulars he might as to her past life and associates, and then take his revenge. God! How she had hoodwinked him!

His face he must, of course, disguise in some simple manner. It was not difficult. In court he took a seat not too far back. Chewing gum, as he had often observed in the subway, had a marvelous power in altering an expression. He sat there, his lower jaw thrust out and his mouth drawn down, ceaselessly chewing. And one eye was partially closed. He had brought the thing to perfection. With shoulders hunched he looked without fear of detection into the fascinating green eyes of "The Countess."

By this time her defense was arranged. Last night, her lawyer explained, she was so overcome with the shock that she could not make even a simple statement to the police.

Miss Violet Benyon, he declared, of London, England, and temporarily at the Plaza, had felt on the previous evening need for a walk. Knowing Fifth Avenue to be absolutely safe she walked North. Passing the Guestwick mansion she saw a man in evening dress stealing down the steps, across the road and into the Park. Fearing robbery she had rung the bell. Getting no answer and finding the door open she went in. The only light was in the library. Of a fearless nature, Miss Benyon of London went boldly in. There was an open safe. This she closed and in the doing of it was imprisoned. That was all. The lawyer swept the finger-prints aside as unworthy evidence. He was appearing before a Neolithic magistrate who was prejudiced against them.

An imposing old lady who claimed to be Miss Benyon's aunt went bail for her niece's appearance to the amount of ten thousand dollars. She mentioned as close friends names of well known Americans, socially elect, who would rush to her rescue ere the day was out. So impressive was she, and so splendid a witness did Miss Benyon make, that the magistrate disregarded Mr. Guestwick's plea and admitted her to bail.

Trent knew very well that Central Office men would dog the steps of aunt and niece, making escape almost impossible. But he was nevertheless convinced that Miss Violet Benyon of London, or the Countess from the Riviera, would never return to the magistrate's court as that trusting jurist anticipated.

And Anthony Trent was right. The two women, despite police surveillance, left the hotel and merged themselves among the millions. The younger woman taking advantage of a new maid's inexperience offered her a reward for permitting her to escape by back ways in order to win, as she averred, a bet. The aunt's escape was unexplained by the police. They found awaiting the elder woman's coming a girl from a milliner's shop. She was allowed to go without examination. Trent read the account very carefully and stored every published particular in his trained memory. There was no doubt in his mind that the milliner's assistant was the so-called aunt. He remembered her as a slim, elderly woman, very much made-up.

On his own account he called at the milliner's and made some inquiries. He found that there was no account with the Benyons and no assistant had been sent to the hotel. It was none of his business to aid police authorities. And he was not anxious that the two should be caught in that way. There would come a time when he was retired from his present occupation when he would feel the need of excitement. Getting even with the clever actress who prevented him from taking the Guestwick money would call for his astutest planning.

CHAPTER X

ANTHONY TRENT SAVES A PIANO

For some months now Trent had been preparing a campaign against the collection of precious stones belonging to Carr Faulkner whose white stone mansion looked across the Park from his home. But whereas Trent's house faced east, the Faulkner abode looked west. And in matter of residence locality there is an appreciable difference in this outlook.

The Faulkner millions were in the main inherited. There was a conservative banking house on Broad Street bearing the Faulkner name but it did not look for new business and found its principal work in guarding the vast Faulkner fortune.

Faulkner's first wife had been a collector of pearls, those modest stones whose assembled value is always worth the criminal's attention. The second wife, a young woman of less aristocratic stock, eschewed pearls, holding the theory that each one was a tear. She wanted flashing stones which advertised their value more ostentatiously. Trent had seen her at the Opera and marked her down as a profitable client.

It was because Trent worked so carefully that he made so few mistakes. He had no friends to ask him leading questions and gossip about his mode of life. He had been half a year collecting information about the Carr Faulkners, the style in which they lived, the intimate friends they had and a hundred little details which a careful professional must know before he can hope to make a success.

The system of burglar alarm installed in the mansion was an elaborate one but he was not unskilled in matters of this sort. For three months he had worked in the shop where they were made and his general inborn mechanical skill had been aided by conscientious study. Attention to detail had saved him more than once, and is an aid to be counted on more than luck.

Yet it was sheer blind, kindly, garrulous luck that finally took Trent unsuspected into the Carr Faulkner mansion. Riding up Madison avenue in a trolley car late one afternoon, he overheard one of the Faulkner's maids discussing the family.

One of the girls had knocked over a vase of cut flowers which stood on a grand piano in Mrs. Carr Faulkner's boudoir and the water had leaked through onto the wire and wood, doing some little damage.

"She was madder'n a wet hen," said the girl.

"Them things cost a lot of money," her companion commented, "and that was inlaid like all the other things in her room. Gee! the way Mr. Faulkner spends the money on her is a crime."

"Second wives have a cinch," said the first girl, sneering. "From all I hear the first was a perfect lady and kind to the maids, but this one is down-right ordinary. You should have heard what she said about me over the 'phone when she told the piano people to send a tuner up, and me standing there. Said I was "clumsy" and "stupid" and "a love-sick fool." I could tell something about love-sick fools if I wanted to! And she knows it."

Her friend cautioned her.

"Be careful," she whispered, "you may want to lose your job but I don't. Don't talk so loud."

It was hardly five o'clock. Anthony Trent left the car and started for a telephone booth. He went methodically through the lists of the better known piano makers. There was one firm whose high-priced instrument was frequently encased in rare woods for specially furnished rooms.

"This is Mr. Carr Faulkner's secretary speaking," he began when the number was given to him. "Have you been instructed to see about a piano here?"

"We are sending a man right away," he was told.

"To-morrow morning will do," said the supposed secretary. "We are giving a small dance to-night and it will not be convenient."

"We should prefer to send now," came the answer. "A valuable instrument might be extensively damaged if not attended to right away."

Trent became confidential. He dropped his voice.

"It's nothing for Mr. Faulkner to buy a new instrument if it's needed, but it's a serious thing if a dance that Mrs. Faulkner gives is interrupted. Money is no consideration here as you ought to know."

The piano man, remembering the price that was exacted for the special case, smiled to himself. It would be better for him to sell a new instrument. It would not surprise him if this affable secretary called in some fine morning and hinted at commission. Such things had been done before in the trade.

"It's just as you say," he returned. "At what hour shall our Mr. Jackson call?"

"As soon as he likes after ten," said the obliging Trent, and rang off.

Then he called up the Carr Faulkner house and told the answering man servant that Mr. Jackson of Stoneham's would call at half past six. He was switched on to the private wire of Mrs. Carr Faulkner.

"It's disgraceful that you can't come before," she stormed.

"Yours is specially made instrument," he reminded her, "and I need special tools."

Then he took the crosstown car to his home and changed into a neat dark business suit. He also arrayed himself in a brand new shirt and collar. Mrs. Kinney always washed these, and many a criminal has had his identity proved by his laundry mark. Trent, like a wise man, admitted the possibility that some day he might be caught but was determined never to take the risks that lesser craftsmen hardly thought of.

Anthony Trent thought it most probable that the Faulkner's butler would be of the imported species. He hoped so. He found that they were more easily impressed by good manners and dress than the domestic breed.

Some day he determined to write an essay on butlers. There was Conington Warren's bishop-like Austin, cold, severe, aloof. There was Guestwick's man, the jovial sportsman type molding himself no doubt on some admired employer of earlier days.

Faulkner's butler was an amiable creature and inclined to associate with a piano tuner on equal terms. He had rather fine features and was admired of the female domestics. His dignity forbade him to indulge in much familiarity with the men beneath him and he welcomed the pseudo-tuner as an opportunity to converse.

"I knew you by your voice," said the butler cordially. "Come in."

There was little chance that the maid servants behind whom he had sat on the car would recognize him. Or if they did there was no reason why they should be suspicious.

Mrs. Carr Faulkner's boudoir was a delightful room on the third floor. A little electric, self-operated elevator leading to it was pointed out by the butler.

"Not for the likes of you or me," said the man. "We can walk."

Mrs. Carr Faulkner was a dissatisfied looking blonde woman. In her opera box surrounded by friends and displaying her famous jewels she had seemed a vision of loveliness to the gazing far-away Trent. Here in her own home and dealing with those whom she considered her inferiors, she made no effort to be even civil.

"Who is this person?" she demanded of the butler.

"The man come to look at the piano, ma'am," he returned.

"You're not Mr. Jackson," she said with abruptness.

It was plain Jackson was known. Trent blamed himself for not thinking of this possibility.

"I am the head tuner," he said with dignity, "we understood it was a case where the highest skill was needed."

She looked at him coldly.

"I don't know that it demands much of what you call skill," she retorted acidly. "You have come at a singularly inconvenient hour. Please get to work at once."

With this she left the room. The butler gazed after her scowling.

"Do you have to put up with that all day?" Trent asked him.

"How the boss stands it I don't know," said the butler.

"Why take it out on a mere piano tuner?" Trent asked.

The butler winked knowingly. He dug Trent in the ribs with a fine, free and friendly gesture.

"Speaking as one man of the world to another," he observed, "I guess you spoiled a little *tête-à-tête* as we say in gay Paree. Mr. Carr Faulkner leaves the Union Club at seven and walks up the Avenue in time to dress for his dinner at eight. There's another gentleman leaves another club on the same Avenue and gets here as a rule at six and leaves in time to avoid the master." The butler leaned forward and whispered in the tuner's ear, "She's crazy about him. The only man who doesn't know is the boss. It's always the way," added the self-confessed man of the world, "I wouldn't trust any woman living. The more they have the worse they are. If ever I marry I'll take a job as lighthouse keeper and take my wife along."

"Will they come in here?" Trent asked anxiously. He wanted the opportunity to do his own work while the family dined and he did not want to be seen by an unnecessary person. He disliked taking even a million to one shot.

The cynical butler interpreted his interest differently.

"You won't understand a word of what they're saying. They talk in French. She was at school in Lausanne and he's a French count, or says he is. I've made a mistake in scorning foreign languages," the butler admitted, "I'd give a lot to know what they talk about." He was not to know that Trent knew French moderately well.

Left to himself Trent called to mind the actions of a piano tuner. He had often watched his own grand being tuned. When Mrs. Carr Faulkner came into the room she beheld an earnest young man delving among the piano's depths. She was interested in no man but Jules d'Aucquier who filled her heart and emptied her purse.

"Is the thing much damaged?" she asked presently.

"I think not," he replied.

"Then you need not stay long?"

"I shall go as soon as possible," he said.

She sank into a deep chair and thought of Jules. And there came to her face a softer, happier look. The butler's talk Trent dismissed as mere servants' gossip. Of Carr Faulkner he knew nothing except that he was years older than his wife. He was, probably, a wealthy roué who had coveted this beautiful woman and bought her in marriage. In high society it was often that way, he mused. Family coercion, perhaps, or the need to aid impoverished parents. It was being done every day. This man of whom the butler spoke was probably her own age. Since the stone age this domestic intrigue must have been going on.

He touched the keyboard—pianissimo at first and then growing bolder plunged into the glorious *Liebestod*. It was not the sort of thing Mr. Jackson would have done but then Anthony Trent was a head tuner as he had explained. He watched the woman's face to see into what mood the music would lead her. He was speedily to find out.

"Stop," she commanded and rising to her feet came to his side. "Why do you do that?"

"I must try it," he answered, a little sheepishly, "we always have to test an instrument."

"But to play the *Liebestod*" she said severely. "I have heard them all play it, Bauer, Borwick, Grainger, d'Albert and Hoffman and you dare to try! It was impertinent of you. Of course if you must play just play those chords tuners always use."

Trent admitted afterwards he had never been more angry or felt more insulted in his life. He had not for a moment supposed this butterfly woman even knew the name of what he played.

"I won't offend again," he said with what he hoped was a sarcastic inflection. She answered never a word. She seemed to be listening. Trent heard a sound that might have been the opening of the elevator door. Then came hurried steps along the hall and Jules d'Aucquier entered.

He was dark to the point of swarthiness, tall and graceful. His rather small head reminded Trent of a snake's. As a man who knew men Trent determined that the newcomer was dangerous. The look that he threw across the room to the intruder was not pleasant.

He spoke very quickly in French.

"Who is this?" he demanded.

"No one who matters," she answered in the same tongue.

"But what is the pig doing here at this hour?" he asked.

"Repairing the piano," she told him, "a poor tuner I imagine for the reason that he plays so well. I had to stop him when he began the *Liebestod*. It affects me too much. That was being played when you first looked into my eyes, dear one."

"Send him away," the man commanded.

"But that would look suspicious," she declared.

Trent noticed that Jules did not respond to the affection which was in the woman's tone.

"You should not telephone to me at the club," he said as he took a seat at her side. "I am only a temporary member and do not want to embarrass my sponsor."

"But you were so cruel to me yesterday," she murmured.

"Cruel?" he repeated and turned his cold, snake eyes on her, eyes that could, when he willed it, glow with fire and passion. "Who is the crueler, you or I?"

"What do you mean?" she cried almost tearfully. "You know I love you."

"And yet when I ask you to do a favor which is easily within your power to perform you refuse. I must have money; that you know."

"It is always money now," she complained. "You no longer say that you love me."

"How can I when my creditors bark at my heels like hungry dogs? Unless I pay by to-morrow it is finished. You and I see one another no more, that is certain."

He looked at her in annoyed surprise when she suddenly smiled. He watched her with an even greater interest than the man gazing from behind the piano. From an escritoire she took a package wrapped in lavender paper. This she placed in the pocket of the coat that he had thrown across a chair.

"What good are cigarettes to me now?" he demanded. "I have told you that unless I have fifteen thousand dollars by noon to-morrow, I am done."

"When you get to your rooms," she said, smiling, "open your cigarettes and see if I do not love you."

Trent admitted this Jules was undeniably handsome now that the dark face was wreathed in smiles. Jules gathered her in his arms.

"My soul," he whispered, and covered her face with kisses. When he attempted to rise and go to the coat his eyes were staring at, she held him tight.

"I got twenty thousand from him," she said. "You will find the twenty bills each wrapped in the cigarette papers. I pushed the tobacco out and they fitted in."

"Wasteful one," he said in tender reproach and sought again to retrieve his coat.

Unfortunately for the debonair Jules d'Aucquier this was not immediately possible. The click of the little elevator was heard. The two looked at one another in alarm.

"It must be Carr," she whispered. "Nobody else could possibly use that elevator now. Somebody has told him." She looked about her in despair. "You must hide. Quick, behind the piano there until I get him away."

Trent working industriously amid the wreckage of what had been a grand piano looked up with polite surprise at the tall man who flung himself almost at his feet and tried to conceal himself behind part of the instrument.

"Hide me, quickly," Jules whispered, "do you hear. I will give you money. Quick, fool, don't gape at me."

For the second time that evening Anthony Trent smothered his anger and smiled when rage was in his heart. And he did so for the second time not because he was conscious of fear but because he saw himself suitably rewarded for his efforts. He felt a note thrust into his hand but this was not the reward he looked for. He was arranging the piano débris around the prostrate Jules when there was a knock on the door and Carr Faulkner entered.

The millionaire's eye fell first of all upon the coat over the chair.

"Who's is this?" he demanded.

The pause was hardly perceptible before she answered.

"I suppose it belongs to the piano man."

Faulkner looked across at the instrument and beheld the busy Trent taking what else was possible from the Stoneman. All the king's horses and all the king's men could not put that instrument together again easily. Trent went about his business with quiet persistence.

Carr Faulkner's voice was very courteous and kind as he addressed the tuner.

"I'm afraid I must ask you to wait outside in the hall for a few minutes until I have had a little private talk with my wife."

"Is that necessary," she said quickly. "I'm just going to dress for dinner. We have people coming, remember."

"There is time," he said meaningly. "I left my club half an hour earlier to-day. Did the change incommode you?"

"Why should it?" she said lightly.

Faulkner was a man of middle age with a fine thoughtful face. It was a face that made an instant appeal to Trent. It mirrored kindliness and good breeding, and reminded him in a subtle way of his own father, a country physician who had died a dozen years before his only son left the way of honest men.

"A few minutes only," he said and Trent passed out into the hall taking care to leave the door opened an inch or so. It was necessary for his peace of mind that he should know what it was Mr. Faulkner had to say to his wife. It might concern him vitally. It was possible that inquiry at Stoneman's might have informed Faulkner of his trickery. While this was improbable Trent was not minded to be careless. This kindly aspect of the millionaire might be assumed to put him off his guard; even now men might be stationed at the exits to arrest him. Very quietly he stole back to the door and listened.

"I have found out for certain what I have long suspected," Faulkner was saying to his wife. "It is always the husband who learns last. Don't protest," he added. "I know too much. I know for example that you have sold many of your jewels to provide funds for a gambler and a rascal."

"I don't know what you mean," she cried white-faced.

"You do," he said, and there was a trace of deep sadness in his voice. "You know too well. This man Jules d'Aucquier is not of a noble French family at all. He is a French-Canadian and was formerly a valet to an English officer of title at Ottawa. It was there he picked up this smattering of knowledge which has made it easy to fool the unsuspecting."

"I don't believe it," she cried vehemently.

He looked at her sadly. The whole scene was crucifixion for him.

"I shall prove it," he said quietly.

"I don't care if you do," she flung back at him.

"You would care for him just the same?" he asked.

"I have not said that I care for him at all," she said, a trace of caution creeping into her manner.

"I shall give you the opportunity to prove it one way or another within a few minutes. We have come to the parting of the ways."

It was at this moment Anthony Trent knocked timidly upon the door. The stage was set to his liking. When he was bidden to enter his quick eye took in everything. There, out of sight d'Aucquier skulked while he prepared to hear his despicable history told to the woman who was his victim. As for the woman she was defiant. She would probably elect to follow a scoundrel who had fascinated her and leave a man behind whose good name she had trailed in the dust. The situation was not a new one but Trent was moved by it. Carr Faulkner had all his sympathy. He registered a vow if ever he met d'Aucquier, or whatever his name might be, to exact a punishment.

"Excuse me," said Anthony Trent, stepping into the room, "but my train leaves in twenty minutes—I live out in Long Island—and I've got to catch it or else the missus will be worrying."

Mrs. Faulkner looked at him frowning. She wanted to get this scene over. He was a good looking piano tuner, she decided, and now his tragedy was plain. He who had no doubt once aimed at the concert stage tuned pianos to support a wife and home in Long Island!

"I'll finish the job to-morrow morning."

She waved him toward the door imperiously. Every moment she and her husband spent in this room added to the chance of the hiding man's discovery.

"Why don't you go?" she cried.

Anthony Trent permitted himself to smile faintly.

"I've come for my coat, Ma'am," he said, and glanced at the raiment d'Aucquier had thrown carelessly over a chair, the coat now laden with such precious cigarettes.

Carr Faulkner was growing impatient at this interruption. He could not understand the look of anger on his wife's face.

"Don't you understand," he exclaimed, "that the man merely wants to go home and take his coat with him?"

He turned to the deferential Trent.

"All right, all right," Trent moved to the chair and took the garment. At the door he turned about and bowed profoundly.

In the lower hall he found the cynical butler whose ideas on matrimony were so decided. He startled that functionary by thrusting into his hand the ten dollars d'Aucquier had forced upon him.

"What's this for?" demanded the butler. When piano tuners came with gifts in their hands he was suspicious. "I don't understand this." He observed that the affability which had made the tuner seem kin to himself was vanished. A different man now looked at him.

"It's for you," said Trent. "I'm not a piano tuner. I'm a detective and I came here after that ex-valet who pretends to be a French nobleman."

The butler breathed hard.

"I 'ate that man, sir," he said simply. "I'd like to dot him one."

"You'll be able to and that within five minutes," Trent assured him. "He is concealed behind the lid of the grand piano I was supposed to repair. Mr. and Mrs. Faulkner are both in the room but *he* doesn't know Jules is there. You take two footmen and yank him out and then if you want to 'dot him one' or two, there's your chance."

The muscles of the butler's big shoulders swelled with anticipation. "Where are you going?" he asked of Trent, now making for the front door.

"To get the patrol wagon," said Anthony Trent.

"How long will you be?" asked the man.

"I shall be back in no time," Trent answered cryptically.

Arrived in his quiet rooms he undid the box of cigarettes. At first he thought he had been fooled for the top layer of cigarettes were tobacco-filled and normal.

But it was on the next row that Mrs. Carr Faulkner had expended her trouble. Each one contained a new thousand dollar bill and their tint enthralled him.

CHAPTER XI

ESPIONAGE AT CLOSE RANGE

Cashing a modest check at the Colonial bank one morning, Trent had fallen in line with a queue at the paying teller's window. He made it a point to observe what went on while he waited. He was not much interested in bank robberies. To begin with the American Bankers' Association is a vengeful society pursuing to the death such as mulct its clients. Furthermore, a successful bank robbery, unless the work of an inside man, needs careful planning and collaboration.

On this particular morning Trent saw a stout and jocund gentleman push his check across the glass entrance to the cashier's cave and received without hesitation a large sum of money. He passed the time of day with the official, climbed into a limousine and was whirled up Broadway.

"Did yer see that?" a youth demanded who stood before Trent.

"What?" he asked quietly. It was not his pose to be interested in other of the bank's customers.

"That guy took out twenty thousand dollars," the boy said, reverence in his tone.

"That's a lot of money," said Trent.

"He lives well," said the lad. "I ought to know, he gets his groceries from us and he only eats and drinks the best."

"He looks like it," the other said genially. If the stout and jocund gourmet had known what was in Trent's mind he would have hied him back to the bank and redeposited his cash. "It's Rudolf Liebermann, isn't it?"

"That's Frederick Williams, and he lives on Ninety-third, near the Drive."

What additional information Trent wanted to know might be obtained from other than this boy. To make many inquiries might, if Frederick Williams were relieved of his roll, bring back the incident to the grocer's boy.

Directly dusk fell Anthony Trent, in the evening garb of fashion, crossed over to Riverside Drive and presently came to the heroic statue of Jeanne d'Arc which stands at the foot of Ninety-third Street. By this time he knew the license number of the Williams' limousine and the address. It was one of those small residences of gray stone containing a dozen rooms or so. Such houses, as he knew, were usually laid out on a similar plan and he was familiar with it.

It was very rarely that he made a professional visit to a house without having a definite plan of attack carefully worked out. This was the first time he sought to gain entrance to a strange house on the mere chance of success. But the twenty thousand dollars in crisp notes tempted him. In his last affair he had netted this sum in notes of a similar denomination and he was superstitious enough to feel that this augured well for to-night's success.

Careful as ever, Trent had made his alibis in case of failure. In one of his pockets was a pint flask of Bourbon, empty save for a dram of spirit. In another was a slip of paper containing the name of the house-holder who occupied a house with the same number as that of Williams, but on Ninety-fifth Street. Once before he had saved himself by this ruse. He had protested vigorously when detected by a footman that he was merely playing a practical joke on his old college chum who lived, as he thought, in this particular house, but was found to be on the next block. And in this case the emptied whiskey flask and the cheerful tipsiness of the amiable young man of fashion—Trent's most successful pose—saved him.

In his pockets nothing would be found to incriminate him. He knew well the folly of carrying the automatic so beloved of screen or stage Raffles. In the first place, the sudden temptation to murder in a tight pinch, and in the second the Sullivan law. In the bamboo cane, carefully concealed, were slender rods of steel whose presence few would suspect. He had left such a cane in Senator Scrivener's Fifth Avenue mansion when he was compelled to make an unrehearsed exit. Once he met the Senator coming down the steps of the Union Club with this cane in his hand. He chuckled to think what might be that worthy's chagrin to know he had been carrying burglar's tools with him.

As there was little light on the lower floor of Frederick Williams' house, Trent let himself in cautiously. There was a dim hanging light which showed that the Williams idea of furnishing was in massive bad taste. At the rear of the hall were the kitchens. Under the swinging door he could see a bright light. The stairs were wide and did not creak. Carefully he ascended them and stood breathless in a foyer between the two main reception-rooms. There were voices in the rear room, which should, if Williams conformed to the majority of dwellers in such houses, be the dining-room. Big doors shut out view and sound until he crept nearer and peeped through a keyhole. He could see Williams sitting in a Turkish rocker smoking a cigar. There were two other men and all three chattered volubly in German. Unfortunately it was a tongue of which the listener knew almost nothing. Reasonably fluent in French, the comprehension of German was beyond him. There was a small safe in the corner and it was not closed. Trent felt certain that in it reposed those notes he had come for.

In the corner of the foyer was a carven teakwood table with a glass top, and on it was a large Boston fern. It would be easy enough to crouch there unobserved. The only possibility of discovery was the remote contingency that Williams and his friends might choose to use this foyer. But Trent had seen that it was not furnished as a sitting-room.

He had barely determined on his hiding place when he found the sudden necessity to use it. Williams arose quickly and advanced to the door. When he threw it open the path of light left the unbidden one completely obscured. The three men passed by him and entered the drawing-room in front. Trent caught a view of a luxuriously over-furnished room and a grand piano. Then Williams began to play a part of a Brahms sonata so well that Trent's heart warmed toward him. But his appreciation of the master did not permit him to listen to the whole movement. He crept cautiously from his cover and into the room the three had just vacated. If there were other of Williams' friends or family here Trent might be called upon to exercise his undoubted talents. One man he would not hesitate to attack since his working knowledge of jiu-jitsu was beyond the average. If there were two, attack would be useless in the absence of a revolver. But if the coast were clear—ah, then, a competence, all the golf and fishing he desired. There would be only the Countess to deal with at his leisure.

The room was empty, but *the safe was closed*! Williams was not devoid of caution. A glance at the thing showed Trent that in an uninterrupted half hour he could learn its secrets. But he could hardly be assured of that at nine o'clock at night. His very presence in the room was fraught with danger. The one door leading from it opened into a butler's pantry from which a flight of stairs led into the kitchen part of the house. Downstairs he could hear faucets running. A dumbwaiter offered a way of escape if he were put to it. To the side of the dumbwaiter was a zinc-lined compartment used for drying dishes. It was four feet long and three in height and a shelf bisected it. This he took out carefully and placed upon the floor of the compartment, making an ample space for concealment. A radiator opened into it, giving the heat desired, and two iron gratings in the doors afforded Trent the opportunity to overhear what might be said. He satisfied himself that the doors opened noiselessly. The burglar's rôle was not always an heroic one, he told himself, and thought of the popular misconception of such activities.

It must have been an hour later when he heard sounds in the adjoining room. By this time he was fighting against the drowsiness induced by the heat of his prison.

The swinging door between the butler's pantry and the dining-room was thrown open and Williams came in. He leaned over the staircase and shouted something in German to some one in the kitchen, who answered him in the same tongue. There was the sound below of locking and bolting the doors. The servants had evidently been sent to bed.

When Williams went back to the other room the door between did not swing to by four or five inches. So far as Williams was concerned this carelessness was to cost him more than he guessed. Even in his hiding place the conversation was audible to Trent, although its meaning was incomprehensible.

He was suddenly awakened to a more vivid interest when he became aware that it was now English that they were talking. There was a new-comer in the room, a man with a nasal carrying voice and a prodigious brogue.

"This, gentlemen," he heard Williams say, "is Mr. O'Sheill, who has done so much good work for us and for the freedom of oppressed, starving, shackled Ireland, which we shall free. I may tell Mr. O'Sheill that the highest personages in the Fatherland weep bitter tears for Ireland's wrongs."

"That's all right," said the Sinn Feiner a trifle ungraciously, "but what's behind yonder door?"

For answer one of the other men flung it open, turned up the lights and permitted Mr. O'Sheill to make his examination. Trent heard the man's heavy tread as he descended the stairway and found at the bottom a locked door.

"You've got to be careful," O'Sheill said when he rejoined Williams and the rest. "These damned secret service men are everywhere, they tell me."

"That is why we have rented a private house," one of the Germans declared. "At an hotel privacy is impossible. We have had our experiences."

These scraps of conversation aroused Anthony Trent immediately. It required only a cursory knowledge of the affairs of the moment for a duller man than he to realize that he had come across the scent of one of those plots which were so hampering his government in their prosecution of the war. Very cautiously he crawled from his hiding place and made his silent way to the barely opened door.

O'Sheill was lighting a large cigar. His was a suspicious, dour face. Williams, urbane and florid, was very patient.

"That I do not tell you the names of my colleagues," he said, "is of no moment. It is sufficient to say that you have the honor to be in the presence of one of the most illustrious personages in my country." Here he bowed in the direction of a small, thin, dapper man who did not return the salutation.

"I came for the money," said O'Sheill.

"You came first for your instructions," snapped the illustrious personage coldly.

"That's so, yer Honor," O'Sheill answered. There was something menacing in the tone of the other man and he recognized it.

"This money," said Williams, "is given for very definite purposes and an accounting will be demanded."

"Ain't you satisfied with the way I managed it at Cork?" O'Sheill demanded.

"It was a beginning," Williams conceded. "Here is what you must do: Wherever along the Irish coast the English bluejackets and the American sailors foregather you must stir up bad blood. I do not pretend to give you any more precise direction than this. Let the Americans understand that the British call them cowards. Let the British think the same of the Yankees. Let there be bitter street fights, not in obscure drinking dens, but in the public streets in the light of day. I will see to it that the news gets back here and let Americans have something to think about when the next draft is raised. Find men in England to do what you must do in your own country. Let there be black blood between Briton and American from Belfast to Portsmouth. Let there be doubt and recrimination so that preparations are hindered here."

The man who passed as Williams looked venomous as he said this. The man to whom he spoke, thinking in his ignorance that he was indeed helping his native land instead of hurting it, and forgetful that in aiding the enemies of America he was stabbing a country which had ever been a faithful friend of Erin's, gave particulars of his operations which Trent memorized as best he might. He was appalled to hear to what length these men were prepared to go if only the good relations between the Allies might be brought to naught.

So engrossed was he with the importance of what he heard that the passing of the large sum of money from Williams to the Sinn Feiner lost much of its entrancing interest. Trent meant to have the money, but he intended also to give the Department of Justice what help he could.

It was not the first time that he had gone from one floor to another by means of a dumbwaiter. It was never an easy operation and rarely a noiseless one. In this instance he was fortunate in finding well-oiled pulleys. It was only when he stepped out in the kitchen that he ran into danger. There was a man asleep on a folding bed which had been drawn across the door. To leave by the front door immediately was imperative. Even were it possible to leave by a rear entrance he would find himself in the little garden at the back and could only get out by climbing a dozen fences. This would be to court observation and run unnecessary risks.

To invite electrocution by killing men was no part of Anthony Trent's practice. It was plain that the servant was slumbering fitfully and the act of stepping over him to freedom likely to awaken him instantly. Even if he had the needed rope at hand binding and gagging a vigorous man was at best a matter of noise and struggle. But something had to be done. He must reach the street in time to follow O'Sheill.

Superimposed on the bed's frame was a mattress and army blanket. Directly behind the sleeper's head was a door which led, as Trent knew from his knowledge of house design, to the cellar. It opened inward and without noise. He bent quietly over the man, put his hands gently beneath the mattress and then with a tremendous effort flung him, mattress, army blanket and all, down the cellar stairs. There was a clatter of breaking bottles, a cry that died away almost as it was uttered, and then the door was shut on silence.

A little later Williams, feeling the need for iced beer and cheese sandwiches, rang the bell for Fritz. When he received no answer he descended to the kitchen with the intention of buffeting soundly a man who could so forget his duties to his superiors. Mr. Williams found only the bare bed. Fritz, with his bedding, had disappeared.

A front door unlocked when instructions had been exact as to the necessity of its careful fastening at all hours, brought uneasy conjectures to his mind. It was only so long as he and his companions were invested with the immunity of neutrality that he was of value to his native land. Of late he had been conscious of Secret Service activities.

Obedient to his training, Williams instantly reported the matter to the thin, acid-faced man under whose instructions he had been commanded to act.

"They have taken Fritz away," he cried.

"Who?" demanded his superior.

"The Secret Service," said Williams wildly. He was now beginning to ascribe aggressive skill to a service at which he had formerly sneered.

Going down to the kitchen, they were startled by a feeble cry from the cellar. There they discovered the frightened Fritz, cut about the face from the bottles he had broken in his fall. His injuries gave him less concern than the admission he had slept at his post. He was, therefore, of no aid to them.

"I do not know," he repeated as they questioned him. "There must have been many of them. One man alone could not do it."

The thin man turned to Williams: "This O'Sheill is in danger. Arm yourself and go to his hotel. It will go badly with you if harm comes to him."

CHAPTER XII

THE SINN FEIN PLOT

Fortunately for O'Sheill's peace of mind, he left the house before Williams made his discovery. He stepped into the street painfully conscious of the large sum of money he carried. It seemed to him that every man looked at him suspiciously. A request for a match was met with an oath and the two women who asked him the location of a certain hotel drew back nervously at his scowl.

He boarded the Elevated at the Ninety-third Street station and alighted at Ninth Avenue and Forty-second Street, still glancing about him suspiciously. It was not until he was in his room on the top floor of a cheap and old hotel on the far West Side that he ventured to feel safe. He sighed with relief as he stuffed a Dublin clay with malodorous shag. Twenty thousand dollars! Four thousand pounds! Some would go to the traitorous work he was employed to prosecute, but a lot of it would go to satisfy private hates. And when it was exhausted there would be more to come. It would be easy to conceal the notes about his person, and, anyway, he reflected, he was not under suspicion.

He was aroused from his reveries by the sudden, gentle tapping on his door. After a few seconds of hesitation he called out:

"What is it ye want?"

The voice that answered him was strongly tinged with the German accent to which he had recently become used. It will not be forgotten that Anthony Trent had a genius for mimicry.

"I'm from Mr. Williams," said the stranger gutturally. He had followed O'Sheill with no difficulty.

"What's your name?" O'Sheill demanded.

"We won't give names," Trent reminded him significantly. "But I can prove my identity. I was in the house at Ninety-third Street when you came. The money was given you to stir up trouble in Ireland and circulate rumors that will embarrass the British government and made bad blood between English and American sailors. You have twenty one-thousand-dollar bills and you put them in a green oilskin package."

"That's right," O'Sheill admitted, "but what do you want?"

He was filled with a vague uneasiness. This young man seemed so terribly in earnest and his eyes darted from door to window and window to door as though he feared interruption.

"Mr. Williams sent me here to see if you had been followed. Directly you went we had information from an agent of ours that your visit was known to the Secret Service. Tell me, did any person speak to you on your way here?"

"No," answered O'Sheill, now thoroughly nervous by the other's anxiety.

"Are you sure?" he was asked.

"There was one fellow who asked me for a light, but I told him to go to hell and get it."

"Anything suspicious about him?" Trent demanded.

"Not that I could see."

"That will be good news for Mr. Williams," Trent returned. "Our agent said the Hunchback was on the job."

"Who's he?" O'Sheill said.

"One of our most dangerous enemies," the younger man retorted. "He's a man of forty, but looks younger. He had one shoulder higher than the other and he limps when he walks. He's the man we're afraid of. I think we have alarmed ourselves unnecessarily."

O'Sheill's face was no longer merely uneasy. He was terror-stricken.

"And I guess we haven't," he exclaimed. *"The man who asked me for a light was a hunchback.* There was two women who asked me the way to some blasted hotel. They looked at me as if they wanted never to forget my face."

"Stop a minute," said Trent gravely. "Answer me exactly about these women. I want to know in what danger we all stand. The only two women known by sight to us who are likely to be put on a case of this kind wouldn't look like detectives. There's Mrs. Daniels and Miss Barrett. They work as mother and daughter. Mrs. Daniels is gray-haired, tall and slight, with a big nose for a woman and eyes set close together. When she looks at you it seems as if the eyes were gimlets. The girl is pretty, reddish hair and laughing eyes." Trent paused for a moment to think of any other attributes he could ascribe to the unknown women he had directed to their hotel just after O'Sheill had scowled at them a half hour back. "And very white little teeth."

"My God!" cried O'Sheill, his arms dropping at his side, "that's them to the life! What's going to happen to me?"

"If they find you with that money you'll be deported and handed over to your British friends. How can you explain having twenty thousand dollars? Mr. Williams thought of that, but he didn't actually know they were on your trail. You must give me the money. I shan't be stopped. You are to stay here. They may be here in five minutes or they may wait till morning, but you may be certain that you won't be allowed to get away. You must claim to be just over here to get an insight into labor conditions." Mr. Williams' messenger chuckled. "I don't believe they can get anything on you."

"But if they do?" O'Sheill demanded. It seemed to him that the stranger's levity was singularly ill-timed.

"If they do," Trent advised, "you must remember that you're a British subject still—whether you like it or not—and you have certain inalienable rights. Immediately appeal to the British authorities. Give the Earl of Reading some work to do. Make the Consul-General here stir himself. Tell them you came over here to investigate labor conditions. That story goes any time and just now it's fashionable. As an Irishman you'll have far more consideration from the British Government than if you were merely an Englishman."

"But what about this money?" O'Sheill queried uneasily.

"I'll take it," Trent told him. "If it's found on you nothing can do you any good. You'll do your plotting in a British jail."

O'Sheill was amazed at the careless manner in which this large sum was thrust into the other man's pocket. Surely these accomplices of his dealt in big things.

"When you're ready to sail you can get it back," Trent continued. "That can be arranged later. Meanwhile don't forget my instructions. Be indignant when you are searched. Call on the British Ambassador." Trent paused suddenly. An idea had struck him. "By the way," he went on, "you have other things that would get you into trouble beside that money."

"I know it," O'Sheill admitted. "What am I to do with them?"

"I'm taking a chance if they are found on me," the younger man commented. "But they are not after me. Give me what you have," he cried.

Into this keeping the frightened O'Sheill confided certain letters which later were to prove such an admirable aid to the United States Government.

It was as Trent turned to the door that he heard steps coming along the passage as softly as the creaking boards permitted.

He placed his fingers on his lips and enjoined silence. The furtive sound completed O'Sheill's distress. He felt himself entrapped. Trent saw him take from his hip pocket a revolver.

"Not yet," he whispered. "Wait."

He turned down the gas to a tiny glimmer. Through the transom the stronger light in the passage was seen. It was but a slight effort for the muscular Trent to draw himself up so that he could peer through the transom at the man tapping softly at the door.

Unquestionably it was Williams, and the hand concealed in his right hand coat pocket was no doubt gripping the butt of an automatic. He was a man of great physical strength, that Trent had noted earlier in the evening. Although of enormous strength himself, and a boxer and wrestler, he knew he would stand no chance if these two discovered his errand. There was no other exit than the door.

Anthony Trent stepped silently to O'Sheill's side.

"It's the Hunchback," he whispered. "If once he gets those long fingers around your throat you're gone. Listen to me. I'm going to turn the gas out. Then I shall open the door. When he rushes in get him. If he gets you instead I'll be on the top of him and we'll tie him up. Ready?"

The prospect of a fight restored O'Sheill's spirits. Every line of his evil face was a black menace to Friedrich Wilhelm outside.

"Don't use your revolver," Anthony Trent cautioned.

"Why?" O'Sheill whispered.

"We can't stand police investigation," said the other. "Get ready now I'm going to open the door."

When he flung it open Williams stepped quickly in. O'Sheill maddened at the very thought that any one imperiled his money, could only see, in the dim light, an enemy. The first blow he struck landed fair and square on the Prussian nose. On his part Williams supposed the attack a premeditated one. O'Sheill was playing him false. The pain of the blow awoke his own hot temper and made him killing mad. He sought to get his strong arms about the Sinn Feiner's throat.

It was while they thrashed about on the floor that Anthony Trent made his escape. He closed the door of the room carefully and locked it from the outside. Then he unscrewed the electric bulb that lit the hall. None saw him pass into the street. It was one of his triumphant nights.

Next morning at breakfast he found Mrs. Kinney much interested in the city's police news as set forth in the papers.

He was singularly cheerful.

"What is it?" he demanded. "Some very dreadful crime?"

"A double murder," she told him, "and the police don't seem to be able to figure it out at all."

Trent sipped his coffee gratefully.

"What's strange about that?" he demanded.

"I don't see," Mrs. Kinney went on, "what a gentleman like this Mr. Williams seems to have been——"

Anthony Trent put down his cup.

"What's his other name?" he inquired.

"Frederick," said the interested Mrs. Kinney. "Frederick Williams, a Holland Dutch gentleman living in Ninety-third Street near the Drive. He aided the Red Cross and bought Liberty Bonds. What I want to know is why he went to a low place like the Shipwrights Hotel to see a man named O'Sheill from Liverpool, England?"

"A double murder?" he demanded.

"Here it is," she returned, and showed him the paper. The two men had been found dead, the report ran, under mysterious circumstances, but the police thought a solution would quickly be found. Anthony Trent smiled as he read of official optimism. He was inclined to doubt it.

When Mrs. Kinney was out shopping he read through the documents he had taken from O'Sheill. They seemed to him to be of prime importance. There was a list of American Sinn Feiners implicating men in high positions, men against whom so far nothing detrimental was known. Outlines of plots were made bare to embroil and antagonize Britain and the United States—allies in the great cause—and all that subtle propaganda which had nothing to do with the betterment of prosperous Ireland but everything to do with Prussian aggrandizement. It was a poisonous collection of documents.

The chief of the Department of Justice in New York was called up from a public station and informed that a messenger was on his way with very important papers. The chief was warned to make immediate search of the premises at Ninety-third Street where a highly important German spy might be captured.

In the evening papers Anthony Trent was gratified to learn that the highly-born, thin, haughty person was none other than the Baron von Reisende who had received his *congé* with Bernstorff and was thought to be in the Wilmhelmstrasse. He had probably returned by way of Mexico.

And certain politicians of the baser sort were sternly warned against plotting the downfall of America's allies. Altogether Trent had done a good night's work for his country. As for himself twenty thousand dollars went far toward making the total he desired.

Consistent success in such enterprises as his was leading him into a feeling that he would not be run to earth as had been those lesser practitioners of crime who lacked his subtlety and shared their secrets with others.

But there was always the chance that he had been observed when he thought he was alone in some great house. Austin, the Conington Warren butler, looked him full in the face on his first adventure. And that other butler who served the millionaire whose piano he had wrecked might, some day, place a hand on his shoulder and denounce him to the world. Yet butlers were beings whose duties took them little abroad. They did not greatly perturb him.

CHAPTER XIII

ANTHONY TRENT INTERESTS
HIMSELF IN POLICE GOSSIP

So far as he knew, none suspected him. His face had been seen on one or two occasions, but he was of a type common among young Americans of the educated classes. Above middle height, slenderly fashioned but wire-strong, he had a shrewd, humorous face with strongly marked features. It might be that the nose was a trifle large and the mouth a trifle tight, but none looking at him would say, "There goes a criminal." They would say, rather, "There goes a resourceful young business man who can rise to any emergency."

Since Trent had calculated everything to a nicety, he knew he must, during these harvesting years, deny himself the privilege of friendship with other men or women. Too many of his gild had lost their liberty through some errant desire to be confidential. This habit of solitude was trying to a man naturally of a sociable nature, but he determined that it could be cast from him as one throws away an old coat when he was a burglar emeritus.

That blessed moment had arrived. He even looked up an old editor friend, the man who had first put into his mind that he could make more money at burglary than in writing fiction.

"It's good to see you again!" cried the editor. "I often wish you hadn't been left money by that Australian uncle of yours, so that you could still write those corking crook yarns for us. There was never any one like you. I was talking about you at the Scribblers' Club dinner the other night."

Trent frowned. Publicity was a thing to avoid and this particular editor had always been ready to sound his praise. The editor had once before asked him to join this little club made up of professional writers. They were men he would have delighted to know under other conditions.

"Be my guest next Tuesday," the editor persisted. "I'm toastmaster and the subject is 'Crime in Fiction. ' I told the boys I'd get you to speak if I possibly could. I'm counting on you. Will you do it?"

It seemed a deliciously ironical thing. Here was an honest editor asking the friend he did not know to be a master criminal to make an address on crime in fiction. Trent laughed the noiseless laugh he had cultivated in place of the one that was in reality the expression of himself. The editor thought it a good sign.

"Who are the other speakers?" Trent demanded.

"Oppenheim Phelps for one. He's over here on a visit. His specialty is high-grade international spy stuff, as you know. E. W. Hornung would be the man to have if we could get him, but that's impossible. I've got half a dozen others, but Phelps and you will be the drawing cards."

"Put me down," Trent said genially, "but introduce me as a back number almost out of touch with things but willing to oblige a pal." He laughed again his noiseless laugh.

Crosbeigh looked at him meditatively. Certainly Anthony Trent was changed. In the old days, before he came into Australian money, he was at times jocund with the fruitful grape, a good fellow, a raconteur, one who had been popular at school and college and liked to stand well with his fellows. But now, Crosbeigh reflected, he was changed. There was a certain suspicion about him, a lack of trust in men's motives. It was the attitude no doubt which wealth brought. The moneyless man can meet a borrower cheerfully and need cudgel his mind for no other excuse than his poverty.

Crosbeigh was certain Trent had a lot of money for the reason he had actually refused four cents a word for what he had previously received only two cents. But the editor admired his old contributor and was glad to see him again.

"I'm going to spring a surprise on you," Crosbeigh declared, "and I'm willing to bet you'll enjoy it."

"I hope so," Trent returned, idly, and little dreamed what lay before him.

The dinner was at a chop house and the food no worse than the run of city restaurants. Anthony Trent, who had fared delicately for some time, put up with the viands readily enough for the pleasure of being again among men of the craft which had been his own.

Oppenheim Phelps was interesting. He was introduced as a historian who had made his name at fiction. It was a satisfaction, he said, to find that modern events had justified him. The reviewers had formerly treated him with patronizing airs; they had called his secret diplomacy and German plot-stuff as chimeras only when they had shown themselves to be transcripts, and not exaggerated ones at that, of what had taken place during the last few years.

Anthony Trent sat next to the English novelist and liked him. It brought him close to the war to talk to a man whose home had been bombed from air and submarine. And Phelps was also a golfer and asked Trent, when the war was over, to visit his own beloved links at Cromer.

It had grown so late when the particularly prosy member of the club had made his yawn-bringing speech, that Crosbeigh came apologetically to Trent's side.

"I'm afraid, old man," he began, "that it's too late for any more speeches except the surprise one. A lot of us commute. Do you mind speaking at our next meeting instead?"

"Not a bit," Trent said cheerfully. But he felt as all speakers do under these circumstances that his speech would have been a brilliant one. He had coined a number of epigrams as other speakers had plowed laboriously along their lingual way and now they were to be still-born.

But he soon forgot them when Crosbeigh announced the surprise speaker.

"I have been very fortunate," Crosbeigh began, "in getting to-night a man who knows more of the ways of crooks than any living authority. Gentlemen, you all know Inspector McWalsh!"

"Well, boys," said the Inspector, "I guess a good many of you know me by name." He had risen to his full height and looked about him genially. He had imbibed just the right amount to bring him to this stage. Three highballs later, he would be looking for insults but he was now ripe with good humor. He had come because Conington Warren had asked him to oblige Crosbeigh. For writers on crime he had the usual contempt of the professional policeman and he was fluent in his denunciation. "You boys," he went on, "make me smile with your modern scientific criminals, the guys what use chemistry and electricity and x-rays and so forth. I've been a policeman now for thirty years and I never run across any of that stuff yet."

Inspector McWalsh poured his unsubtle scorn on such writings for ten full minutes. But he added nothing to the Scribblers' knowledge of his subject.

It chanced that the writer he had taken as his victim was a guest at the dinner. This fictioneer pursued the latest writings on physicist and chemical research so that he might embroider his tales therewith. Personally Trent was bored by this artificial type of story; but as between writer and policeman he was always for the writer.

The writer was plainly angry but the gods had not blessed him with a ready tongue and he was prepared to sit silent under McWalsh's scorn. Some mischievous devil prompted Anthony Trent to rise to his aid. It was a bold thing to do, to draw the attention of the man who had been in charge of the detectives sent to run him to earth, but of late excitement had been lacking.

"Inspector McWalsh," he commenced, "possesses precisely that type of mind one would expect to find in a successful policeman. He has that absolute absence of imagination without which one cannot attain his rank in the force. All he has done in his speech is to pour his scorn of a certain type of crime story on its author. As writers we are sorry if

Inspector McWalsh never heard of the Einthoven string galvanometer upon which the solution of the story he ridicules rests, yet we know it to exist. Were I a criminal instead of a writer I should enjoy to cross swords with men who think as the Inspector does. I could outguess them every time."

"Who is this guy?" Inspector McWalsh demanded loudly.

"Anthony Trent," Mr. Crosbeigh whispered. "He wrote some wonderful crook stories a few years ago dealing with a crook called Conway Parker."

"What one would expect to hear from a man with McWalsh's opportunities to deal with crime is some of the difficulty he experiences in his work. There must be difficulty. We know by statistics what crimes are committed and what criminals brought to justice. What happens to the crooks who remain safe from arrest by reason of superior skill? I'll tell you, gentlemen. They live well and snap their fingers at men like the last speaker. There is such a thing as fatty degeneration of the brain——"

Inspector McWalsh rose to his feet with a roar. "I didn't come here to be insulted."

"I am not insulting a guest," Trent went on equably, "I am asking him to tell us interesting things of his professional work instead of giving his opinion on modern science. I met McWalsh years ago when I covered Mulberry Street for the *Morning Leader*. He was captain then. Let him entertain us with some of the reasons why the Ashy Bennet murderer was never caught. You remember, gentlemen, that Bennet was shot down on Park Row at midday. Then the thoroughbred racer Foxkeen was poisoned in his stall at Sheepshead Bay. Why was that crime never punished? I remember a dozen others where the police have been beaten. Coming down to the present time, there is the robbery of the house of the genial sportsman Inspector McWalsh tells us he is proud to call his friend, Conington Warren. How was it the burglar or burglars were allowed to escape?" Trent was enjoying himself hugely. "I have a right to demand protection of the New York police. In my own humble home I have valuables bequeathed me by an uncle in Australia which are never safe while such men as snap their fingers at the police are at large. Let Inspector McWalsh tell us why his men fail. It will help us, perhaps, to understand the difficulties under which they labor. It may help us to appreciate the silent unadvertised work of the police. The Inspector is a good sport who loves a race horse and a good glove fight as much as I do myself. I assure him he will make us grateful if he will take the hint of a humble scribbler."

The applause which followed gratified the Inspector enormously. He thought it was evidence of his popularity, a tribute to his known fondness for the race tracks. His anger melted.

"Boys," he shouted, rising to his feet and waving a Larranaga to the applauders, "I guess he's right and I hope the fellow who writes that scientific dope will accept my word that it wasn't personal. Of course we do have difficulties. I admit it. I had charge of that Ashy Bennet murder and I'd give a thousand dollars to be able to put my hand on the man who done it. As to Foxkeen I had a thousand on him to win at eight-to-one and when he was poisoned the odds were shortening every minute so you can guess I was sore on the skunk who poisoned him. The police of all countries fail and they fail the most in countries where people have most sympathy with crime. Boys, you know you all like a clever crook to get away with it. It's human nature. We ain't helped all we could be and you know it. We, 'gentlemen of the police, '" he quoted Austin's words glibly, "we make mistakes sometimes. We get the ordinary crook easy enough. If you don't believe me get a permit to look over Sing Sing. The crimes the last speaker mentioned were committed by clever men. They get away with it. The clever ones do get away with things for a bit. But if the guy who croaked Bennet tried murder again the odds are we'd gather him in. Same with the man or men who put strychnine in Foxkeen's oats. The clever ones get careless. That's our opportunity."

The Inspector lighted a new cigar, sipped his highball and came back to his speech.

"Boys, I'm not rich—no honest cop is—but I'd give a lot of money to get my hands on a gentleman crook who's operating right now in this city. I've got a list of seven tricks I'm certain he done himself. He's got technique." Inspector McWalsh turned purple red, "Dammit, he made me an accomplice to one of his crimes. Yes, sir, he made me carry a vase worth ten thousand dollars out of Senator Scrivener's house on Fifth Avenue and hand it to him in his taxi. He had a silk hat, a cane and a coat and he asked me to hold the vase for a moment while he put his coat on. I thought he was a friend of the Senator so I trotted down the hall—there was a big reception on—down the steps past my own men on watch for this very crook or some one like him, and handed it through the window. None of my men thought of questioning him. Why did he do it you wonder. He did it because he thought some one *might* have seen him swipe it. The thing was thousands of years old and if any of you find it Senator Scrivener stands ready to give you five thousand dollars reward. I believe he took the——" Inspector McWalsh stopped. He thought it wiser to say no more. "That's about all now," he concluded. Then with a flourish he added, "Gentlemen, I thank you."

McWalsh sat down with the thunder of applause ringing gratefully in his ears. And none applauded more heartily than Anthony Trent.

CHAPTER XIV

AMBULANCES AND DIAMONDS

There was an opportunity later on to visit the Scribblers again. Crosbeigh begged him to come as he desired a full attendance in honor of an occasion unique in the club's history.

It seemed that some soldier members of the club, foregathering in New York, offered the opportunity for a meeting that might never recur. The toastmaster was a former officer and the speakers were men who had fought through the ghastly early years of the war before the United States came into it.

It happened that Trent had known the toastmaster, Captain Alan Kent, when the two had been newspaper cubs together. In those days Kent had been an irresponsible, happy-go-lucky youngster, liked by all for his carefree disposition. To-day, after three years of war, he was a sterner man, in whose eyes shone steadily the conviction of the cause he had espoused. War had purged the dross from him.

"You boys, here," he said, "haven't suffered enough. You haven't seen nations in agony as we have. The theater of war is still too remote. The loss of a transport wakens you to renewed effort for a moment and then you get back to thinking of other things, more agreeable things, and speculate as to when the war will be over. I've spoken to rich men who seem to think they've done all that is required of them by purchasing a few Liberty Bonds. They must be bought if we are to win the war, but there's little of the personal element of sacrifice in merely buying interest-bearing bonds."

He launched into a description of war as he had seen it, dwelling on the character it developed rather than the horrors he had suffered, horrors such as are depicted in the widely circulated book of Henri Barbusse. This mention of negative patriotism rather disturbed Anthony Trent. All he had done was to buy Liberty Bonds. And here was Alan Kent, who had lived through three years of hell to come back full of courage and cheer, and anxious, when his health was reestablished, to leave the British Service and enroll in the armies of America. It was not agreeable for him to think how he had passed those three years.

He was awakened from these unpleasant thoughts by the applause which followed Kent's speech. The next speaker was an ambulance driver, who made a plea for more and yet more ambulances.

"Lots of you people here," he said, "seem to think that when once a battery of ambulances are donated they are there till the war is over.

They suffer as much as guns or horses. The Huns get special marks over there for potting an ambulance, and they're getting to be experts at the game. I've had three of Hen. Ford's little masterpieces shot under me, so to speak. I'm trying to interest individuals in giving ambulances. They're not very expensive. You can equip one for $5, 000. Men have said to me, 'What's the use of one ambulance?' I tell them as I tell you that the one they may send will do its work before it's knocked out. It may pick up a brother or pal of a man in this room. It may pick up some of you boys even, for some of you are going. God, it makes me tired this cry of what's the use of 'one little ambulance.'"

When the dinner was over Trent renewed his acquaintance with Captain Kent and was introduced to Lincoln, the Harvardian driver of an ambulance. Over coffee in the Pirates' Den Lincoln told them more of his work.

"This afternoon," he said, "I had tea with the Baroness von Eckstein. You know who she is?"

Trent nodded. The Baroness was the enormously wealthy widow of a St. Louis brewer who had married a Westphalian noble and hoped thereby to get into New York and Washington society. The Baron had been willing to sell his title—not an old one—for all the comforts of a wealthy home. He had become naturalized and was not suspected by the Department of Justice of treachery. His one ambition seemed to be to drink himself to death on the best cognac that could be obtained. This potent brew, taken half and half with champagne, seemed likely to do its work. It was rumored that his wife did not hinder him in this interesting pursuit.

"I sat behind him at a theater once," Trent admitted. "He's a thin little man with an enormous head and a strong Prussian accent." He resisted the temptation to mimic the Baron as he could have done. He could not readily banish his professional caution.

"I tried to get the Baroness to buy and equip four ambulances," Lincoln went on. "It would only have cost her twenty thousand dollars—nothing to her—but she refused."

"Before we went into the war," Captain Kent reminded him, "she was strongly pro-German."

"She's had enough sense to stop that talk in New York," Lincoln went on. "She's still trying to break into the Four Hundred and you've got to be loyal to your country for that, thank God!"

"I thought she was in St. Louis," Trent observed.

"She's taken a house in town," Lincoln told him. "The Burton Trent mansion on Washington Square, North. Took it furnished for three months. She had to pay like the deuce for the privilege. *Gotham Gossip* unkindly remarks that she did it so some of the Burton Trents' friends may call on her, thinking they are visiting the Trents. It's the nearest she'll ever get to high society. It made me sick to hear her hard luck story. Couldn't give me a measly twenty thousand dollars because of income tax and high cost of living and all that sort of bunk, while she had a hundred thousand dollars in diamonds on her fat neck. I felt like pulling them off her."

Anthony Trent pricked up his ears at this.

"I didn't know she had a necklace of that value," he mused.

"I guess you don't know much about the fortunes these millionaire women hang all over 'em," said Lincoln. Lincoln had an idea the other man was a bookish scholar, a collector of rare editions, one removed from knowledge of society life.

"That must be it," Trent agreed. He wondered if another man in all America had so intimate a knowledge of the disposition of famous gems. "So she won't give you any money for ambulances?"

"It's known she subscribed largely to the German Red Cross before we got into the war. Leopards don't change their spots easily, as you know. It was one of her chauffeurs at her country place near Roslyn who rigged up a wireless and didn't know he was doing anything the government disapproved of. His mistress lent him the money to equip the thing and she didn't know she ought not to have done it. I tell you I felt like pulling that necklace off her fat old neck. Wouldn't you feel that way?"

"It might make me," Trent admitted, "a little envious."

On the whole, Trent enjoyed his first evening of emancipation immensely. Particularly glad was he to meet his old friend, Alan Kent, again. The repressed life he had led made him more than ever susceptible to the hearty friendship of such men as he had met.

With some of them he made arrangements to go to a costume dance, a Greenwich Village festival, at Webster Hall, on the following evening. He did not know that Captain Kent was attending less as one who would enjoy the function socially than an emissary of his government. It was known that many of the villagers had not registered. Some had spoken openly against the draft and others were suspected of pro-German tendencies that might be dangerous. It was not a commission Kent cared about, but it was a time in the national history where old friendships must count for naught. Treason must be stamped out.

It was not until midnight that Trent dropped into Webster Hall. It was the nearest approach to the boulevard dances that New York ever saw. The costumes were gorgeous, some of them, but for the greater part quaint and bizarre. As a Pierrot he was inconspicuous. There were a number of men he knew from the Scribblers' Club. He greeted Lincoln with enthusiasm. He liked the lad. He envied him his record. It was while he was talking to him that a gorgeously dressed woman seized Lincoln's hands as one might grasp those of an old and dear friend.

"Naughty boy," she said playfully. "Why haven't you asked me to dance?"

"I feared I wasn't good enough for you," Lincoln lied with affable readiness. "You dance like a professional."

While this badinage went on Trent gazed at the woman with idle curiosity. Her enameled face, penciled eyebrows and generally careful make-up made her look no more than five-and-forty. Her hair was henna-colored, with purple depths in it. She was too heavy for her height and her eyes were bright with the light that comes in cocktail glasses. She had reached the fan-tapping, coquettish, slightly amorous stage. Her bold eyes soon fell on Anthony Trent, who was a far more personable man than Lincoln.

"Who is your good-looking friend?" she demanded.

Lincoln was bound to make the introduction. From his manner Trent imagined he was not over-pleased at having to do so.

"Mr. Anthony Trent—the Baroness von Eckstein," he said.

The Baroness instantly put her bejeweled hand within Trent's arm.

"I am sure you dance divinely," she cooed.

Lincoln was a little disappointed at the readiness with which the older man answered.

"If you will dance with me I shall be inspired," said Trent.

"Very banal," Lincoln muttered as the two floated away from him.

"I'm so glad to be rescued from Lincoln," he told her. "He is so earnest and seems to think I have an ambulance in every pocket for him."

"This begging, begging, begging is very tiresome," the Baroness admitted. She wished she might say exactly what she and her noble husband felt concerning it. She had understood that some of these artists and writers in the village were exceedingly liberal in their views. "Mrs. Adrien Beekman has been bothering me about giving ambulances all this afternoon."

"She is most patriotic," he smiled, "but boring all the same."

"I suppose you are one of these delightfully bad young men who say and do dreadful things," she hazarded, a little later.

"I am both delightful and bad," he admitted, "and a number of the things I have done and shall do are dreadful."

"I am afraid of you," she cried coquettishly.

There was about her throat a magnificent necklace, evidently that of which Lincoln had spoken at the Scribblers' dinner. It was worth perhaps half of what the ambulance man had said. The stones were set in platinum.

"I wonder you are not afraid of wearing such a magnificent necklace here," he said later.

"Are you so dangerous as that?" she retorted.

"Worse," he answered.

She looked at him curiously. The Baroness liked young and good-looking men. Trent knew perfectly well what was going on in her mind. He had met women of this type before; women who could buy what they wanted and need not haggle at the price. Her eyes appraised him and she was satisfied with what she saw.

"I believe you are just as bad as you pretend to be," she declared.

"Do I disappoint you?" he demanded.

"Of course," she laughed, "I shall have to reform you. I am very good at reforming fascinating man-devils like you. You must come and have tea with me one afternoon."

"What afternoon?" he asked.

"To-morrow," she said, "at four."

If she had guessed with what repulsion she had inspired Trent she would have been startled. She was a type he detested.

Later he said:

"Isn't it unwise of you to wear such a gorgeous necklace at a mixed gathering like this?"

"If it were real it would be," she answered. "Don't tell any one," she commanded, "but this is only an imitation. The real one is on my dressing table. This was made in the Rue de la Paix for me and only an expert could tell the difference and then he'd have to know his business."

"What are you frowning at?" he demanded when he saw her gaze directed toward a rather noisy group of newcomers.

"These are my guests," she whispered. "I'd forgotten all about them. Doesn't that make you vain? I shall have to look after them. Later on they are all coming over to the house to have a bite to eat." She squeezed his hand. "You'd better come, too."

The Baroness was not usually so reckless in her invitations. She had learned it was not being done in those circles to which she aspired. But to-night she was unusually merry and there was something about Trent's keen, hawk-like type which appealed to her. Lincoln, she reflected, came of a good Boston family with houses in Beacon Street and Pride's Crossing, and his friend *must* be all right.

No sooner had she moved toward her guests than Trent made his way to the street. Over his costume he wore a long black cloak which another than he had hired. Very few people were abroad. There was a slight fog and those who saw him were in no way amazed. Webster Hall dances had prepared the neighborhood for anything.

He was not long in coming to Washington Square. It was in the block of houses on the north side that he was specially interested. From the other side of the road he gazed up at the Burton Trent house. Then going east a little, he came to the door of the only apartment house in the block. It was not difficult for him to manipulate the lock. Quietly he climbed to the top of the house until he came to a ladder leading to the door on the roof.

A few feet below him he could see the roof of the neighboring house. To this he dropped silently and walked along until the square skylight of the Burton Trent mansion was at hand. The bars that held the aperture were rusted. It required merely the exercise of strength to pry one of them loose. Underneath him was darkness. Since Trent had not come out originally on professional business, he was without an electric torch. He had no idea how far the drop would be. Very carefully he crawled in, and, hanging by one hand, struck a match. He dropped on to the floor of an attic used mainly for the storage of trunks.

The door leading from the room was unlocked and he stepped out into a dark corridor. Looking over the balustrade, he could see that the floor below was brilliantly lighted. From an article in a magazine devoted to interior decoration he had learned the complete lay-out of the residence. He knew, for example, that the servants slept in the "el" of the house which abutted on the mews behind. Ordinarily he would have expected them to be in bed by this time. But the Baroness had told him she had guests coming in. There would inevitably be some servants making preparations. They would hardly have business on the second or third floors of the house. The Burton Trents, who had let their superb home as a war-economy measure, would never allow any alteration of the arrangement of their wonderful furniture. And the Baroness would hardly be likely to venture to set her taste against that of a family she admired and indeed envied. It was therefore probable that the Baroness occupied the splendid sleeping chamber on the second floor front, an apartment to which the writer on interior decoration had devoted several pages.

His borrowed cloak enveloping him, he descended the broad stairs until he stood at the entrance of the room he sought. It was indeed a magnificent place. His artistic sense delighted in it. Its furniture had once been in the sleeping room of a Venetian Doge. It had cost a fortune to buy.

The dressing room leading from it was lighted more brilliantly. There was a danger that the Baroness's maid might be there awaiting the return of her mistress.

Peeping through the half-opened door, he satisfied himself that no maid was there. On the superb dressing table with its rich ornaments he could see a large gold casket, jewel-encrusted, which probably hid the stones he had come to get.

Swiftly he crossed the soft Aubusson carpet and came to the table. He was far too cautious to lay hands on the metal box straightaway. Although he was nameless and numberless so far as the police were concerned, he was not anxious to leave finger-prints behind. He knew that in all robberies such as he intended the police carefully preserve the finger-prints amongst the records of the case and hope eventually to saddle the criminal with indisputable evidence of his theft. Usually Parker wore the white kid gloves that go with full evening dress. To-night he was without them. He was also in the habit of carrying a tube of collodion to coat the finger-tips and defy the finger-printers. This, too, he was without since his adventure was an unpremeditated one.

While he was wondering how to set about his business, he was startled by a sound behind him. From the cover of a *chaise longue* at the far end of the room a small, thin man raised himself. Trent knew in a moment it was the Baron von Eckstein. He relaxed his tense attitude and walked with a friendly smile to the other man. He had mentally rehearsed the rôle he was to play. But the Baron surprised him.

"Hip, hip, 'ooray!" hiccoughed the aristocrat.

There was not a doubt as to his condition. He swayed as he tried to sit up straighter. His eyes were glazed with drink.

CHAPTER XV

THE BARON LENDS A HAND

"Hip, hip, 'ooray!" said the Baron again, and sank back into bibulous slumber. By his side on a tray was a half-emptied bottle of liqueur cognac and an open bottle of champagne. He had evidently been consuming over-many champagne and brandy highballs. Anthony Trent considered him for a few moments in silence. He saw a way out of his difficulties and a certain ironical method of fooling investigation which pleased him more than a little.

In a tall tumbler he mixed brandy and champagne—half and half—and poked the little Baron in the ribs. The familiar sight of being offered his favorite tipple made the trembling hand seize the glass. The contents was absorbed greedily, and the Baron fell back on the *chaise longue*.

The well-worn phrase "dead to the world" alone describes the condition of the Baron, who had married a brewery. Trent raised the man—he could have weighed no more than a hundred pounds—in his strong arms and carried him across to the dressing table. And with the Baron's limp hands he opened the jewel case. Therefrom he extracted a necklace of diamonds set in platinum. What else was there he did not touch. He had a definitely planned course of action in view. The Baron's recording fingers closed the box. It would be as pretty a case of finger-prints as ever gladdened the heart of a central-office detective. The Baron was next carried to the *chaise longue*. He would not wake for several hours. It would have been quite easy for Trent to make his escape undetected. But there was something else to be done first. He locked the door of the Venetian bedroom and then took up the telephone receiver. His carefully trained memory recorded the accent and voice of the Baron von Eckstein as he had heard it during an evening at the theater.

He called a telephone number. Fortunately it was a private wire connecting with the central.

"I wish to speak to Mrs. Adrien Beekman," he said when at length there was an answer to his call.

"She is in bed," a sleepy voice returned. "She can't be disturbed."

"She must be," said Trent, mimicking the Baron. "It is a matter of vast importance. Tell her a gentleman wishes to present her ambulance fund with a large sum of money. To-morrow will be too late."

"I'll see what can be done," said the voice. "That's about the only matter I dare disturb her on. Hold the wire."

"Madam," said Trent a minute later, "it is the Baron von Eckstein who has the honor to speak with you."

"An odd hour to choose," returned Mrs. Adrien Beekman with no cordiality.

"I wish to make reparation, Madam," the pseudo Baron flung back. "This afternoon you talked to my wife, the Baroness, about your ambulances."

"And found her not interested in the least," Mrs. Beekman said, a little crossly. So eminent a leader of society as she was not accustomed to refusal of a donation when asked of rich women striving for social recognition.

"We have decided that your cause is one which should have met a more generous response. I have been accused of being disloyal. That is false, Madam. My wife has been attacked as pro-German. That is also false. To prove our loyalty we have decided to send you a diamond necklace. Convert this into money and buy what ambulances you can."

"Do you mean this?" said the astonished Mrs. Adrien Beekman.

"I am never more serious," retorted the Baron.

"What value has it?" she asked next.

"You will get fifty thousand dollars at least," he said.

"Ten ambulances!" she cried. "Oh, Baron, how very generous! I'm afraid I've cherished hard feelings about you both that have not been justified. How perfectly splendid of you!"

"One other thing," said the Baron, "I am sending this by a trusted messenger at once. Please see that some one reliable is there to receive it."

It was safer, Trent thought, to gain the Square over the roofs and down the stairways of the apartment house. It was now raining and hardly a soul was in view. The Adrien Beekman house was only a block distant. They were of the few who retained family mansions on the lower end of Fifth Avenue.

He knocked at the Beekman door and a man-servant opened it. In the shadows the man could only see the dark outline of the messenger.

"I am the Baron von Eckstein," he said, still with his carefully mimicked accent. "This is the package of which I spoke to your mistress."

It seemed, when he got back to Webster Hall, that none had missed him. The first to speak was the Baroness.

"We are just going over to the house," she said cordially.

"I don't want to share you," he said, smiling, "with all these others. I'd rather come to-morrow at four. May I?"

At four on the next day Anthony Trent, dressed in the best of taste as a man of fashion and leisure, ascended the steps to the Burton Trent home and wondered, as others had done before him, at the amazing fowl which guarded its approach.

He was kept waiting several minutes. From the distant reception rooms he heard acrimonious voices. One was the Baron's and it pleased him to note that he had caught its inflections so well the night before. The other voice was that of his new friend, the Baroness. Unfortunately the conversation was in German and its meaning incomprehensible.

When at last he was shown into a drawing room he found the Baroness highly excited and not a little indignant. She was too much overwrought to take much interest in her new acquaintance. Almost she looked as though she wished he had not come. Things rarely looked so rosy to the Baroness as they did after a good dinner and it was but four o'clock.

"What has disturbed you?" he asked.

"Everything," she retorted. "Mainly my husband. Tell me, if you were a woman and your husband, in a drunken fit, gave away a diamond necklace to an enemy would you be calm about it?"

"Has that happened?" he demanded.

"It has," she snapped. "You remember I told you at the dance I had left the original necklace at home for safety?"

"I believe you did mention it," he said, meditating.

"I'd much better have worn it, Mr. Trent. Everybody knows the Baron's passion is for cognac and champagne. No man since time began has ever drunk so much of them. When we got back here last night we had a gay and festive time. It was almost light when I went to my room and found the necklace gone. I sobered the Baron and he could give absolutely no explanation. He said he had slept in the dressing room to guard the jewels. That was nonsense. He came there to worry my maid. She went to bed and left him drinking. The police came in and took all the servants' finger-prints and tried to fasten the thing on them. There were marks on the jewel case where some one's hands had been put. I offered a reward of five thousand dollars for any one who could point out the man or woman who had taken the necklace."

Trent kept his countenance to the proper pitch of interest and sympathy. It was not easy.

"What have the police found?"

"Wait," the Baroness commanded, "you shall hear everything. This morning I received a letter from Mrs. Adrien Beekman. You know who she is, of course. She thanked me, rather patronizingly, for giving my diamond necklace to her Ambulance Fund. She said she had sold it to a Mexican millionaire for fifty thousand dollars, enough to buy ten ambulances."

"How did she get the necklace?" Trent asked seriously.

"That husband of mine," she returned. "The Baron did it. I can only think that in his maudlin condition he remembered what I had told him at dinner about being bothered by the Beekman woman for a cause I'm not very much in sympathy with. There is no other explanation. It all fits in. Actually he took the diamonds to the Beekman place himself. I can't do anything. I dare not tell the facts or I should be laughed out of New York."

"Mrs. Adrien Beekman is very influential," he reminded her, choking back his glee, "it may prove worth your while."

"She hates me," the Baroness said vindictively. "I've never been so upset in my life. You haven't heard all. There's worse. One of my servants is trying to get into the Army and Navy Finger-printing Bureau. She's made finger-prints of every one in the house—me included—from glasses or anything we've touched. It was the Baron's finger-prints on the jewel case, as the police found out, too, and I've got to pay her five thousand dollars reward!"

CHAPTER XVI

THE MOUNT AUBYN RUBY

It was while Trent was shaving that the lamp fell. He started, blessed the man who invented safety razors, that he had not gashed himself, and went into his library to see what had happened.

Mrs. Kinney, his housekeeper, was volubly apologetic.

"I was only dusting it," she explained, "when it came down. I think it's no more than bent."

It was a hanging lamp of Benares brasswork, not of much value, but Trent liked its quaint design and the brilliant flashing of the cut colored glass that embellished it. Four eyes of light looked out on the world when the lamp was lit. White, green, blue and red, eyes of the size of filbert nuts.

He stooped down and picked up the shattered red glass. It was the sole damage done by Mrs. Kinney's activity.

"It will cost only a few cents to have it repaired," he commented, and went back to the bathroom, and speedily forgot the whole matter.

At breakfast Anthony Trent admitted he was bored. There had been little excitement in his recent work. The niceness of calculation, the careful planning and dexterous carrying out of his affairs had netted him a great deal of money with very little risk. There had been risk often enough but not within the past few months. His thoughts went back to some of his more noteworthy feats, and he smiled. He chuckled at the episode of the bank president whom he had given in charge for picking his pocket when he had just relieved the financier of the choicest contents of his safe.

Trent's specialty was adroit handling of situations which would have been too much for the ordinary criminal. He had an aplomb, an ingenuous air, and was so diametrically opposed to the common conception of a burglar that people had often apologized to him whose homes he had looted.

It was his custom to read through two of the leading morning papers after breakfast. It was necessary that he should keep himself fully informed of the movements of society, of engagements, divorces and marriages. It was usually among people of this sort that he operated. To the columns devoted to lost articles he gave special attention. More than once he had seen big rewards offered for things that he had concealed in his rooms. And although the comforting phrase, "No questions asked" invariably accompanied the advertisement, he never made application for the reward.

In this, Trent differed from the usual practitioner of crime. When he had abandoned fiction for a more diverting sport he had formulated regulations for his professional conduct drawn up with extraordinary care. It was the first article of his faith under no circumstances to go to a "fence" or disposer of stolen goods, or to visit pawnshops. It is plain to see such precautions were wise. Sooner or later the police get the "fence" and with him the man's clientèle. Every man who sells to a "fence" puts his safety in another's keeping, and Anthony Trent was minded to play the game alone.

As to the pawnshops, daily the police regulations expose more searchingly the practices of those who bear the arms of old Lombardy above their doors. The court news is full of convictions obtained by the police detailed to watch the pawnbrokers' customers. It was largely on this account that Trent specialized on currency and remained unknown to the authorities.

On this particular morning the newspapers offered nothing of interest except to say that a certain Italian duke, whose cousin had recently become engaged to an American girl of wealth and position, was about to cross the ocean and bear with him family jewels as a wedding gift from the great house he represented. Methodically Trent made a note of this. Later he took the subway downtown to consult with his brokers on the purchase of certain oil stocks.

He had hardly taken his seat when Horace Weems pounced upon him. This Weems was an energetic creature, by instinct and training a salesman, so proud of his art and so certain of himself that he was wont to boast he could sell hot tamales in hell. By shrewdness he had amassed a comfortable fortune. He was a short, blond man nearly always capable of profuse perspirations. Trent knew by Weems' excitement that there was at hand either an entrancingly beautiful girl—as Weems saw beauty—or a very rich man. Only these two spectacles were capable of bringing Weems' smooth cheeks to this flush of excitement. Weems sometimes described himself as a "money-hound."

"You see that man coming toward us," Weems whispered.

Trent looked up. There were three men advancing. One was a heavily built man of late middle age with a disagreeable face, dominant chin and hard gray eyes. The other two were younger and had that alert bearing which men gain whose work requires a sound body and courage.

"Are they arresting him?" Parker demanded. He noticed that they were very close to the elder man. They might be Central Office men.

"Arresting *him?*" Weems whispered, still excitedly, "I should say not. You don't know who he is."

"I only know that he must be rich," Trent returned.

"That's one of the wealthiest men in the country," Weems told him. "That's Jerome Dangerfield."

"Your news leaves me unmoved," said the other. "I never heard of him."

"He hates publicity," Weems informed him. "If a paper prints a line about him it's his enemy, and it don't pay to have the enmity of a man worth nearly a hundred millions."

"What's his line?" Trent demanded.

"Everything," Weems said enthusiastically. "He owns half the mills in New Bedford for one thing. And then there's real estate in this village and Chicago." Weems sighed. "If I had his money I'd buy a paper and have myself spread all over it. And he won't have a line."

"I'm not sure he has succeeded in keeping it out. I'd swear that I've read something about him. It comes back clearly. It was something about jewels. I remember now. It was Mrs. Jerome Dangerfield who bought a famous ruby that the war compelled an English marchioness to sell." The thing was quite clear to him now. He was on his favorite topic. "It was known as the Mount Aubyn ruby, after the family which had it so long." He turned to look at the well-guarded financier. "So that's the man whose wife has that blood-stained jewel!"

"What do you mean—blood stained?" Weems demanded.

"It's one of the tragic stones of history," said the other. "Men have sold their lives for it, and women their honor. One of the former marquises of Mount Aubyn killed his best friend in a duel for it. God knows what blood was spilled for it in India before it went to Europe."

"You don't believe all that junk, do you?" asked Weems.

"Junk!" the other flung back at him. "Have you ever looked at a ruby?"

"Sure I have," Weems returned aggrieved. "Haven't you seen my ruby stick pin?"

"Which represents to you only so many dollars, and is, after all, only a small stone. If you'd ever looked into the heart of a ruby you'd know what I mean. There's a million little lurking devils in it, Weems, taunting you, mocking you, making you covet it and ready to do murder to have it for your own."

Weems looked at him, startled for the moment. He had never known his friend so intense, so unlike his careless, debonair self.

"For the moment," said Weems, "I thought you meant it. Of course you used to write fiction and that explains it."

To his articles of faith Anthony Trent added another paragraph. He swore not to let his enthusiasm run away with him when he discussed jewels. Weems was safe enough. He was lucky to be in no other company. But suppose he had babbled to one of those keen-eyed men engaged in guarding Jerome Dangerfield, the multi-millionaire who shunned publicity! He determined to choose another subject.

"What does he take those men around with him for?" he asked.

"A very rich man is pestered to death," the wise Weems said. "Cranks try to interest him in all sorts of fool schemes and crazy men try to kill him for being a capitalist. And then there's beggars and charities and blackmailers. Nobody can get next to him. I know. I've tried. I've never seen him in the subway before. I guess his car broke down and he had to come with the herd."

"So you tried? What was your scheme?"

"I forget now," Weems admitted. "I've had so many good things since. I followed out a stunt of that crook, Conway Parker, you used to write about. In one of your stories you made him want to meet a millionaire and instead of going to his office you made him go to the Fifth Avenue home and fool the butlers and flunkeys. It won't work, old man. I know. I handed the head butler my hat and cane, but that was as far as I got. There must be a high sign in that sort of a house that I wasn't wise to." Weems mused on his defeat for a few seconds. "I ought to have worn a monocle." He brightened. "Anyway just as I came out of the door a lady friend passed by on the top of a 'bus and saw me. Now you're a good looker, old man, and high-class and all that, but you and I don't belong in places like Millionaires' Row."

"Too bad," said Trent, smiling.

He wondered what Weems would have said if he had known that his friend had within the week been to a reception in one of the greatest of the Fifth Avenue palaces and there gazed at a splendid ruby—not half the size of the Mount Aubyn stone—on the yellowing neck of an aged lady of many loves.

When Weems was shaken off, Dangerfield and his attendants vanished, and Trent had placed an order with his brokers he walked over to Park Row, where he had once worked as a cub reporter. Contrary to his usual custom, he entered a saloon well patronized by the older order of newspapermen, men who graduated in a day when it was possible to drink hard and hold a responsible position. He had barely crossed the threshold when he heard the voice of the man he sought. It was Clarke, slave to the arch-demon rum. He was trying to borrow enough money from a monotype man, who had admitted backing a winner, to get a prescription filled for a suffering wife. The monotype man, either disbelieving Clarke's story or having little regard for wifely suffering, was indisposed to share his winnings with druggist or bartender.

It was at this moment that Clarke caught sight of his old reporter and more recent benefactor. He dropped the monotype man with all the outraged pride of an erstwhile city editor and shook Trent's hand cordially. His own trembled.

"That might be managed," said Trent, listening to his request gravely, "but first have a drink to steady your nerves."

They repaired to a little alcove and sat down. Clarke was not anxious to leave so pleasant a spot. He talked entertainingly and was ready to expatiate on his former glories.

"By the way," said Trent presently, "you used to know the inside history and hidden secrets of every big man in town."

"I do yet," Clarke insisted eagerly. "What's on your mind?"

"Nothing in particular," said the other idly, "but I came downtown on the subway and saw Jerome Dangerfield with his two strong-arm men. What's he afraid of? And why won't he have publicity?"

"That swinehound!" Clarke exclaimed. "Why wouldn't he be afraid of publicity with his record? You're too young to remember, but I know."

"What do you know?" Trent demanded.

"I know that he's worse than the *Leader* said he was when I was on the staff twenty years back. That was why the old *Leader* went out of business. He put it out. A paper is a business institution and won't antagonize a vicious two-handed fighter like Dangerfield unless it's necessary. That's why they leave him alone. The big political parties get campaign contributions from him. Why stir him up?"

"But you haven't told me what he did?"

"Women," said Clarke briefly. "You know, boy, that some men are born women-hunters. That may be natural enough; but if it's a game, play it fair. Pay for your folly. He didn't. You ask me why he has those guards with him? It's to protect him from the fathers of young girls who've sworn to get him. His bosom pal got his at a roof garden a dozen years back, and Dangerfield's watching night and day. He's bad all through. The stuff we had on him at the *Leader* would make you think you were back in decadent Rome."

"What's his wife like?"

"Society—all Society. Handsome, they tell me, and not any too much brain, but domineering. Full of precious stones. I'm told every servant is a detective. I guess they are, as you never heard of any of their valuables being taken. It makes me thirsty to think of it."

Trent, when he had obtained the information he desired, left Clarke with enough money to buy medicine for his wife. With the bartender he left sufficient to pay for a taxi to the boarding-house of Mrs. Sauer, where he himself had once resided. Clarke would need it.

On his way uptown he found himself thinking continuously of Jerome Dangerfield and the Mount Aubyn ruby. There would be excitement in going after such a prize. The Dangerfield household was one into which thieves had not been able to break nor steal. A man, to make a successful coup, would need more than a knowledge of the mechanism of burglar alarms or safes; he would need steel nerves, a clear head, physical courage and that intuitive knowledge of how to proceed which marks the great criminal from his brother, the ordinary crook. If he possessed himself of the ruby there would be no chance to sell it. It was as well known among connoisseurs as are the paintings of Velasquez. To cut it into lesser stones would be a piece of vandalism that he could never bring himself to enact.

It was Trent's custom when he planned a job to lay out in concise form the possible and probable dangers he must meet. And to each one of these problems there must be a solution. He decided that an entrance to the Dangerfield house from the outside would fail. To gain a position in the household would be not easy. In all probability references would be strictly looked up. They would be easy enough to forge, but if they were exposed he would be a suspect and his fictitious uncle in Australia exhumed. Also he did not care to live in a household where he was certain to be under the observation of detectives. No less than Jerome Dangerfield he shrank from publicity.

Mrs. Kinney noticed that he was strangely unresponsive to her well-cooked lunch. When she enquired the cause he told her he wanted a change. "I shall go away and play golf for a couple of weeks," he declared.

CHAPTER XVII

TRENT TAKES A HOLIDAY

At a sporting goods store that afternoon he ran into Jerome Danger-field again. He had just brought a dozen balls when he saw the million-aire and his two attendants. He was not minded to be observed of them, so slipped into the little room where putters may be tried and drives be made into nets. From where he was he could hear Dangerfield's dis-agreeable, rasping voice. His grievance, it seemed, was that other golfers were able to get better balls than he. He badgered the clerk until the man found spirit to observe: "If there was a ball that would make a dub play good golf it would be worth a fortune to any one."

Trent was able to see the look of anger the capitalist threw at him. And this anger he saw reflected on the faces of the two attendants. Decid-edly any lone man pitting his courage and wit against the Dangerfield entourage would need sympathy.

"Send me a half-gross up to Sunset Park Hotel," he heard Dangerfield say as he walked away, still frowning.

"I hope you don't have many of that kind to wait on," Trent said sympathetically. He was always courteous to those with whom he had dealings.

"He's the limit," said the clerk; "and from the way he looked at me I guess the boss will hear of it. Seemed to think there was a ball that would make him drive two hundred and fifty and hole a twenty-foot putt and I was trying to hide it from him. You wouldn't think it, but he's one of the richest men living. Gee, it makes me feel like a Socialist when I think of it!"

The clerk wondered why it was a superb golfer, as he knew Trent to be, was modest and courteous, while a man like Dangerfield was so overbearing.

Before he went home Trent looked up Sunset Park in a golfer's guide. It was a little-known course among the Berkshires, with only nine holes to its credit. The rates of the hotel were sufficiently high to make it clear only the rich could play. It was probably one of these dreary courses where a scratch player would be a rara avis, a course to which elderly men, playing for their health, gravitated and made the lives of caddies miserable.

It was a curious thing, Trent thought, that while this morning he knew nothing of Dangerfield, by night he knew a great deal. An evening paper told him why the millionaire was going to the Berkshires. There was to be a wedding in high society and the bride was a niece of Mrs. Jerome Dangerfield. The ceremony would take place at the Episcopal Church of the Good Shepherd, and a bishop would unite the contracting parties. The fancy dress ball to be held would be the most elaborate ever held outside New York. A great pavilion was to be erected for the occasion in the grounds of the bride's magnificent home, and Newport would be for the moment deserted. It was rumored that the jewels to be worn would exceed in value anything that had ever been gathered together this side the Atlantic, and so on, two columns long.

It explained very clearly why the Jerome Dangerfields were going to Sunset Park. The collective value of the jewels appealed particularly to Trent. He wondered if the Mount Aubyn ruby would shine out on that festal night. And if so how would it be guarded? It would be less difficult to disguise the detectives in fancy costume than in evening dress. Of course the owner of such a world-famous gem might wear an imitation as the Baroness von Eckstein had done. But if Clarke had painted her aright this was an occasion when an ambitious woman would be willing to take risks.

The proprietors of the Sunset Park Hotel were glad to accommodate Mr. Anthony Trent with a bed and bathroom for a little over a hundred dollars a week. It was a very select resort, they explained, attracting such people as the Jerome Dangerfields and their friends.

The golf course was owned by the hotel and the first tee was on the lawn a few yards from the front piazza. On the morning following his arrival, Trent, golf clubs already allotted to a caddy, waited to see what kind of golf was played. They were indifferently good but he betrayed little attention until he saw Dangerfield coming. Immediately he went to the tee but did not make his first shot until the millionaire was near enough to see. Playing alone as was the capitalist—for few were yet on the links—he had not to wait as he must have done had the other been playing with a partner. The first green was distant one hundred and sixty yards from the tee. A brook with sedgy reeds was a fine natural hazard, and as the green was on an elevated plateau with deep grass beyond, it was not an easy one to reach. Dangerfield dreaded it.

Dangerfield saw a tall, slim young man correctly clad in breeches and stockings, using a mashie, drop his ball neatly on the green within putting distance of the hole. Later he saw the hole done in two which was one under par.

"Who is that man?" Dangerfield demanded of his caddie.

"Never seen him before," the lad answered.

Dangerfield took his brassey and went straightway into the brook. He saw, however, as he was ball hunting, this stranger make a wonderful drive to the second—two hundred and fifty yards, the enthusiastic caddie swore. Meanwhile the millionaire continued to press and slice and pull and top his ball to such effect as to do the double round in one hundred and forty-two. Nothing exasperated him so much as to find the game mock his strength and desire. A power wherever money marts were, he was here openly laughed at by caddies. He was discovering that rank on the links is determined by skill at the game alone. What mattered it that he was the great Jerome Dangerfield. What had he done the round in? What was his handicap?

He particularly wanted to humble Stephen Goswell, president of the First Agricultural Bank of New York City. Goswell was a year ahead of him at the game and had the edge on him so far. Goswell could manage short approaches occasionally, strokes that were beyond his own inflexible wrists. Now this tall, dark stranger had such strokes to perfection. The ball driven up into the air skimmed tree, wall or bunker and rolled up to the pin sweetly. Dangerfield quickly made up his mind. He would invite the stranger to play with him and then get hints which would improve his game fifty per cent.

"Morning," he said later at the "Nineteenth Hole" where the stranger was taking a drink.

"Good morning," said the stranger rather stiffly. "It is evident," thought Dangerfield, "he does not know who I am."

"Going 'round again after lunch?" Dangerfield demanded.

"I think so," the stranger responded.

"We might play together," said Dangerfield. "I haven't a partner."

"I'm afraid that won't make a good match," Trent told him. "Surely there is some one more your strength who would make a better match of it?"

"Huh!" grunted the other, "think I don't play well enough, eh?"

"I know it," said Trent composedly.

Dangerfield regarded him sourly.

"You're not overburdened with modesty, young man."

"I hope not," the other retorted, "nothing handicaps a man more in life. I happen to know golf, though, and my experience is that if I play with a much inferior player I get careless and that's bad for my game. I'm perfectly frank about it. You know next to nothing about the game. In your own line of work you could no doubt give me a big beating because you know it and I don't."

"And what do you suppose my line of work is?" snapped the annoyed mill-owner.

"I don't know," Trent commented. "Either a dentist or a theatrical producer." As he spoke up sauntered one of the two men with whom he had seen Dangerfield in the subway.

"I'd like to hire some one to take the starch out of you," Dangerfield said as he rose to his feet.

"Quite easy," Trent returned, "almost any professional could."

He watched the two walk away and chuckled. He had attracted the millionaire's attention and he had rebuffed him. So far his programme was being carried out on scheduled time. The attendant had not looked at him with any special interest. It was unlikely in different clothes, under other conditions and in a strange place he would recognize him.

He did not play again that day. Instead he paid attention to some elderly ladies who knitted feverishly and were inclined to talk. He learned a great deal of useful news. For example, that the Dangerfields always had meals in their big private suite and rarely without guests from nearby homes. That they quarreled constantly. That Mr. Dangerfield never went to bed wholly sober. That he was given to sudden gusts of temper and only last year had beaten a caddie and had been compelled to settle the assault with a large money payment. That he was not above pocketing a golf ball if he could do so without being observed. That he had several times been seen to lift his ball out of an unfavorable lie into one from which he could play with greater chance of making a good stroke.

These petty meannesses Trent had already surmised. Dangerfield seemed to him that sort of a man. He was more interested in the dinner parties. But a man in such a position as he was had to be careful as to what questions he asked. People had a knack of remembering them at inopportune moments. Fortunately one of the ladies, who was a Miss Northend of Lynn, came back to it. She was a furious knitter and knitted best when her tongue wagged.

"Of course this hotel belongs to Mr. Dangerfield," she babbled, "and that explains why they have a palatial suite here and can entertain even more readily than if they had a summer home, as their friends have. This is a very fashionable section. The women dress here as if they were in Newport. Every night Mr. Dangerfield goes down to the hotel safe and brings something gorgeous in the jewelry way for his wife to wear. There's a private stairway he uses. I wandered into it once by mistake."

"And sister was so flustered," the other Miss Northend of Lynn told him, "that when he accused her of spying on him she couldn't say a word. It really did look suspicious until he knew we were Northends and our father was his counsel once when he controlled the Boston and Rangely road."

When these estimable maidens had finished, Anthony Trent knew all those particulars he desired. It was not the first time amiable gossips had aided him. But he played his part so well that Miss Fannie chided her sister.

"He wasn't a bit interested in the Dangerfield wealth," she said. "All a young man like that thinks of is golf."

"Well," said her sister, "I am interested and I'm frightened, too. When I think of all that amount of precious stones in the hotel safe, I'm positively alarmed. Every night she wears something new, her maid told the girl who looks after our rooms."

CHAPTER XVIII

THE GREAT BLACK BIRD

There was exactly one week to the night of the fancy dress dance at the Uplands from the time that the Northend sisters gave the abstractor so much information. Every moment of it was carefully taken up by that calculating gentleman.

For example, on the following morning, Wednesday he played a round with the club's champion, an amateur of some skill. Dangerfield posing for the moment as a warm admirer of the local player, followed the two on their match, betting freely on Blackhall, his club-mate. Also, he violated every rule of the royal and ancient game by speaking as Trent made his strokes. Never in his ten years of golf had Trent played such a game. It was characteristic of him to do his best when conditions were worst.

When the game was over at the thirteenth hole Dangerfield turned crossly to Blackhall.

"You played a rotten game!" he said.

"I never played a better," that golfer exclaimed. "The whole trouble with me was that I was up against a better man."

It may be observed that Blackhall was a sportsman.

Dangerfield was astonished and gratified next day when he was essaying some approaching to find Trent watching his efforts in a not unfriendly spirit.

"The trouble with you," said the younger player graciously, "is that you chop your stroke instead of carrying through. I'll show you what I mean."

In the half hour he devoted to Dangerfield he improved the millionaire's game six strokes a round.

"It would be no fun to play with you," he said when Dangerfield again invited him, "but I hate to see a man trying to approach as you did when a little help could put him right."

Thus were any Dangerfield suspicions disarmed. He helped him once or twice more and on every occasion insisted that the hovering attendant be sent away.

"Your keeper," said Trent genially, "puts me off my stroke."

"Keeper," grinned Dangerfield, "I'm not as bad as that. He's my valet."

Two days before the ball at the Uplands it was observed that Anthony Trent visited the Nineteenth Hole more frequently and stayed there longer. He was playing less golf now. The bartender confided in Mr. Dangerfield, who was also a consistent patron, that he was drinking heavily.

"I guess," said the tender of the bar with the sapience of his kind, "that he's one of these quiet periodic souses. They tell me he has the stuff sent up to his room."

"Too bad!" said Mr. Dangerfield, shaking his head as he ordered another.

It was true that to Trent's room much dry gin and lemon juice found its way, together with siphons of iced carbonic. The carbonic and the lemon juice was drunk since a belated heat wave was visiting the Sunset Park Hotel. The gin found its way into his flower laden window boxes, which should have bloomed into juniper berries. Trent liked a drink as well as any other golfer, but he found that it just took the keen edge off his nerves. He was less keen to realize danger and too ready to meet a risk when he drank. As a conscientious workman he put it behind him when professionally engaged.

On the night of the ball he was, to quote a bell boy, dead to the world, which proves that bell boys may be deceived by appearances. On the night of the ball he was keyed up to his highest personal efficiency.

Physically he was at his best. His muscles were always hard and his wind good. The resisting exercises he practised maintained the former and a little running every day aided the latter.

The great costume ball was to take place on the third of September, when the sun would set at half-past six. The Uplands was no more than a half hour motor spin distant from the hotel. The time set was half-past nine, which meant few would be there before ten. It was plain then that Mrs. Jerome Dangerfield would not commence her preparations for dressing until after the dinner. She was devoted to the pleasures of the table, as her maid lamented when she harnessed her mistress within her corsets.

Looking from his window, Trent saw that the sun had retired behind clouds early in the afternoon. Darkness would not be delayed, and the success of his venture depended upon this.

Reviewing the amazing events of the evening of September the third, it is only fair to let Jerome Dangerfield relieve his feelings in a letter to his closest friend, the president of the First Agricultural Bank of New York.

"You were right in warning me not to bring the Mt. Aubyn ruby up to this place. It was Adele's fault. She wanted it for the wedding. The damned thing has gone, Steve, vanished into thin air. If you told me what I'm going to tell you, I should say you were crazy. The people here and the fool police thought I'd been drinking. I'd had three or four cocktails, but what is that to me—or you? I was absolutely in possession of my senses.

"We dined early and we dined alone. At eight I went down for the jewels Adele wanted to wear. The ruby was the *pièce de résistance* of course. I went down my own private stairway as usual and unlocked the door leading from it to the hotel lobby. Devlin is here, and O'Brien, but they were both outside keeping tabs on strangers. The papers have played this costume ball up so much that every crook in the land knew what we had to offer in the way of loot. Graham, the hotel clerk, came with me to the private stairway and swears he pushed the door to as I started to go up the stairs. And he swears also that, although it wasn't lighted as well as usual, there was nobody in sight. They are steep stairs, Steve, but they save me rubbing shoulders with every man or woman who might want to get acquainted in the public elevators; and, naturally, I wasn't carrying a fortune where any crook could get a crack at me.

"Read this carefully. I was on the fifteenth step of the flight of twenty-two steps when the thing happened. The light was dim because one of the bulbs wasn't working and the only illumination came from a red light at the head of the stairway.

"I was holding the jewel box in both hands resting it almost on my chest when the thing happened. There was suddenly a noise that might have been made by the beating of wings and something swooped out of nowhere and hit me on my wrists with such violence that I went backwards down the stairs and was unconscious for more than ten minutes. On each wrist there is an abrasion that might be caused by the sharp bill of a big bird. I'm bruised all over and have three stitches over one eye.

"I found the box lying on one of the steps closed as I had held it. *The only thing that was missing was the Mt. Aubyn Ruby!*

"Devlin and O'Brien have all kinds of theories but I told them I wanted the stone back and if they didn't get it I wouldn't have them any longer in my employ.

"Devlin says he will swear a car passed him on the Boston road yesterday containing some Continental crooks who used to operate along the Italian and French Riviera. He's full of wild fancies and swears I shall get the ruby back. I'm not so sure. I've given up the theory that it was a great black bat which hit me, but whatever it was it was a stunt pulled by a master craftsman who is laughing at Devlin and his kind. Can you imagine a crook who would leave behind what this fellow did?

"I wish you'd go to the Pemberton Detective Agency and get them to send some one up here capable of handling the situation. I shall be coming down to New York as soon as I'm able. I'm too much bruised to play golf but when I do I shall win some of your money. I've had some lessons from a crackerjack golfer up here who goes round the eighteen holes in anything from seventy-two to seventy-eight. My stance was wrong and I wasn't gripping right."

So much for Jerome Dangerfield. When Devlin and O'Brien examined the scene of the crime they immediately noticed that some fifteen feet above the ground level a stained glass window lighted the stairway. "Of course," they exclaimed in unison, "that is the solution." But the theory did not hold water, as the soil of the flower-beds showed no sign of a ladder or any footmark. They had been raked over that afternoon and the gardener swore no foot but his had set foot in this enclosed garden which supplied the hotel tables with blooms. An examination of the window showed no helpful finger marks. It was an indoor job, they declared, amending their first opinion.

But they were thorough workmen in their way. For instance: Anthony Trent, reclining fully dressed across his bed with cigarette stubs and emptied glasses about him within thirty minutes of the robbery, was evidently in fear of interruption. An onlooker would have seen him take three gin fizzes in rapid succession until indeed his face wore a faint flush. He listened keenly when outside his door footsteps lingered. And he was snoring alcoholically when the hotel clerk entered, bringing with him Messrs. Devlin and O'Brien.

"He's been like this for days," Graham, the clerk, asserted. "If it wasn't that he was no trouble and made no noise I should have told him to get out. A pity," Graham shook his head, "one of the pleasantest-spoken men in the hotel, and some golfer, they tell me."

"You leave us," Devlin commanded. "We are acting for the boss and it'll be all right."

Out of the corner of his eye Trent watched the two trained men make a thorough examination of his room and effects. Indeed, their thoroughness gave him ideas which were later to prove of use. But they drew blank. They examined the two fly rods he had brought with him and a collapsible landing net with great care, tapping the handles and balancing the rods. They sighed when nothing was found.

"This guy is all right," said O'Brien.

"I don't know," said Devlin. "He looks a little too much like a moving-picture hero to suit me. He may have it on him."

At this moment Trent sat up with an effort and looked from one to the other of the visitors. As drunken men do, it appeared not easy to get them in proper focus.

Devlin was not easily put in the wrong. His manner was most respectful.

"Mr. Dangerfield wants you to join him in a little game of bridge," he began ingratiatingly.

"Sure," said the inebriate. "Any time at all." He attempted to get up.

"You can't go like this," Devlin assured him. "You'd better sober up a bit. Take a cold bath."

O'Brien obligingly turned the water on and five minutes later Devlin assisted him into the tub, while O'Brien examined the clothes he had left in his sitting-room.

Then the two left him abruptly and made no more mention of bridge or Dangerfield. Trent rolled on the bed chuckling. The honors were his.

The great black bird swooping from nowhere to relieve Dangerfield of his great ruby and other stones of value, to strike that worthy upon his strong wrists with such startling effect as to make him fall down a dozen steps, was capable of a simpler explanation than he had supposed.

Trent, a week before the robbery, had observed with peculiar attention the window leading to Dangerfield's private stairway. He could see one easy approach to it and one of greater difficulty. The first was approach by a step-ladder. The second was a great arm of the enormous tree that reared its head above the hotel roof. This arm hung down from the roof almost twenty feet above the little window. He believed that his weight would bring it swaying down to the window-ledge. He tried it one moonless night and found the scheme feasible. Already the chiller mountain breezes following the heat spell were making visitors close their windows. On the evening of the third of September he stole from his room by climbing over the roof until he came to the side where the big tree was. In one hand he held a coil of rope to hold the branch when his weight was taken off it. This rope he tied to the iron staple of the shutter outside the window. It was easy to open this.

Dropping silently on to the stairs, he unscrewed the bulb of the light until the staircase was in partial darkness. Tense, he knelt on the edge of the window and waited for the millionaire. And as the man came in sight he suddenly lifted from a step his landing net, the same collapsible one Devlin had examined with such care. But this time it was draped in dark material to conceal its form. The brass rim, sharp and heavy, struck Dangerfield's wrists as he held the box by both hands on a level with his heart. Into the open net the precious casket fell silently. Trent was in his room ten minutes ere Dangerfield came to consciousness. His next move seemed strange and unnecessary. With a used golf ball in his pocket, he slid down the veranda posts until he came, by devious routes, to the shed in which the lockers were of those who used the links. It had long since been closed for the night. Parker unfastened Dangerfield's locker and placed the ball in the pocket, where it lay with others of similar age and make.

He was able to return to his room unobserved. It was less than a half hour afterward that he received his call from the two detectives.

Although he was anxious to get on the links again and breathe the air of the pine woods, he was careful not to undo his artistic preparations. It was noticed that no more drink was sent to his room. There came instead ice water and strong coffee. He was getting over it, they said. Two days later he was out on the links and made a peculiarly bad round, taking ten more strokes than usual. Dangerfield watched him from the piazza. One of his arms was in a sling.

"Cut the rough stuff out," said Dangerfield, "that's the second time you topped your ball."

Trent passed a hand across his face, possibly to hide a smile.

"I guess I'll have to," he returned simply. "It was that damned heat wave that got me going."

It happened that the Dangerfields and Trent returned to New York on the same train. Devlin and O'Brien were in attendance. Trent noticed that when Devlin's eye fell on the golf bag over his shoulder he frowned. So far the ruby had not been recovered and here was a piece of baggage that might hold crown jewels. Over Devlin's broad shoulders his master's golf bag was suspended. Cheerily and with respect he approached the crack player.

"Let me hold your golf bag, sir," he said with a ready smile. "I'll put it on the train for you."

Trent relinquished it with relief. "Thank you," he returned, "it will be a help."

He had long ago noticed that his own bag and Dangerfield's were alike save for the initials. They were both of white canvas, bound with black leather. Watching the smiling Devlin with a well-disguised curiosity, he saw that Dangerfield's bag had been substituted for his own. Devlin had done exactly as Trent expected him to do and had, in the doing of it, saved him much trouble.

There were not many people in his Pullman. Dangerfield had his private car. None saw Anthony Trent open the ball pouch on the Dangerfield bag and extract therefrom an aged and somewhat dented ball. He balanced it almost lovingly in his hand. Never in the history of the great game had a ball been seen with the worth of this one. And yet he had so cunningly extracted its core and repaired it when once the Mount Aubyn ruby was nestling in its strange home that detection was unlikely, even were an examination made. A porter had the Dangerfield bag and Trent's suitcase when Devlin came up to him. He was no longer obliging. He had spent wearisome hours in the privacy of the Dangerfield car examining every part of the Trent impedimenta. The task had wearied him and had been fruitless.

"You got the boss's clubs," he said shortly.

Languidly Trent examined what his porter carried.

"You're to blame for it," he answered, and as Mr. Dangerfield came up raised his voice a little. He knew Devlin suspected him, and he sensed that some day the two would meet as open foes.

"This man of yours," cried Trent, "tried to give me your clubs instead of my own. I wouldn't lose mine for anything."

"You crack golfers couldn't do anything without your own specially built clubs," jeered the millionaire, "I believe it's half the game."

Trent smiled.

"There's something in the ball, too," he admitted, and had difficulty in keeping his face straight.

Mrs. Kinney was delighted to see her employer home again, and hurried to a convenient delicatessen store so that he might be fed. It was when she came back that her eye caught sight of the brass lamp from Benares.

Where had been the unsightly gap caused by her breaking of the red glass was now a piece which glittered gaily.

"Why, you've had it mended, sir," she cried. "I feel I ought to pay for it, since it was my carelessness which broke it."

"I'm glad you did," he laughed. "If you hadn't I shouldn't have got this." He looked at it with pride. "Do you know, Mrs. Kinney, I like this one better."

"It makes the other ones look common though," she commented.

"You're right," he admitted. "I think I shall have to replace them, too."

CHAPTER XIX

TRENT ACQUIRES A HOME

One day, months before the affair of the ten ambulances, Horace Weems had seen Anthony Trent about to enter Xeres' excellent restaurant. Lacking no assurance Weems tacked himself on to his friend.

"Say, do you feed here?" he demanded and looked with respect at his friend's raiment.

"Only when I'm hungry," Trent retorted. He knew it was useless to try to get rid of Weems. "Have you dined?"

"Thanks," said Weems, "I don't mind if I do."

In those days Weems was proud as the owner of the finest camp on Lake Kennebago. He was high stomached and generous of advice. He told Trent so much of a certain stock—a gold mine in Colorado—that at last he purchased a considerable interest in it. Later he learned that Weems had unloaded worthless stock on him. Trent bore no sort of malice. He had gone into the thing open-eyed and Weems, as he knew of yore, never sold at a loss.

Weems had been wiser to have held his stock for tungsten in large quantities was discovered and what cost Trent five thousand dollars was now worth ten times that amount.

It was one evening shortly after his adventures with the Baron von Eckstein that Weems called him up on the telephone. That he was able to do so annoyed Trent who had carefully concealed his number. But Horace Weems had secured it by a use of mendacity and with it the number and the address. He said he was 'phoning from a nearby drug store and was about to pay a visit.

Weems was ill at ease. And he was unshaven and his shoes no longer shone with radiance. His disheveled appearance and attitude of dejection swept away his host's annoyance. He took a stiff Scotch and seltzer.

"Little Horace Weems," he announced, "has got it in the neck!"

"What's happened?" Trent demanded.

"Got that Wall Street bunch sore on me and hadn't the sense to see the danger signals." Weems soothed his throat with another stiff drink. "The trouble with me is I'm too courageous. I knew what I was up against but did that frighten me? No siree, no boss, I went for 'em like you used to go through a bunch of forwards in a football game. I'm like a bull terrier. I'm all fight. Size don't worry me. They pulled me down at last but it took all the best brains in the 'Street' to do it. They hate a comer and I'm that. Well, this is the first round and they win on points but this isn't a limited bout. You watch little Horace. I'll have a turbine steam yacht yet and all the trimmings. Follow me and you'll wear diamonds or rags—nothing between. Rags or diamonds."

Weems was a long time coming to the point. When he did it was revealed as a loan, a temporary loan.

"It's like this," said the ingenuous Weems, "when I sold you those shares in a tungsten mine I did it because you were a friend."

"You did it," Trent reminded him, "because you hadn't a faint idea there was tungsten there and you thought you'd done something mighty clever. What next?"

"You needn't be sore about it," Weems returned, "you made money."

"I'm not sore," Trent said smiling. "You did me a good turn but I don't have to be grateful all things considering. How much do you want?"

"I shall get back," Weems said a little sulkily. "I only want a hundred or maybe two hundred, although five hundred would see me through till I get the money for the camp."

"You are not going to sell that?" Trent cried. It was of all places the one he craved.

"Got to," Weems asserted.

"Who is going to buy it?"

"A fellow from Cleveland named Rumleigh."

"I remember him," Trent said frowning, "he's a hog, a fish hog. All the guides hate him. What's he going to give you?"

"Forty thousand," said Weems.

"Constable, grand piano and all?"

"The piano's there," Weems told him, "but the picture is sold. Honest, Tony, that picture surprised me. Senator Scrivener gave me ten thousand dollars for it. Just some trees, an old barn and some horses looking over a gate. What do you know about that? That helped me some."

"You're such a damned liar, Weems, that I never believe you but I'll swear Rumleigh isn't paying you forty thousand dollars for that camp. It's a good camp but if you've got to sell in a hurry he'll hold you down to less than that. Be honest for once and tell me what he's going to give."

"Twenty-two thousand," Weems said sullenly.

"I'll give you twenty-five," said Trent carelessly.

"His is a cash offer," Weems said shaking his head, "and that's why I'm selling so cheap."

Trent took a roll of bills from his pocket and peeled off before Weems' astounded eyes five and twenty thousand dollars.

"Mine is also a cash offer," he observed.

"Come right off to my lawyer," Weems cried springing to his feet. "Gee, and I thought you hadn't as much money as I have."

Thus it was that Anthony Trent came into possession of his camp. It was a beautiful place and there were improvements which he planned that would cost a lot to execute. He decided that it might be unwise to retire yet from a profession which paid him such rewards. Another year and he could lay aside his present work satisfied that financial worries need never trouble him. He admitted that many unfortunate things might happen in twelve months but he was serene in the belief that his star was in the ascendant.

CHAPTER XX

"WANTED—AN EMERALD"

Since Anthony Trent had replaced the red glass in his Benares lamp with the Mount Aubyn ruby, the other pieces of cut glass seemed so dull by comparison that had his visitors been many, suspicion must have arisen from the very difference they exhibited. The lamp was discreetly swung in a distant corner and the button which lighted the lamp carefully concealed.

Reading one morning that owing to the financial trouble into which the war had plunged a great West of England family, the celebrated Edgcumbe sapphire had been purchased by a New York manufacturer of ammunition—one of the new millionaires created by the war to buy what other countries had to sacrifice.

The papers gave every necessary particular. At ten o'clock one morning Anthony Trent sallied forth to loot. By dinner time the Edgcumbe sapphire had replaced the blue cube of cut glass and in his lamp the papers were devoting front page space to its daring abduction. How he accomplished it properly belongs to another chapter in the life of the master criminal. So easy was it of consummation that he planned to use the same technique for a greater coup.

When these two great stones were making his brazen lamp a thing of flashing beauty they threw into infinite dullness the cube of green. Looking at it night after night when Mrs. Kinney was long abed and the grateful silences had drowned the noise of day, Anthony Trent longed for an emerald to bear these lordly jewels company.

There was an excellent second-hand book store on Thirty-second street, between Seventh avenue and Sixth, where he browsed often among waiting volumes. One day he picked up a book, written in French, "Romances of Precious Stones." It was by a Madame Sernin, grandniece of the great Russian novelist Feoder Vladimir Larrovitch. Trent remembered that he had read her translation of *Crasny Baba* and *Gospodi Pomi*, and looked at this original work with interest. It was published in Paris just before the war.

He knew well that most of the great stones which had became famous historically were still in Europe. And Europe, until the long war was over, was closed to him. He hoped Madame Sernin had something to say about American-owned jewels. There was a reference in the index and later, in his rooms, he read it eagerly. There were, Mme. Sernin announced, but two of the great emeralds in the United States. One belonged to the wife of the Colombian minister and was found in Colombia. Trent considered this stone carefully. It might not be in the United States after all. Mme. Sernin was doubtful herself. But of the second stone she was certain. It was known as the Takowaja Emerald. A century and a half before it had been dug from the Ural Mountains. That great *"commenceuse,"* the second Catherine of Russia, had given it to her favorite, Gregory Orlov, who had sold it to a traveling English noble in a day before American gold was known in Continental Europe.

It was now the property of Andrew Apthorpe, of Boston in Massachusetts. Presumably the man was a collector, and assuredly he was wealthy, but Anthony Trent had never heard of him. A trip by boat to Boston would make a pleasant break and a day later he was steaming north. His inevitable golf clubs accompanied him. Trent was one of those natural-born players whose game suffer little if short of practice. And of late he had not stinted himself of play. He told Mrs. Kinney he was going to Edgartown for a few days. He had sometimes played around these island links; and his bag of clubs was always an excellent excuse for traveling in strange parts.

Directly he had registered at the Adams House he consulted a city directory. Andrew Apthorpe's town house was in the same block on Beacon street which held the Clent Bulstrode mansion.

It was a vast, forbidding residence of red brick running back to the Charles embankment. The windows were small and barred and the shades drawn. An empty milk bottle and a morning paper at a basement door gave evidence of occupancy. And at the garage at the rear a burly chauffeur was cleaning the brass work of a touring car. Looking wisely and suspiciously at Trent as he sauntered by was an Airedale. The family, Trent surmised, was absent and the caretaker, who rose late if the neglected Post was a sign, and this man and dog were left to guard the place.

If the Takowaja emerald were housed here with two such guardians its recovery might not be difficult. But the more Trent thought of it the more improbable it seemed that the owner of such a gem should leave it prey to any organized attack. The curious part about this Ural emerald was that Trent had never before heard of it and he knew American owned stones well. Most of the owners of famous jewels were ready to talk of them, lend them for exhibition purposes when they were properly guarded, but he had never seen a line about the Apthorpe emerald.

A few minutes before midday Anthony Trent strolled into the Ames building and saw that Andrew Apthorpe, cotton broker, occupied very large offices. A little later he followed one of the Apthorpe clerks, a well-dressed, good-looking young man, to the place where he lunched. It was curiously unlike a New York restaurant. Circular mahogany counters surrounded self possessed young women who permitted themselves to attend to those who hungered. To such as they knew and liked they were affable. To others their front was cold and severe.

The Apthorpe employee was a favorite, apt at retort and not ill pleased if others noted it. Soon he drifted into conversation with Trent, who with his careful mind had read through the column devoted to cotton in the morning papers and was ready with a carefully remembered phrase or two for the stranger who responded in kind.

Gradually, by way of the Red Sox, the beauties of Norumbega Park and the architectural qualities of Keith's, the young man lapsed into personalities and told Anthony Trent all he desired to know of Andrew Apthorpe. Andrew, it seemed, was not beloved of his employees. He was unappreciative of merit unless it accompanied female beauty. He was old; he was ill. His family had abandoned him with the sincere reluctance that wealth is ever abandoned.

"He lives up at Groton," said Trent's loquacious informant, "in a sort of castle on a hill fitted with every burglar resisting device that was ever invented."

"What's he afraid of?" Trent demanded.

"He's got a lot of valuables," the other answered, "cut gems and cameos and intaglios and things that wouldn't interest any one but an old miser like him. I have to go up there once in a while. The old boy has an automatic in his pocket all the while. I think he's crazy."

There were two or three men at Camp Devens whom Trent knew slightly. The Camp was within walking distance of Groton, he learned. By half past nine on the following morning Anthony Trent left Ayer behind him and breasted the rising ground towards Groton. He could go to the Camp later. He might not go at all but if questioned as to his presence the excuse would be a just one. He was always anxious that his motives would pass muster with the police if ever he came in contact with them.

After a couple of miles he came in sight of the beautiful tower of Groton School Chapel. Two or three times he had played for his school against this famous institution in the years that seemed now so far behind him. The town of Groton, some distance from the more modern school, charmed his senses. Restful houses among immemorial elms, well kept gardens and a general air of contentment made the town one to be remembered even in New England.

He hoped he would be able to find something about Apthorpe from some local historian without having to lead openly to the matter. A luncheon at the famous Inn might discover some such informant. But he was not destined to enter that admirable hostelry for coming toward him, with dignified carriage and an aura of fragrant havana smoke about him, was Mr. Westward whom he had known slightly at Kennebago. This Mr. Westward was the most widely known fisherman on the famous lake, an authority wherever wet-fly men foregathered.

Trent would have preferred to meet none who knew him by name. This was a professional adventure and not a trout fishing vacation. But the angler had already recognized him and there was no help for it. Westward rather liked Anthony Trent as he liked all men who were skilled in the use of the wet-fly and were, in his own published words, "high-minded, fly-fishing sportsmen."

"Why, my dear fellow," said Westward genially, "what are you doing in my home town?"

"I'd no idea you lived here," Trent said, shaking his hand. "I thought you were a New Yorker."

Westward pointed to a modest house. "This is what I call my office," he explained. "I do my writing there and house my fishing tackle and my specimens."

"I wish you'd let me see them," Trent suggested smiling. "I've often marveled at the way you catch 'em."

It was past twelve when he had finished talking over what Mr. Westward had to show. He realized he had forgotten the matter which brought him to Groton. When Mr. Westward asked him to luncheon he hesitated a moment. This hesitation was born not of a disinclination to accept the angler's hospitality but rather to the feeling that he was out for business and if he failed at it might be led as a criminal to whatever jail was handy. And were he thus a prisoner it would embarrass a good sportsman. But Mr. Westward gained his point and led Trent to a big rambling house further down the street that was a rich store house of the old and quaint furniture of Colonial days.

Mrs. Westward proved to be a woman of charm and culture, endowed with a quick wit and a gift of entertaining comment on what local happenings were out of the ordinary.

"Has Charles told you of the murder?" she asked.

"We've been talking fish," Anthony Trent explained.

"Oh you fishermen!" she laughed. "I often tell my husband he won't take any notice of the Last Trump if he's fishing or talking of trout. We actually had a murder here last night."

"I hope it was some one who could be easily spared," Trent returned, "and not a friend."

"I could spare him," Mrs. Westward said decisively. "I know his wife and she has my friendship but for Andrew Apthorpe I have never cared."

"Apthorpe?" Trent cried. "The cotton man?"

"The same," Mrs. Westward assured him.

Anthony Trent was suddenly all attention. He surmised that the murder of so rich a man was actuated by a desire for his collection. And if so, where was the Takowaja emerald?

"Please tell me," he entreated, "murders fascinate me. If the penalty were not so severe I should engage in murder constantly. What was it? Revenge? Robbery?"

"Yes and no," Charles Westward observed with that judicial air which confounded questioners. "Revenge no doubt. Robbery perhaps, but we are awaiting the arrival of Mrs. Apthorpe and her daughter. We shall not know until then whether his collection of valuables has been stolen."

"What about the revenge theory?" Trent inquired.

"Apthorpe made many enemies as a younger man. Physically he was violent. There are no doubt many who detested him. Personally I had no quarrel with him. I sent him a mess of trout from the Unkety brook this season and had a little talk with him over the phone but he saw few except his lawyer and business associates."

"Is any one suspected in particular?" Trent asked.

"The whole thing is mysterious," Mrs. Westward declared with animation. "Last night at eight o'clock I received a telephone message from his nurse, a Miss Thompson, a woman I hardly know. Once or twice I have seen her at the Red Cross meetings but that is all. She apologized for calling but said she felt nervous. It seems that Mr. Apthorpe had let all the servants go off to the band concert at Ayer. There were two automobiles filled with them. The only people left were Miss Thompson in the house and a gardener who lives in a cottage on the grounds. They left the house just after dinner—say half past seven. At a quarter to eight a stranger called to see Mr. Apthorpe."

"Accurately timed," commented Mr. Westward.

"Miss Thompson declined to admit him. You must understand, Mr. Trent, that Andrew Apthorpe was a very sick man, heart trouble mainly, and she was within her rights. The man who would not give his name put his foot in the door and said he would see Mr. Apthorpe if he waited there all night. While she was arguing with him, begging him, in fact, to go away, her employer came to the head of the stairs that lead from the main rooms to the hall. Miss Thompson explained what had happened. To her surprise he said, 'I have been expecting him for twenty years. Let him in.'"

"Why should she call you up?" Trent asked.

"Merely because she was nervous and knew other people even less than she did me." Mrs. Westward hesitated a moment. "There have been rumors about her and Mr. Apthorpe which were not pleasant. They were probably not true but when a man has lived as he had it was not surprising. She called me up at eight because the two men were quarreling. My husband told you he was a man of violent temper. That is putting it mildly. I told her there was nothing to be alarmed about. At nine she called me up again to say that she would be grateful if Mr. Westward and my nephew Richmond, who is staying with me, would go up there as she had heard blows struck and Mr. Apthorpe was too ill to engage in any sort of tussle. I told her my two men were out but that the police should be called in. While I was talking she gave a shriek—it was a most dramatic moment and I could hear her steps running from the telephone."

"My nephew and I came in at that moment," Westward interrupted, "and went up the hill to the house as fast as possible. Mrs. Westward meanwhile had telephoned for the police. Miss Thompson was waiting on the steps. She was hysterical and afraid to go back into the lonely house."

"Richmond said he thought she had been drinking," his wife interjected.

"That meant nothing," Westward observed, "she was hysterical and I don't wonder in that great lonely house. When we went in with the police we found the big living room door locked with the key on the inside. We had to break it open and found it bolted. Evidently the stranger had seen to that. Old Apthorpe was lying dead shot through the head with a bullet from his own revolver. The window was open. There was a twelve-foot drop to the grass outside and the man had lowered himself by a portiere. So far not a trace has been found of him. A great many people pass through here on the way to or from Boston and we have become so used to strangers that no heed is paid to them any more."

"Was there any evidence of robbery?" Trent asked.

"Not a trace so far as we could see. I mean by that there was no disorder. Things of value might have been taken but nothing had been broken open. We shan't know until Mrs. Apthorpe comes."

"It was evidently," Mr. Westward declared, "some man whom he had been expecting. Miss Thompson, according to her story, did not know the man's name and yet was told to admit him. It may be the police will find it from correspondence."

"I doubt it," Trent observed shaking his head. "If it was a man Apthorpe had dreaded for a score of years he wouldn't be corresponding with him."

"Then why was he admitted?" asked Mrs. Westward.

"Consider the circumstances," Anthony Trent reminded her. He was becoming thoroughly interested. "Here he was almost in the house, his foot in the door. All the servants were away. No matter what Apthorpe said he would have got in. What more likely than that the proud over-bearing old man felt sufficient confidence in his nerve and his revolver? Or if he didn't he would not admit it. The curious part to my mind was how this unknown timed it so exactly. He turned up just as the servants were going out for the evening." He turned to Mrs. Westward, "Why didn't Miss Thompson telephone for police aid do you suppose? Does it seem strange to you that she telephoned to you instead?"

"Knowing Andrew Apthorpe it does not," she answered. "He would have been furious if she had done so. To begin with he has had many squabbles with the local authorities over trumpery matters. He was most unpopular. The last thing he would have desired would be to have them in his house. None of the servants were from Groton and he would not have them associating with local people."

Anthony Trent ruminated for a little. So far nothing had been developed which offered a reasonable solution of the problem. And the problem for him was a different one from that which would confront the police. Trent's problem was to secure the Takowaja emerald. So far neither of the Westwards had mentioned it. Probably for the reason that they did not know of its existence. It would be unwise, he decided, to try to lead them to talk of the dead man's collection of jewels. But he felt reasonably certain in his own mind that in this carefully guarded house, replete with burglar alarms and safety appliances, the treasure from the Ural Mountains had been reposing within a dozen hours. The stranger who had come after a score of years and had left murder in his trail, was more likely to have come for the great green stone than anything else.

"I wish I could have a look at the place," he said presently.

"Amateur detective?" laughed Mrs. Westward.

"I can't imagine anything being more exciting," he admitted, "than to follow this mysterious man except, perhaps, to be the man himself and outwit the detectives."

"Why not take Mr. Trent up there, Charles?"

Plainly Mr. Westward was not eager to do so. This was due to a dis-like to invade premises under police supervision to which he had no business except a friendly curiosity. Still there would be no harm done. He had known the Apthorpes for years and perhaps Anthony Trent might be an aid. Some one had told him Trent was an expert in the oil market. He had no reason to believe him anything but a man of probity.

"It might be arranged," he said slowly.

CHAPTER XXI

THE MURDER OF ANDREW APTHORPE

The Apthorpe estate ran parallel to the main street of the town but the house itself was perched on a hill almost a mile distant from it. A long winding ascent led to a big stone, turreted mansion commanding an extensive view of the country that lay about it. A well kept lawn three hundred yards in width surrounded the house.

"The place was built," Mr. Westward explained, "by Colonel Crofton, the railroad man. On this lawn were great beds of rhododendrons which cost a great deal of money. When Apthorpe bought it he had them torn up and sown in grass. He said the flower beds and shrubberies were places where burglars might conceal themselves by day to break in by night."

"He was certainly suspicious," Trent commented.

Westward pointed to the house which rose like a fortress above them.

"When Crofton had it there were windows on the ground level and several entrances. Apthorpe had them filled with granite all except that big doorway opposite."

By this time Trent was near enough to see that the house was not remote from buildings such as the stables and garages which are adjacent to most such residences. He remarked on the peculiarity.

"The automobiles are kept in the basement of the house," Westward explained. "The big doors I pointed out to you cannot be opened by the chauffeurs. When they want to go out or come in they have to phone for permission. Then Mr. Apthorpe or some one else would touch a button in his big living room and the gates would swing open. He had a searchlight on the tower until the Federal authorities forbade it."

"It seems to me he must have lived in dread of violence," Trent observed, "and yet why should he? He was a well known Boston broker of an old New England family, not the kind one would think involved in crime. In fiction it is the man who comes home after spending half his life in the mysterious East that one suspects of robbing gods of their jeweled eyes and incurring the sworn vengeances of their priests."

"All men who collect precious stones live in dread," Charles Westward said. "I've never seen any of his things. I'm not interested in them particularly. I've always talked about fishing when I've been there, but it's common knowledge that he was going to leave his valuables to the Museum of Fine Arts. One of the things which incensed his wife was that he wouldn't give her or her daughter any of the jewels but preferred to keep them locked away."

A flight of twenty granite steps led to the main entrance, two heavily built, metal studded doors. A lofty hall was disclosed with a circular stairway around it. Leading from the hall to what seemed the main room on that floor was a flight of six steps. The chestnut doors had been shattered. Obviously it was the room in which Apthorpe had met his death. For the rest it looked in no way different from half a hundred other rooms in big houses which Trent had investigated professionally. Bookshelves not more than four feet in height lined three sides of the apartment. Making a pretense of reading the titles Trent looked to see whether they were indeed volumes or mere blinds. The policeman in charge, knowing Mr. Westward well, was only too willing to show him and his friend what was to be seen. The body, he explained, was in an upper chamber.

One peculiarity Trent noted in the book cases. Apparently there was no way to open them. They were of metal painted over. If keyholes existed they were hidden from view. Fearing that the policeman in charge would notice his scrutiny, he walked over to the open window and looked out. It was from this that the murderer made his escape. Twelve feet below the green closely cropped turf touched the granite foundation of the walls.

When Mr. Westward offered him a cigar he took out his pipe instead and knocked out the ashes against the window ledge. Mr. Westward heard an exclamation of annoyance and asked its cause. Then he saw that while the stem of the pipe remained in its owner's hand the bowl had fallen to the lawn below.

"I won't be a minute," Trent said, and went down the main steps to the grounds. It was no accident that led him to drop his favorite briar. His keen eyes had seen footprints in the grass as he looked down. They might well be the marks of him who had stolen the famous emerald and Trent had decreed a private vendetta against one who might have robbed him for what he came into Massachusetts. Searching for the pipe bowl which he had instantly detected he made a rapid examination of the ground.

There were indeed footprints made undoubtedly by some one dropping from the end of the portiere to the soft turf. And as he gazed, the mysterious man whom he had suspected faded into thin air. They were the imprints of the high heels that only women wear! Carefully he followed them as far as the big gates of the garage. They were not distinct to any but a trained observer. They were single tracks leading from the grass beneath the window to the garage. Not an unnecessary step had been taken. Apparently the local police had pulled in the portiere from the window and had made no examination of the grass below.

Trent noticed that a man, evidently a gardener, was approaching him. Quickly he dropped the bowl of his pipe again among some clover. The man was eager and obliging. Furthermore he had heavily shod feet which were already making their impression on the turf to the undoing of any who might seek, as Anthony Trent had done, to make a careful examination. Already the high heeled imprints were obliterated.

When the pipe was found the man insisted on speaking of the murder. He declared that for an hour on the fatal night a big touring car had been drawn up near his cottage in a lane nearby and that two men got out of it leaving another in charge.

Trent shook him off as soon as he could and returned to the house, his previously held theories wholly upset. He had built them in the facts or falsities carefully supplied by Miss Thompson and he was anxious to see the lady. It was most likely that the woman who had lowered herself from the window was the woman who had committed the murder. And for what could the crimes have been committed so readily as the Takowaja emerald?

He recalled now that there had been a certain reserve in the Westwards' manner when they had spoken of Miss Thompson. Might they not have suspected her and yet feared to voice these suspicions to a stranger?

As he thought it over he came to the conclusion that it was not of the crime of murder they suspected her but perhaps because of her relations with so notorious a man as the late Andrew Apthorpe. He remembered that the dead man's family was alienated from him, possibly for this very reason.

He was given an opportunity very shortly to see the nurse. She came along the hall, not seeing him as he stood in the entrance, and made her way toward Mr. Westward. She was a tall woman, quietly dressed and not in nurses' uniform. Her walk was studied and her gestures exaggerated. She was that hard, blond type over-laden with affectation to one who observed carelessly. But Trent could see she had a jaw like a prize fighter and her carefully pencilled eyes were intrinsically bellicose. She had a big frame and was, he judged, muscularly strong. And of course nurses must have good nerves. If she had the emerald he was determined to obtain, it would not be an easy conquest.

Her greeting of Mr. Westward was effusive. Indeed it seemed too effusive to please him. He was courteous and expressed sympathy. She talked volubly. She related in detail the events of the previous night and the listener noticed that she was letter perfect. The only new angle he got was a description of the supposed murderer. According to Nurse Thompson he was about fifty, wore a short grizzled moustache, was of medium height but very broad, and dressed in a dark gray suit. In accent she judged him to be a Westerner. She would recognize him, she declared dramatically, among ten million.

Trent had no wish to meet her—yet. He had seen her, recognized a predacious and formidable type and had observed she wore expensive shoes with fashionably high heels.

Presently Charles Westward joined him.

"I've been talking to Miss Thompson," he volunteered.

"I saw you," Trent said, "but supposed it was one of the family. She wasn't dressed as a nurse."

"She doesn't act like one," Westward answered. "Richmond was right. That woman drinks. I don't like her, Mr. Trent."

"I suppose she needs sympathy now that her position is lost?"

The more Anthony Trent thought over the matter the more thoroughly he became convinced that the mysterious stranger of whom the nurse spoke had no existence. If she had killed her employer she would not have done so unless it were to her advantage. And what better reason could there be, were she criminally minded, than some of his famous jewels? Trent determined to follow the thing up. He chuckled to think that he was now on the opposite side of the fence, the hunter instead of the hunted. But that was no reason that he should aid his enemy the law. If he devoted his talents to the running down of the murderer he wanted the reward for himself.

Supposing that she had planned the crime, the opportunity was hers when she had the old man alone in the house. She would have been far too clever to use her knowledge of drugs to poison him. By such a ruse she would inevitably have incurred suspicion. If his assumption were correct she had been very clever. At eight o'clock she had started the ball rolling. At nine she had strengthened her position by some acting clever enough to deceive Mrs. Westward. And when they had reached her primed by her story of the threatening stranger they had found her waiting hysterically for their aid. No doubt she had been drinking. Most women hate using firearms for violent purposes unless the act is one of suddenly inspired fury when the deed almost synchronizes with the impelling thought.

She had planned the thing carefully. She had, if his theory held, probably shot the old man as he sat reading. Then she had locked and barred the great doors and lowered herself to the ground and entered by the garage door which she could have opened from above. Thus the men coming to her aid found a scene prepared which her ingenuity had led them to expect as entirely reasonable.

"By the way," he demanded suddenly, "how long was the doctor or coroner in getting to Mr. Apthorpe?"

"He didn't get there until midnight. His motor broke down."

It was thus impossible to fix accurately the time of Apthorpe's death.

As they turned from the drive into Groton's main street a big limousine passed them. To its occupants Mr. Westward raised his hat.

"Mrs. Apthorpe," he explained, "her daughter and son-in-law, Hugh Fanwood. The other man was Wilkinson the lawyer who acts for Mrs. Apthorpe." He paused as another car turned into the drive. "Look like detectives," he commented. "We are well out of it."

That night Anthony Trent went back to New York. Twenty-four hours later his fast runabout drew up at the Westward's hospitable home.

"I brought my car over from Boston," he explained untruthfully, "on my way back to New York by way of the Berkshires and dropped in to see if there was any news in the Apthorpe murder case. The Boston papers had very little I didn't already know."

He learned a great deal that interested him. First that Nurse Thompson had been left fifty thousand dollars in the Apthorpe will. This, on the advice of counsel, would not be contested, as the widow desired, on the ground of undue influence. Her daughter Mrs. Hugh Fanwood was not desirous of publicity.

Secondly one of the most famous jewels in the world had been stolen.

"Imagine it," Mrs. Westward exclaimed, "for five years an emerald that was once in a Tsarina's crown has been within a mile of us and not a soul in Groton knew of it. It was worth a fortune. *Now* we know why the poor man was done to death."

"Have they any clue?" he demanded.

"They have offered a reward of ten thousand dollars. Miss Thompson's description of the man has been circulated widely and caused arrests in every town in the state. The house is being searched by a detective agency but we all believe it's useless. I don't think Amelia Apthorpe behaved at all well. She insisted on having everybody searched who was in the house. Not Charles of course but every one she didn't know and some whom she did."

"I was in the house," Trent reminded them, "perhaps I ought to offer myself."

"No, no," Westward exclaimed, "I told Mrs. Apthorpe who you were. I said you bought the Stanley camp on Kennebago and that I could vouch for you."

"That's mighty nice of you," Trent responded warmly. It was at a moment like this when he realized he was deceiving a good sportsman that he hated the life he had chosen. It was one of the reasons that he denied himself friends. "Did she have any sort of scrap with Miss Thompson?"

"It's too mild a word," said Westward. "After the nurse's things were searched she was told to go. Then she said she should bring an action against Mrs. Apthorpe for defamation of character and illegal search.

She promised that there would be enough scandal unearthed to satisfy even the yellow press. I don't suppose poor Amelia Apthorpe knew there were such lurid words in or out of the dictionary until the Thompson woman flung them at her."

"Will she bring action, do you think?"

"I think she's too shrewd. From what Hugh Fanwood told me they had looked up her record and found it shady. She *was* a graduate nurse once. Her diploma is genuine and the doctor here tells me she knew her business, but there are other things that she wouldn't want in print. I think we've seen the last of her. She'll get her fifty thousand dollars and when she's gone through that she'll find some other old fool to fall for her."

So far, Trent's conjecture as to her character had been accurate. The death of Apthorpe meant a large sum of money to her while the legacy remained unrevoked. He could not marry her since he was not divorced from his wife. Perhaps he had believed in her sufficiently to show her his peerless emerald. Or perhaps he had only hinted at its glories and she had become possessed of the secret of its whereabouts. In any case Anthony Trent firmly believed she had it. It was quite likely that she had secreted it somewhere in the grounds of the mansion to retrieve it without risk later on. What woman except Nurse Thompson would have lowered herself from the room to the turf below on the night of the murder? And was it not likely that the emerald was the cause of the tragedy? The whole history of precious stones could be written in blood. In any case it was a working hypothesis sound enough for Trent to have faith in.

In accordance with the advice of lawyers and relatives Mrs. Andrew Apthorpe decided to place no obstacle in the way of the departure of Nurse Thompson. She told Mrs. Westward she was certain the woman had taken the diamond ring she flaunted and that it had not been a gift, as she claimed, from her employer. Furthermore it was evident that she had made a good deal of money in padding the household expenses.

Detectives, meanwhile, clinging faithfully to the description so generously amplified by Miss Thompson of the thief in the night, were hunting everywhere for him and his loot.

The *West Groton Gazette* supplied Anthony Trent with some much needed information. It printed in its social columns the news that Miss Norah Thompson was to make an extended stay in the West, making her first long stop at San Francisco. Until then she was staying with a married sister in East Boston. Since the name was given in full Anthony Trent had little difficulty in finding what he needed. An operative from a Boston detective agency gleaned the facts while Trent made a pleasant stay at the Touraine. To the operative he was a Mr. Graham Maltby of Chicago.

When he went West on the same train as the now resplendent Miss Norah Thompson he was possessed of a vast amount of information concerning her. In St. Louis six years before she had badly beaten a man whom she declared had broken his engagement to marry her. She was a singularly violent disposition and had figured in half a dozen cases which wound up in police courts.

CHAPTER XXII

A THIEF TO CATCH A THIEF

It was not a matter of much difficulty for Trent, still Mr. Maltby, to become acquainted with male members of the set in San Francisco which Miss Thompson affected. He knew that she dined each night at a café which attracted many motion picture people. And he learned that there was a producer from Los Angeles now looking for easy money in San Francisco who was very friendly with her. Since this man Weiller was easy of approach to such as seemed prosperous it was not difficult for Trent to strike up an acquaintance one day at the St Charles. Weiller first of all, as became a loyal native son, spoke of climate. Then with even greater enthusiasm he spoke of the movies as money-makers. He wanted to get a little money together, put on a feature and sell it. He arranged all the details on the back of a St. Charles menu card. He had an idea which, if William Reynard of New York could learn of it, would bring that eminent producer of features a cool million.

Anthony Trent hung back with the lack of interest a man with money to invest may properly exhibit. Weiller was sure he had money. He lived at a first class hotel, he dined well and he was a "dresser" to be admired. Also Weiller had seen a sizeable roll of bills on occasion.

There came a night when at Anthony Trent's expense, Miss Norah Thompson, Weiller and a svelte girl called by Weiller California's leading "anjenou," partook of a sumptuous repast. Had it not been that Trent was out for business the whole thing would have disgusted him. Weiller and Norah were blatantly vulgar and intent on impressing their host. The "anjenou" said a hundred times that he was like one of her dearest "gentlemen friends" now being featured by the Jewbird Film company. Her friend was handsome but she liked Anthony's nose better.

With coffee came the great scheme. Weiller wanted to make a five reel feature of the Andrew Apthorpe murder. Norah Thompson was to play the lead!

"It'll knock 'em dead!" cried Weiller. "Gee! What press agent stuff!" He helped himself with a hand trembling from excitement to another gulp of wine. "My boy, you're in luck. We'll go into this thing on equal shares. I'm putting up fifty thousand dollars and you shall put up a like sum. We'll clear up five hundred per cent."

"You've put up fifty thousand in actual cash?" Trent demanded.

"That's what I capitalize my knowledge of pictures at," Weiller explained.

"George is one of the best known producers in the game," Miss Thompson said, a trifle nettled at what she thought was a smile of contempt on the other's face. "He don't need your money. I've got enough in this bag right here to produce it." She waived a black moiré bag before Trent's eyes.

George Weiller looked at her and frowned. What a foolish project, he thought, to spend one's own money when here was a victim.

"You keep that, little one," he said generously. "We're gentlemen; we don't want to take a lady's money. We'll talk it over later."

A keen salesman, he noted Trent was growing restive. If the matter were persisted in he might either take a fright or take offence. All this he explained later. "You see, Norah," he remarked, "that guy has a chin on him that means you can't drive him."

"He's got a cold, nasty eye," said Norah who was not without her just fears of strangers.

"I'm going to play the game so he'll beg me to let him in on it," Weiller boasted. "I know the way to play that sort of bird."

The negotiations resulted in Trent's seeing a great deal more of this precious couple than he cared for. The "anjenou" finding her charms made no impression on him was rarely included in the little dinners and excursions.

It was when Trent had met Miss Thompson a dozen times that he consulted the notes he had made on each occasion. It was a method of working unique so far as he could learn. It might yield no results in a thousand cases. In the thousand and first it might be the clue. It was nothing more than a list of the costumes he had seen the ex-nurse wear.

On going through the list he saw that whereas Miss Thompson had worn a new dress on each occasion of the dinners in public restaurants with shoes and hosiery to harmonize or match the color scheme of her gown she had always carried the black moiré bag. And since it was a fashion of the moment for women to own many and elaborate bags of this sort to match or harmonize with the color scheme or details of their costumes, it seemed odd that Norah Thompson, who had been buying everything that seemed modish, should fail to follow the way of the well dressed.

The bag as he remembered it was about seven inches wide and perhaps ten inches long. It was closed by a silver buckle and a pendant of some sort swung at each corner. Concentrating upon it he remembered they were not beads but made of the same material as the bag itself and in size about that of an English walnut. He called to mind the fact that he had never seen her without this bag. Why should she cling so closely to what was already demodé? Were he a genuine detective the problem had been an easy one. He could seize the bag, search it and denounce her. But that would entail giving up a priceless stone for a few thousand dollars of reward.

On the pretext of having to buy a present for a Chicago cousin, Anthony Trent led the willing Weiller into one of the city's exclusive department stores. Weiller was anxious to do anything and everything for his new friend. That night he, Norah and some other friends were to be Trent's guests at a very recherché dinner. He felt, as the born sales-man senses these things, that he would get his answer that night and that it would be favorable. And with fifty thousand dollars to play with he might do anything. Probably the last project would be to make a picture himself.

Trent asked to be shown the very latest thing in bags. The counter was presently laden with what the salesgirl claimed to be direct importations from Paris. Trent selected one which he said would suit his cousin.

"You ought to get one for Norah," he said. "What color is she going to wear to-night?"

"Light blue," Weiller returned almost sulkily. He had been with her when she purchased the gown and resented the extravagance. If she went on at that rate there would be nothing left for him. "What they call gen-tian blue."

The salesgirl picked out an exquisite blue bag on which the lilies of France had been painted daintily by hand. It was further decorated with a border of fleur-de-lis in seed pearls.

"This is the biggest bargain we have," the girl assured them. "The government won't allow any more to be brought over. It's marked down to a hundred dollars." She looked at George Weiller, "Will you take it?"

"I'm not sure it's the shade my friend wants," he prevaricated. In reality he cursed Trent for dragging him into a proposition which could cost such a sum. He had not a tenth of the amount upon him.

"I'll take it," Trent said carelessly, pushing a hundred dollar bill over the counter, "I've plenty of cousins and girls always like these things."

Weiller sighed enviously. He often remarked if he could capitalize his brains he would pay an income tax of a million dollars; but that did not prevent him from being invariably short of ready money.

He was looking forward to the dinner Trent was to give him and his friends that night. Besides Norah there were five other moving picture people who were to be used to impress Trent with their knowledge of the game and the money he could make out of it. They would be amply repaid by the dinner; for there are those who serve the screened drama whose salaries are small. These ancilliary salesmen and women were to meet at half past six in the furnished flat Norah Thompson had rented. There they were to be drilled.

It was while they were receiving the finishing touches that Anthony Trent knocked upon the door, blandly announcing that he had brought an automobile to take Norah and George to the hotel where he was staying.

Instantly the gathering registered impatience to start. Weiller, always suspicious, feared that Trent might think it curious that so many were engaged in earnest conversation, and he wondered if their voices had carried to the hall where Trent had waited.

Suave and courteous, Trent made himself at home among the crowd of people who were, so they informed him, world famous in a screen sense.

Trent, as usual, had timed things accurately. It was part of his scheme that Norah should want to banish from his mind the idea that there had been any collusion. She was bright and vivacious in her manner toward him.

"You are a sweet man," she exclaimed, "I'm dreadfully hungry—and thirsty. Come on boys and girls."

He noticed that although arrayed in a new costume of blue, she clung to her back moiré bag. He called Weiller aside while Norah mixed a last cocktail for the men.

"George," he whispered, "that blue bag I bought is just the thing to give Norah." George felt a parcel thrust into his hand. "It's a little present from me to you and she mustn't know I bought it."

"She shan't from me," Weiller said almost tremulously. Nothing could have happened more delightfully. Not ten minutes ago in the presence of his even less prosperous motion picture colleagues, Norah had called him a tightwad who didn't think enough of the woman he was to marry to buy her a ring. He explained that easily enough by saying nothing in San Francisco was good enough for her and that he was ordering one from New York. This present from a rich and careless spender would prove affluence no less than affection. "Thanks, old man, a million times."

Norah was at the door when he presented it. She was genuinely affected by the gift. Perhaps her thanks were even warmer when one of her friends picked up the sales slip which had fluttered to the ground and read aloud the price. "I'm tired of that black bag," George complained.

"Norah's never going to carry that when she's got this," one of the other women cried. "It matches her gown exactly."

"I took care of that," George said complacently. "I told the saleswoman to get me the best she had but it must be gentian blue."

There seemed a momentary hesitation before the black bag was discarded. To cling to it at such a moment would be to court suspicion. This was Trent's strategy. Her manner was not lost upon one of the others, a character woman named Richards.

"Why, George," she laughed, "I believe a former lover gave Norah that bag and she hates to part with it. I was in a picture once where the heroine carried the ashes of her first sweetheart around with her. I'd look into it if I was you."

Nonchalantly Norah emptied the contents of the black bag into the new one. Then she pitched the old one onto a chair.

"Now for the eats," she said cheerily.

CHAPTER XXIII

THE SECRET OF THE BLACK BAG

The dinner was a wearisome affair to Trent. His companions were vulgar, their conversation tedious and the flattery they offered him nauseous. It was exactly half-past nine when a waiter came to his side and told him there was a long distance call for him from Denver. Apologizing he left the table.

"His brother is a mining man out in Colorado," Weiller informed the company. "They're a rich bunch, the Chicago Maltbys."

"They can't come too rich for us," one of his friends chuckled. "Pass me the wine, George."

"This is a great little opportunity for rehearsing," Weiller reminded them. "I've got to sign this bird up to-night. If I do we'll have another little dinner on Saturday with a souvenir beside each plate."

Directly Trent reached the hotel lobby he slipped the waiter a five dollar bill. "If they get impatient," he cautioned the man, "say I'm still busy on the long distance and must not be interrupted."

Five minutes later he opened the door of Norah's flat and turned on the light. There, upon a chair, was the bag on which he had built so many hopes. His long sensitive fingers felt each of the pendants. Then with the small blade of a pocket knife he cut a few stitches and drew out the Takowaja emerald. For a full minute he gazed at its green glittering glory. Then from a waistcoat pocket he took the brilliant which had been purchased with the Benares lamp. They were much of a size and he placed the glass where the jewel had been and with a needle of black silk already prepared sewed up the cut stitches. The whole time occupied from entering the apartment to leaving it was not five minutes. He was back with his guests within a quarter of an hour.

"You must have had good news," Norah exclaimed when he took his seat. His face which had been expressionless before was now lighted up. He was a new man, vivacious, witty and bubbling over with fun.

"I had very good news," he smiled, "I put through a deal which means a whole lot to me. Let's have some more wine to celebrate."

The dinner was taking place in a private room and he had insisted that the service be of the best. Now he was free from the tension that inevitably preceded one of his adventures he could enjoy himself. For the first time he looked at the omnibus by the door behind him. It was not the youthful fledgling waiter he expected to see but a big, dark man with a black moustache and imperial. Norah observed his glance.

"George offered to star him as the mysterious count but the poor wop don't speak English."

"I'll bet he left spaghetti land because he done a murder," George commented, "a nasty looking rummy I call him."

"I'll swear he wasn't here when I went to the 'phone," said Trent. "I should have noticed him."

None heard him. The new bottle demanded attention. There was something vaguely familiar about the face but for the life of him Trent could not place it. Uneasily he was aware that the man of whom this strange waiter reminded him had come at a moment of danger. The more he looked the more certain he was that imperial and moustache were the disguising features. But it is not easy to strip such appendages off in the mind's eye and see clearly what lies beneath. But there was a way to do so. On the back of an envelope Trent sketched the waiter as he appeared. It was a good likeness. Then with the rubber on his pencil end he erased moustache and imperial. The face staring at him now was beyond a question that of Devlin, the man who had run foul of him over the case of the Mount Aubyn ruby. He remembered now that Devlin had left Jerome Dangerfield's employ to join a New York detective agency.

What was Devlin doing here disguised as a waiter if not on his trail? And pressed against his side was a stone of world fame. There was no possibility of escape. The dining room was twenty feet from the street below and he had no way of reaching it. The door was guarded by Devlin and outside in the corridor waiters flitted to and fro. "Old Sir Richard caught at last."

He was roused from his eager scheming by a waiter asking what liqueur he would have. Automatically he ordered the only liqueur he liked, green chartreuse. Would Devlin allow the party to break up? If so he had a place of safety already prepared for the emerald. But if arrest and search were to take place before he could reach his room there was no help. He would be lucky to get off with fifteen years.

Something told him that Devlin was about to act. Waiters were now grouped about the door. He knew that Devlin must long ago have marked him down and this was the final scene. And yet, oddly enough, when suddenly the door closed and a truculent detective advanced to the table tearing off moustache and imperial, Anthony Trent, who had not left his seat, had no longer the incriminating stone upon him. He felt, in fact, reasonably secure.

"Quiet youze," Devlin shouted and flashed a badge at them. Five of the eight felt certain he had come for them. Weiller owed much money in the vicinity of Fort Lee, New Jersey and was never secure. And more than that he had passed many opprobrious remarks concerning the waiter whom he supposed did not understand him.

"I'm employed," said Devlin, "to recover the emerald stolen from the home of the late Andrew Apthorpe of Groton, Massachusetts, on the third of last month, and you can be searched here or in the station house."

"It's an outrage," exclaimed Miss Richards the character woman.

"Sure it is," Devlin agreed cynically, "but what are you going to do about it?"

A woman operative was introduced who took the ladies of the party into an adjoining room for search. The emerald was not found. The search revealed merely, that Miss Richards had been souvenir hunting and her spoils were a knife, spoon and olive fork.

The men had passed the ordeal successfully. That they had made the most of their host's temporary absence the pockets full of cigars, cigarettes and salted almonds testified. Anthony Trent seemed hugely amused at the procedure. Alone of them he did not breathe suits for defamation of character and the like.

"I have rooms here," he reminded Devlin, "by all means search them."

"I have," snapped the other, showing his teeth.

"I regret I didn't bring my golf clubs," Trent taunted him.

"I hope I'll put you in a place where they don't play golf," Devlin cried angrily. "I'm wise to you."

"It's good he's wise to something," shouted Miss Richards.

"Isn't it?" Trent returned equably. "I've had no experience of it so far." He resumed his seat and beckoned a waiter, "Some more coffee. Sit down, ladies, the ordeal is over."

"Not by a long shot," snarled Devlin, "I've got a search warrant to search the apartment rented by Norah Thompson and I want you, Weiller, to come with me." He turned to the moving picture celebrities—self confessed celebrities—"as for you, you'd better beat it quick."

Devlin's last impression of the ornate dining room was the sight of the debonair Trent sipping his green chartreuse. Devlin ground his strong teeth when the other raised the green filled glass and drank his health.

He was not to know that in the glass invisible amid the enveloping fluid was the Takowaja emerald, slipped there in the moment of peril.

CHAPTER XXIV

DEVLIN'S PROMISE

Half an hour later the stone, reposing in a tin box of cigarettes, was in the mails on the way to Trent's camp at Kennebago. Mrs. Kinney had instructions to hold all mail and its safety was thus assured. There was nothing more to fear. He wanted very much to know what had happened at Miss Thompson's apartment and proposed to call after breakfast.

But Devlin called first upon him. It was a depressed Devlin. Not indeed a Devlin come to be apologetic, but one less assured.

"Well?" said Trent affably, "come to search me again. I'm getting a little tired of it, my good man."

"I want to know why you pass here under the name of Maltby of Chicago when your name is Trent and you live in New York City."

"A private detective has no right to demand any such knowledge. Last night you took upon yourself powers and authority which we could have resisted if we chose. You had no legal right to search us. I submitted first because I had nothing to fear and secondly to see if the others had the stone. I didn't think they had."

"What do you know about the stone?" Devlin demanded suspiciously.

"Everything except just where it is at this present moment. Between you and me, Devlin, I'm here after it too. I was at Groton, as can easily be proved, on the day after the murder." Trent smiled as a curious look passed over the detective's face, "I'm going to disappoint you. I passed the day and night in Boston when the murder was done. I have just as much use for that ten thousand dollars as you have. By the way I suppose you got the stone?"

"Like hell I did," Devlin cried red in the face, "I got this." He showed Trent the piece of cut glass which had hung in his room for so long. "Glass, that's what it is." Devlin leaned forward and looked hard into Anthony Trent's eyes. "You know more about this than you pretend. It ain't accident that brings you around when two such stones as Dangerfield's ruby and this here emerald get stolen. There's something more to it than that. There's something mighty queer about you, Mister Anthony Trent, and I'm going to see what it is."

Trent looked at him for a moment and then smiled. It was the tolerant smile of the superior. It angered Devlin. His red face grew redder still.

"My good Devlin," said Trent, "stupidity such as yours may be a good armor but it is a poor diving suit."

"Talk sense," Devlin commanded.

"If you wish," Trent agreed easily. "I mean that you haven't the mental equipment to live up to your desires. You have the impertinence to think *you* can outwit *me*. I'm your superior in everything. Mentally, morally and physically I can beat you and in your heart you know it. I think I've stood about as much from you as I care to take from any man. For a time you amused me. At Sunset Park you thought you were being very subtle searching my room with your twin ass, O'Brien, but I was laughing at you."

"You was drunk," said Devlin slowly.

"That's how gin takes me," said the other, "I see the ludicrous in men and things. Just listen to me. My past and present bears investigation. You looked me up and you know." Trent drew his bow at a venture. "You found that out, didn't you?"

"Because I couldn't find anything against you doesn't prove you're what you pretend," Devlin admitted grudgingly.

"The point I wish to make is this," Anthony Trent said incisively, "I'm tired of you. You bore me. You weary me. You exasperate me. I am willing to overlook your blundering stupidity this time but if you worry me again I shall go after you so hard you'll wish you'd never heard my name. I've got money and that means influence. You've neither. Think it over. Now get out."

Devlin looked at him doubtfully. There was a strong personal animus against Anthony Trent. He hated anything suave, smiling or polite. And when these qualities were in conjunction with physical prowess they spelled danger. But for the moment nothing was to be gained by violence. Devlin essayed a genial air.

"We all of us make mistakes," he admitted. "I'm willing to say it. I'm sorry I've gone wrong over this case." He held out a big short fingered hand. "Good-bye."

"What's the use?" Trent demanded. "You will always be my enemy and I never shake hands with an enemy if I can get out of it."

Devlin was at a loss for the moment. It had been his experience that when he offered a hand it was grasped gladly, eagerly. There was something in this harder unsmiling Trent which impressed him against his will.

"They shake hands before the last round of a prize fight," he reminded the other man.

"So they do," said Trent smiling a little, and offered his hand.

Two weeks later he was compelled to concede that Devlin's pertinacity sometimes won its reward.

Devlin had always been an advocate of the third degree. Together with some operatives from his agency he staged a gruesome drama into which hysterical and frightened the drink-enervated Norah Thompson was dragged. Under the pitiless cross-examination of these hard men she broke down. Andrew Apthorpe's murderer was found. But the triumph was incomplete. She convinced them that although the emerald had been hers for a time, of its destination or present ownership she had no idea. She went into penal servitude for life with a newspaper notoriety that made the Takowaja emerald the most famous stone in existence.

CHAPTER XXV

ON THE TRAIL OF "THE COUNTESS"

The expert has usually a critical sense well developed. It was so with Anthony Trent. He read the details of all the crimes treated in the daily press almost jealously. What the police regarded as clever criminals were seldom such in his eyes. There were occasionally crimes which won his admiration but they were few and far between. Violence to Trent's mind was a confession of incompetency, the grammar school type of crime to a university trained mind. One morning the papers were unusually full of such examples of robberies with attendant assaults. Clumsy work, he commented, and then came to a robbery in Long Island of jewels whose aggregate value was more than a hundred thousand dollars.

The home of Peter Chalmers Rosewarne at the Montauk Point end of Long Island was the victimized abode. All Americans knew Peter Chalmers Rosewarne. He was the "Tin King," enormously wealthy, splendidly generous and fortune's favorite. His father had been a Cornish mining captain who had come from Huel Basset to make a million in the United States. His son had made ten millions.

His Long Island place, known as St. Michael's Mount after that estate in Cornwall near where his father had been born, was a show place. The gardens were extraordinary. The house was filled with treasures which only the intelligent rich may gather together. Rosewarne was a convivial soul in the best sense of the phrase. He loved company and he loved display and more than all he loved his wife on whom he showered the beautiful things women adore. Abstractors of precious stones would gravitate naturally to such a home as his.

Anthony Trent remembered that the Rosewarne strain of Airedales was the best the breed had to show. He had read once that Rosewarne turned his dogs loose at nights and laughed burglars to scorn. And well he might, for of all dogs, the gods have blessed none with such sense as the Airedales possess. Theirs not to bark indiscriminately or bite their master's friends. Theirs to reason why: to know instinctively what is hidden from the lesser breeds.

A dozen such dogs roaming their master's grounds, their guardian instincts aroused, would effectually bar out strangers. That a robbery had been committed at St. Michael's Mount spelled for Trent an inside job. The papers told him that a large house party was gathered under the hospitable Rosewarne roof. Rosewarne himself indignantly denied the possibility of his guests' guilt. The servants seemed equally satisfactory.

Sifting the news Anthony Trent learned that the suspected person was a girl who had been member of a picnic party using the Rosewarne grounds. There was a space of nearly ten acres which the mining man had reserved for parties, suitably recommended, who made excursions from the Connecticut side of the Sound. Here Sunday Schools passed blameless days and organized clambakes. The party to which the suspected girl belonged was a camp for working girls situated on one of the Thimble Islands.

Nearly forty of them, enjoying the privilege of the Rosewarne grounds, had spent the day there. Mrs. Rosewarne herself had seen them depart into the evening mist. Then she had seen, thirty minutes later, a girl running to the water's edge. She was dressed, as were the others of her party, with red trimmed middy blouse and red ribbons in her hair. A brunette, rather tall and slight, and awed when the chatelaine of the great estate asked what was the matter. It seemed she had become tired and had slept. When she awoke the boat was gone; she had not been missed.

Mrs. Rosewarne was not socially inept enough to bring the simple girl to her own sophisticated dinner table. Instead the girl had an ample meal in the housekeeper's room. At nine o'clock a fast launch was to be ready to take her to her camp. It might easily overtake the sail boat if the breezes died down.

At nine-fifteen the mechanician in charge of the boat came excitedly into the house to relate his unhappy experiences. The girl, wrapped in motor coat, was safely in the boat when she begged the man to get her a glass of water from the boat house at the dock. It was while he was doing so that the boat disappeared. He heard her call to him in fright and then saw the boat—one capable of twenty knots an hour—glide away with the girl holding her hands out to him supplicatingly. She had fooled with the levers, he averred, and would probably perish in consequence. It was while Rosewarne considered the matter of sending out his yacht in pursuit that the discovery was made that a hundred thousand dollars worth of jewels had been taken.

The mechanician had been fooled, of that they were now assured, and the working girl became a fleeing criminal. The sudden temptation through seeing sparkling stones in profusion was the result. A number of boats went in pursuit and the ferries were watched, but the fast motor launch was not found.

Considering the case from the evidence he had at command Trent was certain it was no genuine member of the working girls' camp who had done this thing. Every move spoke of careful preparation. Some one had chosen a moment to appear at the Mount when suspicion would be removed and her coming seem logical. And no ordinary person would have been able to drive a high powered boat as she had done. Another thing which seemed conclusive proof of his correctness was the fact that the girl had overlooked—this was as the police phrased it—Mrs. Simeon Power's pearl necklace and the diamond tiara belonging to Mrs. Campbell Glenelg. This omission supported the police theory that it was the work of an inexperienced criminal.

Anthony Trent chuckled as he read this. He also had rejected the Power's pearls and the Glenelg tiara. They had been in his appraising hand. *They were both extraordinarily good imitations!* Assuredly a timid working girl could not be such a judge of this. She was a professional and a clever one. Probably she had sunk the launch and swam ashore.

Later reports veered around to his view. The camp people were highly indignant at being saddled with a criminal. They had counted noses before embarkation and none was missing. Mrs. Rosewarne described the girl and so did the housekeeper. The latter, remarking on the slightly foreign intonation, was told by the girl herself that she came from New Bedford where her father was employed in a textile mill belonging to Dangerfield. Like so many of the inhabitants of this mill town he was of French Canadian stock and habitually spoke French in the home. But the housekeeper who had served the wealthy in England and Continental Europe would have it that this intruder come of a higher social class than New Bedford mills afford.

Interviewing the housekeeper in the guise of a Branford newspaper man Trent asked her a hundred questions. And each one of her answers confirmed the belief that had grown in him. This clever woman was "The Countess." He felt certain of it. That slight intonation was hers. The figure, the height, the coloring. And of course the exact knowledge of what stones were good and what were not. This was another count against her for Trent had marked St. Michael's Mount for his hunting ground and now precautions against abstractors would be redoubled.

He felt almost certain that this was the Countess's first exploit since her escape from the hotel after the Guestwick robbery. He had followed the papers too closely to miss any unusual crime. A woman of her breeding need never drop to association with the typical criminal. Since she was marooned in the United States during the war she was of necessity cut off from her favorite Riviera hunting grounds. Where, then, might she meet the wealthy set if not among the owners of big estates on Long Island? Trent felt it probable that she was near some such social center as Meadowbrook or Piping Rock. How was he to find her?

To begin with he decided to attend the Mineola Horse and Dog show. This country fair, held during late September, invariably attracted, as he knew, all the horse-loving polo-riding elements of the smart set. Not to go there, not to be interested intelligently in horses, hounds and dogs was a confession of ineligibility to the great Long Island homes.

Although he entertained a bare hope of seeing her and passed the first day in disappointment, he saw her almost directly he entered the show grounds on the second morning. She looked very smart in her riding habit, her hair was done in a more severe coiffure than he had noticed before. She was talking to a well known society woman, also in riding kit, a Mrs. Hamilton Buxton, famous for her horses and her loves. But he could not judge from this whether or not the Countess was on friendly terms with her or not. There is a *camaraderie* among those who exhibit horses or dogs which is of the ring-side and not the salon. Outside it was possible Mrs. Hamilton Buxton might not recognize her.

Later on he saw that both women were riding in the class for ladies' hunters, to be ridden side saddle by the owners. So the Countess owned hunters now! Well, he expected something of the sort from a woman who had outwitted so astute a craftsman as himself. In a sense he was glad of it. It was better to find her in such a set as this. When she rode around the ring he saw by the number she bore that she was a Madame de Beaulieu of Old Westbury. She rode very well. There was the *haute école* stamp about her work and she was placed second to Mrs. Hamilton Buxton whose chestnut was of a better type.

Anthony Trent went straightway to New York. He did not want to be seen—yet. He called up a certain number and made an appointment with a Mr. Moor. This man, David Moor, was a private detective without ambition and without imaginative talent. It always amused Trent when he employed a detective to find out details that were laborious in the gathering. In some subtle manner Trent had given Moor the impression that he was a secret service agent exceedingly high in the department.

"Moor," he said briskly as the small and depressed David entered the room, "I want to find all about a Madame de Beaulieu who lives in Old Westbury, Long Island. I suspect her of being a German spy. Find out what other members of the household there are, and who calls. Whether they are in society or only trying to be. I want a full and reliable report. The tradesmen know a whole lot as a rule and servants generally talk. I want to know as soon as possible but keep on the job until you have something real." He knew that Moor by reason of an amazingly large family was always hard up. He handed him fifty dollars. "Take this for expenses."

Moor went from the room with tears in his eyes. He looked at Trent as a loving dog looks at its master. Two years before his wife lay at the point of death, needing, more than anything, a rest from household worries and the noise of her offspring. Trent sent her to a sanitarium and the children to camps for the whole of a hot summer. In his dull, depressed fashion, Moor was always hoping that some day he could do something to help this benefactor who waved his thanks aside.

The report, written in Moor's small, clear writing, entertained Trent vastly. Madame de Beaulieu was a daughter of France whose husband was fighting as an officer of Chasseurs and had been decorated thrice. Many pictures adorned the house of her hero. She had a French maid who allowed herself to be very familiar with her mistress. Undoubtedly she was the "aunt" of the Guestwick occasion. The men of the household were doubtful according to Moor. One was Madame's secretary, an American named Edward Conway, who looked after her properties, and the other an Englishman, Captain Monmouth, a former officer of cavalry who had broken an ankle in a steeple chase, so the report ran, and was debarred from military service. He was a cousin by marriage. The servants asserted that he was an amazingly lucky player at bridge or indeed of any card game. So much so indeed that the neighboring estate owners who had been inclined to be friendly were now stiffly aloof. The captain's skill at dealing was uncanny. Bills were piling up against them all. It was due largely to this that Moor was able to get so much information. A vituperative tradesman sets no watch on his tongue. Conway, the secretary, confined his work almost entirely to drinking. There were many bitter wrangles at the table but the English tongue was never adopted on such occasions. The part of Moor's screed which interested Trent most was that there had been a discussion overheard by a disgruntled maid to take in some wealthy paying guest and offer to get him into Long Island's hunting set. It would be worth a great deal to an ambitious man to gain an entrée into some of these famous Westbury homes. Of course the odd household could probably not live up to such promises but its members had done a great deal. For example, a Sunday paper in its photogravure supplement had snapped Madame de Beaulieu talking with Mrs. Hamilton Buxton; and Captain Monmouth was there to be seen chatting with Wolfston Colman, the great polo player. An excellent beginning astutely planned.

It was while Anthony Trent debated as to whether he dare risk the Countess's recognition of him that a wholly accidental circumstance offered him the opportunity.

Suffering from a slightly inflamed neck he was instructed to apply dioxygen to the area. This he did with such cheerful liberality that his shaving mirror next day showed him a man with black hair at the front and a vivid blond at the back. The dioxygen had helped him to blondness as it had helped a million brunettes of the other sex. For a moment he was chagrined. Then he saw how it might aid. It was his intention to go back to Kennebago for the deer hunting and accordingly he despatched Mrs. Kinney post haste. She was used to these erratic commands and saw nothing out of the ordinary in the fact that he was in a bath robe with a turkish towel wound about his head. He was in dread of becoming bald and was continually fussing with his hair. In a day or so Anthony Trent was a changed being. His eyes had a hazel tint in them which formed not too startling a contrast to his new blondness. He was careful to touch up his eyebrows also.

Shutting up his flat he registered at a newly built hotel as Oscar Lindholm of Wisconsin. He would pass for what we assume the handsome type of Scandinavian to be. It was at this hotel Captain Monmouth stayed when he came to indulge in what he termed a "flutter" with the cards. There were still a few houses in the city where one could be reasonably sure of quiet. Hard drinking youths were barred at these houses. They became quarrelsome. The men who played were in the main big business men who could win without exhuberance or lose without going to the district attorney. They were invariably good players and lost only to the professionals. And their tragedy was that they could not tell a professional until the game was done. Captain Monmouth always excited in players of this type a certain spirit of contempt. He was so languid, so gently spoken, so bored at things. And he consumed so much Scotch whiskey that he seemed primed for sacrifice. But he was never the altar's victim. He was always so staggered at his unexpected good fortune that he readily offered a revenge. A servant had told David Moor that the household was supported on these earnings.

Captain Monmouth, stepping through the lounge on the way to his taxi, caught sight of Oscar Lindholm. Oscar was leaning against the bar rail talking loudly of the horse. Five hours later Oscar was still standing at the bar and the horse was still his theme. Monmouth was a careful soul for all his gentle languors and sauntered into the tap room and demanded an Alexander cocktail. As became a son of Wisconsin, Oscar was free and friendly. The "Alexander" was a new one on him, he explained, dropping for a moment themes equine.

Monmouth never made the mistake of offering friendship to a barroom stranger unless he knew exactly what he was and how he might fit into the Monmouth scheme of things. He referred Mr. Lindholm to the guardian of the bottles. It was the size of the Lindholm wad that decided Captain Monmouth to accept an invitation to a golden woodcock in the grill room. There it was that Lindholm opened his heart. He wanted to follow hounds from the back of a horse.

"Well, why don't you, my good sir?" Monmouth replied languidly. For a moment a light of interest had passed across the dark blue eyes of the ex-cavalryman. Trent knew he was interested.

Trent explained. He said that the following of hounds near New York was only possible to one who passed the social examination demanded by these who controlled the hunting set.

"You're quite right," Monmouth admitted, "for the outsider it's impossible."

"I'll show 'em," Oscar Lindholm returned chuckling. Then he took the proof of an advertisement from the columns of a great New York daily and passed it over to Monmouth.

"Wealthy westerner wants to share home among hunting set of Long Island. Private house and right surroundings essential. References. O. L."

And that light passed over the Englishman's eyes, and was succeeded by a look of boredom.

"You don't suppose, do you," he asked, "that the kind of people you want to know will admit a stranger from Wisconsin into their family?"

"Why not?" the other cried, indignantly. "Isn't this a free country and ain't I as good as any other man?"

"In Wisconsin, undoubtedly: I can't speak for Westbury. By the way, can you ride?"

"I could ride your head off," Lindholm bragged.

"Yes?" said Monmouth softly. "Now that's very interesting. Perhaps we could arrange a little match somewhere?"

"Any time at all," Trent returned. He did not for a moment believe he had a chance against Monmouth but he could afford to lose a little money to him. In fact he was anxious for the opportunity.

"You are staying here?" Monmouth demanded.

Trent pushed a visiting card toward him. It was newly done. "Oscar Lindholm, Spartan Athletic Club, Madison, Wisconsin."

"Yes, I'm staying here," he admitted. "Are you?"

"My home is in Westbury," Captain Monmouth replied.

"Then you could get me right in to the set I want?"

"Impossible," cried the other, rising stiffly to his feet. "One owes too much to one's friends."

"Bull!" said Oscar Lindholm rudely. "You only owe yourself anything. If I have a lot of money and you want some of it why consult your friends? What have they done for you?"

"I don't care to discuss it," Captain Monmouth exclaimed. "Good night, Mr. Lindholm." He limped away.

Assuredly he was no simpleton. He was not sure of this blond lover of cross-country sport. If Lindholm were genuine in his desire to break into the sort of society he aimed at he would come back to the attack. If he were not genuine it were wiser to shake him off.

As for Trent, he felt reasonably sure things would come his way. But there was a certain subtlety about these foreign gentlemen of fortune which called for careful treading. Were he once to win his way to the establishment of Madame de Beaulieu he would be in dangerous company. The man who had just left him was dangerous, he sensed. The Countess already commanded his respect. Then there was the so-called secretary and the woman who posed now as a maid. And in the house there might be a treasure trove that would make his wildest expenditures justified. Looked at in a cool and reasonable manner it was a very dangerous experiment for Anthony Trent to make. He would be one against four. One man against a gang of international crooks, all the more deadly because they were suave and polished.

It was while he was breakfasting that Captain Monmouth took a seat near him. Trent commanded his waiter to transport his food to Monmouth's table.

"What about that horse race?" he demanded.

"Let me see," the other murmured. "Oh yes, you say you can ride?"

"I can trim you up in good style," Trent said cheerfully, "any old time."

"What stakes?" Monmouth asked, without eagerness. "What distance? Over the sticks or on the flat?"

"Stakes?" Trent said as though not understanding.

"I never ride or play cards for love," Monmouth told him.

"That can be arranged later," Trent said, "the main thing is where can we pull it off? Out west there's a million places but here everything is private property."

Captain Monmouth reflected for a moment.

"I shall be in town again in three days' time. You'll be here?"

"Depends what answers I get to my advertisement."

"Oh yes," Monmouth returned, "they will be very amusing. Very amusing indeed."

"Why?" Trent demanded.

"Because the people who will answer will not suit your purpose at all. There may be many who would be glad of help in running a house in these hard times but they dare not answer an advertisement like yours for fear it might be known. And then again think of the risk of taking an unknown into the home?"

"I offer references," Trent reminded him.

"But my dear sir," Monmouth protested, "what are athletic clubs in Madison to do with those who have the entrée to Meadowbrook?"

"Supposing," Trent said presently, "a family such as I want did get into communication with me, how much would they expect?"

Captain Monmouth looked at him appraisingly. Trent felt certain that if a figure were named it would be the one he would have to pay for the privilege of meeting the charming Madame de Beaulieu.

"One couldn't stay at a decent hotel under two hundred and fifty a week," the cavalryman returned. "You'd have to pay at least five hundred."

"That's a lot," Trent commented.

"I imagined you'd think that," Monmouth said drily.

"But I could pay it easy enough," the pseudo-Scandinavian retorted.

CHAPTER XXVI

ANTHONY TRENT—"PAYING GUEST"

And in the end, he did. When Captain Monmouth suggested that the match between the two be ridden off on his own grounds near Westbury, Anthony Trent felt certain that he was taken there to be inspected by the other members of the household.

Edward Conway was a taciturn, drink-sodden man not inclined to be friendly with the affable Oscar Lindholm. Of the match little need be said. Trent, a good rider, had engaged to beat a professional at his own game. Captain Monmouth was the richer by a thousand dollars.

In the billiard room of Elm Lodge after the race Monmouth offered his guest some excellent Scotch whiskey and grew a little more amiable.

"I presume, Mr. Lindholm," he said, "that you would have no objection to my man of business looking up your rating in Madison?"

"Go as far as you like. What you will find will be satisfactory."

"It is," Monmouth smiled. "I wish I had half the money that you have. I should consider myself rich enough and God knows my tastes are not simple."

"So you had me investigated?" Trent smiled a little. "When?"

"When we made this match."

Trent had found that the assumption of a name might be dangerous if investigations were made concerning it. It was with his customary caution that he had taken Lindholm's name. David Moor, his little detective, often spoke of his cases to his patron. He had spoken at length about the case of Oscar Lindholm of Madison, Wisconsin. A lumber millionaire, Oscar came to New York to have a good time in the traditional manner of wealthy men from far states. A joyride in which a man was run down figured prominently in his first night's entertainment. Fearing that the notoriety of this would affect his political aspirations in the west he was sentenced to a month on Blackwell's Island under an assumed name. During this month his name could safely be used. The day that Trent became a member of the household at Elm Lodge the real Lindholm had ten days more to serve.

The wardrobe which Trent had gathered about him was utterly unlike his own perfect outfit. He conceived Oscar Lindholm to be without refinements and he dressed the part. He could see Captain Monmouth shudder as he came into the drawing room on the night of his arrival. Lindholm wore a Prince Albert coat and wore it aggressively.

His patent leather shoes had those hideous knobs on them wherein a dozen toes might hide themselves.

"My dear man," gasped Monmouth, "we dress for dinner always."

"What's the matter with me?" the indignant guest asked.

"Everything," Monmouth cried. "You look like an undertaker. Fortunately we are very much of a size and I have some dress clothes I've never worn. If Madame de Beaulieu had seen you I don't know what would have happened."

In ten minutes Trent was back in the drawing room this time arrayed as he himself desired to be. Madame de Beaulieu had not yet come down.

"Madame is particular then?" Trent hazarded.

"She has a right to be," Monmouth said a little stiffly, "she belongs to one of the great families of France."

Trent, watching him, saw that he believed it. This was a new angle. She had deceived Monmouth without a doubt. For the first time, and the last, Trent observed a certain confusion about Captain Monmouth.

"In confidence," he said, "Madame de Beaulieu and I are engaged to be married. Captain de Beaulieu and she were negotiating for divorce when the war broke out and we must wait therefore."

Trent remembering Moor's report as to the members of the household pointed to Edward Conway sipping his third cocktail. "That's the chaperon, eh?"

"Madame de Beaulieu's aunt, Madame de Berlaymont, is here," Monmouth said affably. "It is our custom to use French at the table as much to starve the servants of food for gossip as anything else. You speak French of course?"

"Not a word," Trent lied promptly, "now if you want to talk Danish or Swedish I'm with you."

Madame de Berlaymont! No doubt the French maid resuming the aunt pose. At the Guestwick affair she had been an English lady of fashion. Had they put themselves to this bother simply for his sake? He doubted it.

"We've not been here long," Captain Monmouth went on, "and we know very few people. Of course we could easily know the wrong sort but that's dangerous. To-night one of the most popular and influential men in the country is coming."

Captain Monmouth had no time to mention his name for Madame de Beaulieu came in. It was the first time Trent had met her face to face since that night at the Guestwick's. He was not without a certain nervousness. Looking at himself in the mirror he seemed so much the product of peroxide that it must easily be recognized. But Madame de Beaulieu gave him the most cursory of glances. There was a certain nervousness about her and Monmouth which had little enough to do with him.

This visit of the influential neighbor plainly was what concerned them. Trent assumed, shrewdly enough, that they were trying, for reasons of their own, to break into the wealthy hunting set and had not found it easy.

Madame de Beaulieu was beautifully gowned. She looked to be a woman of thirty, whereas when he had first seen her she looked no more than two and twenty. She carried herself splendidly. Her French accent was marked. In the police court she spoke as the English do. When the little bent, gray-ringletted but distinguished aunt came in, he could not recognize her at all. Assuredly he had stumbled upon as high class band of crooks as had ever bothered police. He could sense that they regarded him as a necessary nuisance whose five hundred dollars a week helped the household expenses. And he knew, instinctively, that Captain Monmouth and Edward Conway would plan to get some of the millions he was supposed to have.

Trent's Swedish accent was copied faithfully from his janitor who had been of a superior class in his own country before he had fallen to furnace tending. He did not overdo it. To those listening, he appeared anxious to overcome his accent and lapsed into it only occasionally.

Trent heard Monmouth tell Madame de Beaulieu that Lindholm's dress was terrible and that by God's grace their measurements were identical or they would have been disgraced by a guest in a frock coat. He spoke in rapid French and in an undertone but Trent's ears were sharp and had ere this warned him of danger where another man would have heard nothing.

The guest of honor was no less than Conington Warren. He was ripely affable. He had come to this dinner more to report on the behavior of the strangers occupying Elm Lodge than anything else. A bachelor may sit at a table—or a divorced man—where the married man cannot go. At the Mineola Show Madame de Beaulieu had made a good impression on the women but they were not sure of her. They had found that Captain Monmouth was indeed the second son of Sir John Monmouth, Bart, and formerly an officer of Lancers. He had wasted his money at the race track and the gaming table; but then that was not wholly frowned upon by the young bloods of American society.

Trent could see that Warren was impressed. There was an air of breeding about his hostess and host he had not thought to see. The dinner was good enough to win his distinguished commendation. He unbent so far as to question Mr. Lindholm about political conditions in his native state. He congratulated Madame de Beaulieu on the single string of exquisite pearls that were about her white throat. And well he might. Cartier had charged Peter Chalmers Rosewarne a pretty penny for them not so long ago.

Had he but known it he would have been even more interested in the ring which Oscar Lindholm wore. It was a plain gold band in which a single ruby blazed. He had never worn it till now. He felt Lindholm might easily allow himself the luxuries of which Anthony Trent was denied. The stone had adorned a stick pin which Conington Warren once loved and lost.

Monmouth's knowledge of horses commended itself to the owner of thoroughbreds. Two men such as these could not play a part where horses were concerned. Conington Warren remembered seeing Monmouth win that greatest of all steeplechases the Grand National. A *camaraderie* was instantly established. It was a triumphant night. Undoubtedly the household at Elm Lodge would be accepted.

Thinking over the situation in his own room that night Trent admitted he was puzzled. Why this struggle for social recognition? His first theory that it was in order to rob wealthy homes was dismissed as untenable. To begin with it was an old trick and played out. Directly an alien household in a colony of old friends attracts attention it also attracts suspicion. And if this section of Westbury were to suffer an epidemic of burglaries Madame de Beaulieu's home would come under police supervision.

There was little doubt in Trent's mind that this Captain Monmouth was a member of the family he claimed as his. Conington Warren and he had common friends in England. What was his game?

And yet Madame de Beaulieu, or "The Countess," had been notorious as the leading member of a gang of high class crooks. She had even been fingerprinted and had he believed served a sentence. Not a month before she had taken a hundred thousand dollars' worth of jewels from St. Michael's Mount and an amount of currency not specified. As the days went by Trent made other discoveries. He found for one thing that the man whose name he had taken had a reputation for drinking for he found a decanter and siphon ever at his elbow. By degrees he and Edward Conway gravitated together. This Conway, whose part in the game he could not yet guess, was drinking himself steadily to death.

One morning Trent came upon Conway scribbling on a pad of paper. He stared hard at what he wrote and then tossed the crumpled paper into a nearby open fire. The day was chilly and the blazing logs were cheerful. When Conway was gone Trent retrieved the paper and saw the signature he had assumed copied to a nicety. Conway probably had his uses as a forger. The gang of the Countess had accomplished notable successes by these means.

Trent had not been an hour in the house when he discovered that Monmouth and Madame de Beaulieu had eyes only for one another. It was a vulgar intrigue Trent supposed and explained the situation. But as day succeeded day he found he was wrong. Here were two people, a beautiful woman accomplished and fascinating and a man of uncommon good looks and distinction, head over ears in love with one another. Conceivably such people, removed from the conventions of society, would pay small attention to the *convenances* and yet he saw no gesture or heard no word in French or English that was not proper. Sometimes he felt he must have mistaken the aristocratic Madame de Beaulieu and her Empire aunt for the wrong women. But he could not mistake the Rosewarne pearls which he had viewed in Cartier's only a week before the mining man bought them as a birthday present for his wife.

The night that Monmouth and the woman he loved were asked to a dinner party at Conington Warren's home, Oscar Lindholm had two more days to serve on Blackwell's Island. So far Anthony Trent had accomplished nothing. He had lost a thousand dollars on a horse race, two weekly payments of five hundred dollars for board and another thousand in small amounts at auction and pool. He was most certainly a paying guest.

Conway and Trent were not asked. Madame de Berlaymont was indisposed. It was the opportunity he had wanted. It was Conway's habit to sleep from about ten in the evening until midnight. Every night since Trent had been at Elm Lodge the so-called secretary had done so. In a large wing chair with an evening paper unopened on his knees he would fall into sleep. He could be counted upon therefore not to interrupt. The servants retired no later than ten to their distant part of the rambling house. Only Madame de Berlaymont might be in the way. In reality this amiable chaperone was a woman in the early twenties Trent believed and could not be counted upon to remain unmoved if she heard strange noises in the night as of burglars moving.

Trent already knew the lay-out of the house. It was just past ten when the servants went to bed and Conway sunk in his two hours' slumber that Oscar Lindholm went exploring.

Stepping very carefully by Madame de Berlaymont's room he listened a long while. No sound met his ears. Then with a practiced skill he turned the door knob and entered an unlighted room. Still there was no sound of breathing. And when he switched on the light the apartment was empty. The indisposition which had kept the aged lady two days confined to her chamber was plainly a ruse. Trent could return to it later.

Never before to-night had Trent carried an automatic pistol and been prepared to use it if necessary. He was now in a house whose inmates were, like himself, shrewd, resourceful and strong. For all he knew Conway might long ago have suspected him.

Madame de Beaulieu and her chaperone occupied the bedrooms of one wing of the low rambling house. In the other wing Monmouth, Lindholm and Conway slept. Over this bachelor wing as it was called were some smaller rooms where the four maid servants slept.

The rooms of Madame de Beaulieu were beautifully furnished. It was a suite, with salon, bedroom and a large bathroom. Trent determined to allow himself an hour and a half. Skilled as he was in searching he felt he would discover something in those ninety minutes.

But the time had almost gone by and he was baffled. There was nothing. He probed and sounded and measured as he had seen Dangerfield's detectives do but nothing rewarded him. What jewels Madame de Beaulieu owned she had probably worn. But how dare she wear at a dinner party where the Rosewarne's might conceivably be, so well known a string of pearls? And what of those other baubles which were missing from St. Michael's home?

A carved ivory jewel box on her dressing table revealed only a ball the size of a golf ball made of silver paper. She had begged him to save the tinsel in the boxes of cigarettes he smoked so that she might bind this mass until it became worthy of sending to the Red Cross.

Anthony Trent balanced the silver sphere in his hand. Naturally it was heavy. "If I," he mused, "wanted to hide my three beauties I couldn't think of anything safer than this. She's clever, too. Why shouldn't she use it for something she's afraid of anybody seeing?"

A steel hat pin was to his hand. Exerting a deal of wrist strength he thrust it through the mass. In the middle it met with a resistance that the pin could not pierce. It was twelve o'clock as he put it in his pocket and locked the door of his own room. It seemed minutes before his eager fingers could strip off piece after piece of silver paper. And then the palm of his hand cupped one of the most beautiful diamonds he had ever seen.

It was fully a hundred carats in weight and its value he could hardly approximate. No stone of this size had ever been lost in the United States. He remembered however some four years ago the Nizam of Hyderabad—one of the greatest of Indian potentates and owner of an unparalleled collection of diamonds—had bought a famous stone in London. It was never delivered to him. The messenger had been found floating in the Thames off Greenhithe. The reputed price of purchase had been thirty-five thousand pounds. The Nizam's had been a blue-white diamond and Anthony Trent believed he held it in his hand. He thought of his Benares lamp and chuckled. If he desired to avenge himself on Madame de Beaulieu for the loss of the Guestwick money he was amply rewarded now. The blazing thing in his hand would fetch at least two hundred thousand dollars if he dared dispose of it.

Obviously the correct procedure for the supposed Oscar Lindholm was to make his escape at once. He would have little chance to do so were the abstraction to become known. Of course Madame de Beaulieu would look in her ivory casket directly she came in. Did he himself not always glance anxiously at his lamp whenever he had been away from it for a few hours?

Cautiously he made his way down to the hall where his coat and hat were.

As he passed the door it opened and Madame de Beaulieu entered with Monmouth. She was pale, so pale indeed that Trent stopped to look at her.

"Back early, aren't you?" he asked.

"Madame has had bad news," said Monmouth and looked at her anxiously. She sank into a big chair before the open fire. Certainly she was very beautiful. Looking at her it seemed incredible that she could be one of the best known adventuresses in the world. Perhaps, after all, much of the anecdote that was built about her was legendary. Presently she spoke in French to Monmouth.

"Bear with me, my dear one," she said, "but I must see him alone. I am a creature of premonitions. Let me have my way."

The look that Captain Monmouth bent upon Anthony Trent was not a friendly one. There was a new quality of suspicion and antagonism in it.

"Madame de Beaulieu," he said stiffly, "wants to speak with you alone. I see no occasion for it but her wish is law. I shall leave you here."

When they were alone she did not speak for some minutes. Then she turned to him and looked at him searchingly. He felt the necessity of being on his guard.

"Mr. Lindholm," she said quietly, "I do not understand you."

"Why should you bother to?" he asked.

"Because I am afraid of everything I do not trust. You say you are a naturalized Swede. That would explain your hair." She leaned forward and looked him full in the face, "Mr. Lindholm, you have made one very silly mistake which no woman would make."

"And that is—what?" he demanded.

"You have let your bleached hair get black at the roots. You are a black-haired man. Why deny it?"

"I don't," he said. "I admit it."

"Then why are you here?"

"Captain Monmouth knows. A desire to break into society if you like."

"Will you answer me one question truthfully," she asked, "on your honor?"

"Yes," he said. There was no reason why he should not.

"Are you a detective?"

"On my honor, no. Why should Madame de Beaulieu fear detectives?"

There was a faint flush in her cheeks now and a brighter color in her eyes. She was enormously relieved at his answer.

"Why are you here, then?"

"If you must know," he told her, "it was for revenge."

"Not to harm Captain Monmouth?" she cried paling.

"I came on your account," he said quietly. "You don't remember me?"

She shook her head. "When did we meet? In Europe?"

"No less a place than Fifth avenue."

"Ah, at some social function? One meets so many that one has no time for recalling names or even faces."

"Later I saw you at a police court. You were an indignant young English-woman accused of robbing Mr. Guestwick or trying to. You may recall a man who opened the Guestwick safe for you, a man upon whose good nature you imposed." He looked very somber and stern. She shrank back, and covered her face with her white hands.

"I knew happiness was not for me," she said brokenly. "I said, when I found the man I loved was the man who loved me. 'It is too wonderful, too beautiful. It is not for me. I am born under an unlucky star.' And you see I was right."

Trent considered her for a moment. Here was no acting. Here was a woman whose soul was in agony.

"You forget," he said, "that I don't know what you mean."

"I had better tell you," she said with a gesture of despair. "Captain Monmouth and I love each other. It has awakened the good in us that we both thought was buried or had never existed. While my husband, Captain de Beaulieu, lived there was no chance of a divorce. He is Catholic. To-night after dinner one of Mr. Warren's guests brought a late paper from New York and I saw that my husband was killed. I could stay there no longer. Coming home in the motor I asked myself whether it would be my fate to win happiness. I doubted it even though I repented in ashes. Then it was I began to think of you, the stranger whose money we needed, the stranger who reminded me vaguely of some day when there was danger in the air. Under the light as I came in I saw your hair. Then I knew that in the hour of my greatest hope I was to experience the most bitter despair."

"You forget, Madame," he said harshly, "that I have had the benefit of your consummate acting before."

"And you think I am acting now?"

"Why shouldn't I?" he retorted, "you have everything to gain by it. I can collect the Guestwick reward, and send you back to prison."

"I can pay you more than the ten thousand dollars he offered," she cried quickly.

"With the sale of the Rosewarne jewels?"

She shrank back. "Ciel! How could you know?"

"I do," he said brusquely, "and that's enough. You see you are trying to fool me again. You say your love has brought out the good in you that you didn't know you possessed and yet a few weeks back you are at your old tricks again. Is that reasonable?"

"I'll tell you everything," she cried wildly. "You must understand. It was I who took the Rosewarne jewels. Why? Because I am fighting for my happiness. Captain Monmouth knows nothing of what my life has been. I have told him that after the war I shall go back to France and sell my property and with it help him to buy a place that was once a seat of his family. There, away from the world, we shall live and die. I want only him and he wants only me. We have known life and its vanities. We want happiness. You hold it in your hands. If you take your revenge by telling him, you break my heart. Is that a vengeance which satisfies you, Monsieur l'Inconnu? If so, it is very easy. He is in the next room. Call him. You have only to say, 'Captain Monmouth, this woman whom you love is a notorious criminal. All Europe knows her as the Countess. The money that she wants to build her house of love with is stolen money. She will assuredly disgrace your name as she has that of the great family from which she sprang. '"

She looked supplicatingly at Anthony Trent. "You have only to tell him that and there is no happiness left for me in all the world."

"Do you think I would do that?" he demanded.

"How can I tell? Why should you not? I am in your power."

There was no doubting the genuineness of her emotion. Formerly she had tricked him but here was her bared soul to see.

"I came here," he said slowly, "angry because you had played upon my sympathies and outwitted me. I schemed to gain an entrance to this house for no other reason. I shall leave it admiring you and Monmouth and hoping you will be happy."

It was as though she could scarcely believe him.

"Then you will not tell him?" she exclaimed. "You will go without that for which you came?"

She did not understand his smile.

"I shall not tell him," Anthony Trent declared. "As for the rest—we are quits, Madame."

At the hour when the real Oscar Lindholm left Blackwells Island the pretender was lovingly setting the fourth jewel in the Benares lamp. It would have been difficult to find two happier men in all America that morning.

CHAPTER XXVII

MRS. KINNEY MAKES A CONFESSION

Anthony Trent looked about his well-furnished rooms with a certain merited affection. In a week he would know them no more. Already arrangements had been made to send the furniture to his camp on Kennebago. A great deal of the furniture Weems had gathered there was distressfully bad. Weems ran to gilt and brocade mainly.

As Trent surveyed his apartment it amused him to think that never was a flat in a house such as this furnished so well and at so great a cost. The things might seem modest enough at first glance. There was, for example, a steel engraving, after Stuart, of George Washington. A fitting and a worthy picture for any American's room but hardly one which required a large amount of money to obtain.

None save Anthony Trent knew that behind the print was concealed one of the most beautiful examples of that flower of the Venetian Renaissance, Giorgione. A few months before the Scribblers' Club had invited motion picture magnates to its monthly dinner. Only a few of these moulders of public taste had accepted. There were good enough reasons for declination. The subject incensed those who held that writers had no grudge against the "movies." Others lacked speech-making ability in the English tongue. And there were some high-stomached producers who feared the Scribblers' fare might be unworthy.

One big man consented to speak. He was glib with that oratory which comes from successful selling. Before he had sprung into notoriety he had been a salesman in a Seventh Avenue store, one of those persuasive gentlemen who waylay passersby. His speech was, of course, absurd. It was interesting mainly as an example that intelligence is not always necessary in the making of big money.

It was when he began to speak of the material rewards that his acumen had garnered, that Anthony Trent awoke to interest. The producer told his hearers that they had assuredly read of the sale to an unnamed purchaser of a Giorgione. "I am that purchaser!" said the great man. "I give more money for it than—" his shrewd appraising eye went around the table. He saw eager unsuccessful writers, starveling associate editors and a motley company of the unarrived. There were a few who had gained recognition but in the main it was not a prosperous gathering as commerce reckons success. "I give more money for it," he declared, "than all this bunch will make in their lifetime. It'll be on view at the Metropolitan Museum next week when you boys can take an eyefull. It's on my desk at this present moment in a plain wooden case. It ain't a big picture; this Giorgione"—his "G" was wrongly pronounced—"didn't paint'em big. My wife don't know anything about it but she's got the art bug and she'll get it to-morrow morning as her birthday present."

However, the lady was disappointed. The wooden case was brought to the table and the magnate unwrapped it with his own fat fingers. Instead of the canvas representing a Venetian fête and undraped ladies, was the comic sheet of a Sunday paper. The motion picture magnate used his weekly news-sheet (produced in innumerable theatres) to advertise his loss by a production of the missing picture. It was good advertising and made the Venetian master widely known. But it still reposed behind the sphinx-like Washington.

The Benares lamp was naturally his *pièce de résistance*. Never in history had such value been gathered together in a lamp. Trent remembered seeing once in the British Museum a lamp from the Mosque of Omar at Jerusalem on which was inscribed, "The Painter is the poor and humble Mustafa." As he looked at his own lantern he thought, "The Decorator is the unknown Anthony Trent."

Collectors of china would have sneered at a single vase on the top of a bookcase. It was white enameled and had a few flowers painted on it. And the inscription told the curious that it was a souvenir of Watch Hill, R. I.

In reality it was the celebrated vase of King Senwosri who had gazed on it twenty-five centuries before Christ. Senator Scrivener had bought it at a great price in Cairo. Some day the white enamel which Trent had painted over the imperishable glass would be carefully removed and it would gladden his eyes in Maine where visitors would be infrequent.

There were a dozen curious things Trent looked at, things hidden from all eyes but his, which aroused exciting memories of a career he fully believed had drawn to a close. He doubted if ever a man in all the history of crime had taken what he had taken and was yet personally unknown. Some day, if possible, he might be able to learn from the police what mental estimate they had formed of him. He must loom large in their eyes. They must invest him with a skill and courage that would be flattering indeed were he to learn of it. The occasional mentions of him he read in daily papers were too distorted to be interesting and McWalsh's tribute to the unknown master was his only reward so far.

The life that was coming, was to be the life he desired. Leisure, the possession of books, the opportunity to wander as he chose through far countries when the war was over. And he liked to think that later he might find love. Often he had envied men with children. Well, he could offer the woman that he might find comforts that fiction would never have brought him. He was getting to have fewer qualms of conscience now. He often assured himself that he was honest by comparison with war profiteers. He had taken from the rich and had not withheld from the poor.

His immunity from arrest, the growing certainty that his cleverness had saved him from detection led him on this particular night to speculate upon his new life with an easy mind. He had been wise to avoid the dangers of friendship. He had been astute in selecting a woman like Mrs. Kinney who distrusted strangers. She believed in him absolutely. She looked to his comforts and cared for his health admirably. She would assuredly be happy in Maine.

And then he remembered that during the last week or so she had been strangely moody. She had sighed frequently. She had looked at him constantly and gazed away when he met her eye. She was old, and the old were fanciful as he knew. Perhaps, after all she regretted leaving the New York which filled her with exquisite tremblings and fear. In Maine she would be lonely. She should have a younger woman to aid her with the house work. A physician should look her over. Trent was genuinely fond of the old woman.

He was thinking of her when she came into the room. Undoubtedly there was something unusual about her. There was no longer the pleasant smile on her face. He was almost certain she wore a look of fear. Instantly he sensed some danger impending.

"There's a man been here three times to-day," she began.

"What of it?" he demanded. So far as she could judge the news did not disconcert him.

"Is there anybody you might want to avoid?" she asked, and did not look at him as she spoke.

"A thousand," he smiled. "Who was it?"

"He wouldn't leave his name."

"What was he like?"

"A man," she told him, "sixty. Well dressed and polite but I didn't trust him. He'll be back at ten."

It was now almost half past nine.

"I don't see everybody who calls," he reminded her.

"You must see him," she said seriously.

"Why?" he demanded.

"He said you would regret it if you did not."

"Probably an enterprising salesman," he returned with an appearance almost of boredom.

"No, he isn't," she said quickly.

There was no doubt that Mrs. Kinney was terribly in earnest. He affected the air of composure he did not feel.

"Who then?" Anthony Trent demanded.

"I think it's the police," she whispered.

Then suddenly she fell to weeping.

"Oh, Mr. Trent," she said brokenly, "I *know*."

"What?" he cried sharply, suddenly alert to danger, turned in that moment from the debonair careless idler to one in imminent risk of capture.

"About you," she said.

"What about me?" he exclaimed impatiently.

"I know how you make your living. I didn't spy on you, sir, believe me, I just happened on it." Timidly she looked over to the Benares lamp gracefully swinging in its dim corner. "I know about that."

For a moment Anthony Trent said nothing. A few minutes ago he had sat in the same chair as he now occupied congratulating himself on a new life that seemed so near and so desirable. Now he was learning that the little, shrinking woman, who so violently denounced crime and criminals, had found him out. What compromise could he effect with her? Was it likely that she was instrumental in denouncing him to the authorities, tempted perhaps by the rewards his capture would bring? For the moment it was useless to ask how she had discovered the lamp's secret.

"What are you going to do?" he demanded. He was assuredly not going to wait for the police to arrest him if escape were possible. He might have to shut the old woman in a closet and make his hurried exit. He always had a large sum of money about him. Of late the banks had been aiding the government by disclosing the names of those depositors who invested sums of a size that seemed incompatible with their positions and ways of living. He feared to make such deposits that might lead to investigation and of late had secreted what money his professional gains had brought him.

"What am I going to do?" she echoed. "Why help you if I can."

He looked at her, suspicion in his gaze. Her manner convinced him that by some means or other she had indeed stumbled upon what he had hoped was hidden. It was not a moment to ask her by what means she had done so. And, equally, it was no moment for denial.

"Why should you help me?" he demanded. He could not afford blindly to trust any one. "If you think you have found something irregular about me why do you offer aid? In effect you have accused me of being a criminal. Don't you know there's a law against helping one?"

"I'm one, too," she said, to his amazement.

"Nonsense!" he snapped. He was too keen a judge of character to believe that this meek old creature had fallen into evil ways.

"Do you remember," she said steadily—and he could see she was intensely nervous—"that I told you I had no children when I applied for this place?"

"Yes, yes," he answered impatiently. It seemed so trivial a matter now.

"Well, I lied," she returned, "I had a daughter at the point of death. I needed the position and I heard you telling other applicants you wanted some one with no ties."

"That's hardly criminal," Anthony Trent declared.

"Wait," she wailed, "I did worse. You remember when you furnished this place you sent me to pay for some rugs—nearly two hundred dollars it was?"

"And you had your pocket picked. I remember."

"I took the money," she confessed. "If I had not my girl would have been buried with the nameless dead."

He looked at the sobbing woman kindly.

"Don't worry about that, Mrs. Kinney. If only you had told me you could have had it."

"I know that now," she returned, "but then I was afraid."

"You'll stand by me notwithstanding that?" he pointed to the jeweled lamp.

"Why of course," she said simply, and he knew she was genuine.

Almost as she spoke the bell rang.

"Go to the head of the stairs," he commanded, "and I will let him in. Be certain to see how many there are. If there are two or more, call out that some men are coming. If it is the one who called before, say 'the gentleman is here. ' Listen carefully. If there are two or more I shall get out by the roof. Meet me to-morrow by Grant's Tomb at ten o'clock in the morning. You've got that?"

Mrs. Kinney was perfectly calm now and he was certain that her loyalty could be depended upon. Presently she called out, "The gentleman is here."

Anthony Trent rose slowly from his chair by the window as his visitor entered. It was a heavily built man of sixty or so dressed very well. At a glance the stranger displayed distinguished urbanity.

"What a charming retreat you have here, Mr. Trent," he observed.

"It is convenient," said Anthony Trent shortly. The word "retreat" sounded unpleasantly in his ear. It had a sound of enforced seclusion. He continued to study the elder man. There was an inflection in his voice which we are pleased to term an "English accent." And yet he did not seem, somehow, to be an Englishman. His accent reminded Trent of a man he had met casually two years before. It was at a Park riding school where he kept a saddle horse that he encountered him. From his accent he believed him to be English and was surprised when he was informed that it was Captain von Papen he had taken to be British. He learned afterwards that the Germans of good birth generally learned their English among England's upper classes and acquired thereby that inflection which does not soothe the average American. This stranger had just such a speaking voice. Obviously then he was German and one highly connected. And at a day when German plots and intrigue engaged public attention what was he doing here?

"Mine is a business call," said the stranger.

"You do not ask if this is a convenient hour," Trent reminded him.

"My dear sir," the other said smiling, "you must understand that it is a matter in which my convenience is to be consulted rather than yours." The eyes that gleamed through the thick glasses were fixed on Trent's face with a trace of amusement in them. The stranger had the look of one who holds the whip-hand over another.

"I don't admit that," Anthony Trent retorted. "I don't know your name or your errand and I'm not sure that I want to."

"Wait," said the other. "As for my name—let it be Kaufmann. As for my errand, let us say I am interested in a history of crime and want you to be a collaborator."

"What qualifications have I for such an honor?"

Anthony Trent rammed his pipe full of Hankey and lit it with a hand that did not tremble. Instinctively he knew the other watched for signs of nervousness.

"You have written remarkable stories of crime," Mr. Kaufmann reminded him. "I regret that the death of an Australian uncle permitted you to retire."

"You will not think it rude, I hope," Trent said with a show of politeness, "if I say that you seem to be much more interested in my business than I am in yours."

"I admire your national trait of frankness," Kaufmann smiled, "and will copy it. I am a merchant of Zurich, at Bahnhof street, the largest dyer of silk in Switzerland. This much you may find through your State Department if you choose."

"And owing to lack of business have taken up a study of crime?" Trent commented. "Your frankness impresses me favorably, Mr. Kaufmann. I still do not see why you visit me at this hour."

"We shall make it plain," Mr. Kaufmann assured him cordially. "First let me tell you that my business is in danger. This dye situation is likely to ruin me. I have, or had, the formulae of the dyes I used. They were my property."

"German formulae!" Trent exclaimed.

"Swiss," Kaufmann corrected, "bought by me, and my property. They have been stolen from my partner by an officious amateur detective—one of your allies—and brought here. The ship should be in shortly. He will stay in New York a day or so before going to Washington. When he goes he will take with him my property, my dye formulae. He will enrich American dyers at my expense."

"You can't expect me to feel grieved about that," Anthony Trent said bluntly.

"I do not," said Kaufmann. "But I must have those formulae." He leaned forward and touched Trent on the arm. "You must get them."

Trent knocked the gray ashes from his pipe. The merchant of Zurich gazed into a face which wore amusement only. He was not to know the dismay into which his covert threat had thrown the younger man. Without doubt, Trent told himself, this stranger must have stumbled upon something which made this odd visit a logical one, some discovery which would be a sword over his head.

"In your own country," said Trent politely, "I have no doubt you pass for a wit. To me your humor seems strained."

Kaufmann smiled urbanely.

"I had hoped," he asserted, "that you would not have compelled me to say again that you *must* get them. I fancied perhaps that you would be sensitive to any mention of, shall we say, your past?"

"My past?" queried Trent blandly. He did not propose to be bluffed. Too often he had played that game himself. It might still be that this man, a German without question, had only guessed at his avocation and hoped to frighten him.

"Your past," repeated the merchant. "The phrase has possibly too vague a sound for you. Let me say rather your professional activities."

"I see," Trent smiled, "you are interested in the writing of stories. My profession is that of a fiction writer."

"You fence well," Kaufmann admitted, "but I have a longer and sharper foil. I can wound you and receive never a scratch in return. You speak of fiction. Permit me to offer you a plot. Although a Swiss I have, or had, many German friends. We are still neutral, we of Switzerland, and you cannot expect us to feel the enmities this war has stirred up as keenly as you and your allies do."

"That I have noticed," Trent declared.

"Very well then. I have a close friend here, one Baron von Eckstein. You have perhaps heard of him—yes?"

Anthony Trent knitted his brow in thought.

"Married a St. Louis heiress, didn't he?"

"A very delightful lady, and rich," Kaufmann returned. "Charitable too, and loyal. My friends are all very loyal. Did you know that she donated ten fully-equipped ambulances to this country?"

"I saw it in the papers," said Anthony Trent. And for the life of him he could not help smiling.

Mr. Kaufmann begged permission to light a cigar. It would have been difficult to find a more urbane or genial gentleman in all Switzerland.

"The Baron and Baroness von Eckstein are close friends."

Since he offered no other remarks Anthony Trent spoke.

"And I am to derive a story from so slender a plot."

"That is but the beginning," Kaufmann assured him. "One night the Baroness had a very valuable necklace stolen. It was worth a great deal more than was supposed. Diamonds have gone up in price. She told me about it. In my native land I had some little skill as an amateur detective. She had been to a ball and had met many strangers. At my request she mentioned those to whom she had spoken at length. Among them was your name. That means nothing. There were twenty others. Now I come to another interesting thing. Do I entertain you?"

Anthony Trent simulated a yawn. He gave the appearance of one who listens because a guest in his house speaks and politeness demands it. In reality a hundred schemes went racing through his head and in most of them Herr Kaufmann played a part that would have made him nervous had he guessed it.

"Indeed yes," Anthony Trent assured him. "Please continue."

"Very well," said the other cheerfully. "Next, my plot takes me to New Bedford. You know it?"

"A mill town I believe?"

"Many of the mills are owned by my friend Jerome Dangerfield who used to purchase my dyes. We are friends of thirty years. He was the owner of the celebrated Mount Aubyn ruby. It was stolen from him, knocked out of his very hands. A most mysterious case. You have heard of it?"

"I saw that ten thousand dollars was offered for the return of the stone and capture of the thief."

"I made my little list of those to whom Dangerfield had talked during his stay at Sunset Park. Your name was there, Mr. Trent."

"If you are thinking of writing it up," Trent said kindly, "I must advise you that editors of the better sort rather frown on coincidence. Coincidence in fiction is a shabby old gentleman to-day with fewer friends every year. What next?"

"Nothing, now," Kaufmann admitted readily. "Since then I have investigated you. I find you write no more; that you live well; that while your money supposedly comes from Australia you never present an Australian draft at your bank. Now, my dear Mr. Trent, I may misjudge you. Possibly I do. But in the interests of my friends the Baron and Baroness, to say nothing of my customer Jerome Dangerfield, I may be permitted to investigate any man whose way of living seems suspicious. I ought perhaps to put the matter into the hands of the police."

"Have you?" Trent demanded sharply.

"Not yet. It may be that I shall when I leave here. You may be thinking what a fool I am to come here and tell you these startling things when you are so much younger and stronger than I. I should answer, if you asked me, that I have a permit to carry a revolver and that I have availed myself of it."

Blandly he showed the other a. 38 automatic Bayard pistol.

"You may be misjudged," he said cordially. "If so I offer you the apology of a Swiss gentleman. But consider my position. Suppose we abide by the decision of the police." He looked keenly at Anthony Trent, "Are you willing to leave it to them? Shall I call up Spring 3100?"

Kaufmann gave Trent the idea that he knew very much more about his life than he had so far admitted. There was a certainty about the man that veiled disquieting things. If he knew the Von Ecksteins and Dangerfield as he claimed, it was one of those unfortunate coincidences which life often provides to humble supercilious editors like Crosbeigh. Police investigation was a thing Trent feared greatly. Under cross-examination his defense would fall abjectly. It was no good to inquire how Kaufmann had found out that he had never offered an Australian check at his bank. It was sufficient that his charge was true.

"It is rather late to bother the police," he said smiling.

Kaufmann breathed relief, "Ah," he said genially, "we shall make excellent collaborators, I can see that. To-day is Tuesday. On Thursday at this hour I shall come with particulars of what I expect you to do for us?"

"Us?" Trent exclaimed.

"Myself and my partners," Kaufmann explained. "Yes, at this hour I shall come and you will serve your interest by doing in all things as I say. The alternative is to telephone police headquarters and say an elderly merchant from Zurich threatens you, slanders you, impels you to perform unpleasant offices."

Kaufmann smiling benignly backed toward the door. He closed it behind him. A little later Anthony Trent saw him on the sidewalk five stories below.

He started as he heard footsteps behind him. It was Mrs. Kinney.

"Was it anything serious?" she asked.

"I'm afraid it was," he answered. "I want you to go up to Kennebago with me to-morrow afternoon. I shall take only my personal baggage. The furniture can wait. The apartment will be locked up."

She spoke with a certain hesitation.

"I listened to what he was saying, Mr. Trent."

"I hoped you would," he answered, "I may need a witness."

"Don't you think it would be wiser to wait and do what he wants you to?"

"Perhaps," retorted her employer, "but I don't see how he can find me out in Kennebago. Who knows about it but you and Weems? You haven't mentioned it to any one and Weems isn't anxious his financial condition should be suspected. And, beside that, he's in Los Angeles. I shall pay the rent of this flat up till Christmas and tell the agent I may be back for a few days any time. I must leave the furniture." He looked about him regretfully. "That could be traced easily enough." He decided to take the Benares lamp, Stuart's picture of Washington, the vase of King Senwosri, and one or two things of price. They could go in his trunks.

"But, sir," Mrs. Kinney persisted timidly, "if he finds you out it may go badly with you and it wouldn't be difficult to get what he wants."

"Perhaps not," he said gravely, "but if I were to do one such thing for them they would use me continually."

"But he only wants his dye formulae," she reminded him.

"Don't you understand," he said, "that he is a German spy and wants me to betray my country?"

CHAPTER XXVIII

THE GERMAN SPY MERCHANT

Anthony Trent rode into Kennebago by the corduroy road from Rangely. It took longer but it seemed a less likely way of being seen than if he had taken the train to Kennebago. It had been his intention before Kaufmann had come across his horizon to make the call upon Mr. Westward his first action. As he stood at the window of the big dining room he could see the genial angler, and John his guide, rowing over to the edge of a favorite pool. There he sat in the stern, rod in hand, no doubt thinking of the chapter he was writing on the "Psychology of Trout."

For years Anthony Trent had looked forward to days like this in his new home. But the thrill of it was gone. He had hoped to look over the lake to the purple hills beyond with a serenity of mind that might now never be his. How much did Kaufmann know? Would he lodge information with the police? Dare he? Probably he would not dare to call. But anonymous information of so important a character would speedily bring detectives on his trail. Beyond a question he should have bought a camp on some far Canadian lake under another name, and reached it by devious ways.

He had betrayed much ingenuity in bringing himself, Mrs. Kinney and their baggage, to Kennebago as it was. Successions of taxis from hotel to station, and from station to hotel, crossing his own tracks a half dozen times would make pursuit difficult. He had no way of estimating Kaufmann's skill at following a clue. But the man had impressed him, Anthony Trent, who had foiled so many.

Next morning he determined to fish and was attending to his rods with the loving care of the conscientious angler when a knock came at the door. It opened on to the big screened piazza.

"Come in," he shouted, thinking Mrs. Kinney wished to consult him.

Instead there entered Mr. Westward who greeted him heartily. It was indeed an honor, for the piscatorial expert called upon few.

"Glad to see you, my dear fellow," said Westward, shaking him by the hand. "I happened to meet a friend of yours who was coming to see you and lost his way so I've brought him along."

Kaufmann also wrung his hand. He seemed no less delighted to see Trent than had been Mr. Westward.

"What a charming retreat you have here," he exclaimed cordially.

There followed a conversation concerning trout and salmon which under normal conditions would have been delightful to Trent. Kaufmann was affable, genial, and talked of the finny spoils of his native lakes. It was only when Westward's erect form had disappeared down the path that his manner became forbidding.

"Why did you leave New York?" he snapped.

"Because I chose to," said the other.

"What a fool! what a fool!" cried Kaufmann, "and how fortunate that I am good tempered."

"Why?" Trent demanded.

"Because I might have had you investigated by the police. Instead I followed you here—not without difficulty I admit—and renew my offer." He looked about the luxurious house that was miscalled a "camp." It was not the kind of home a man would lose willingly. "I ask very little. I only want a certain package of letters which a man who lands tomorrow in New York has in his possession. One so skilled as you can get it easily. You have presence, education, ready wit. I confess it is difficult for me to believe you have sunk so low."

Anthony Trent flushed angrily.

"There are lower depths yet," he exclaimed.

"Yes?" the other returned, "as for instance?"

"Your sort of work!" he cried. "Do you suppose I imagine you to be a Swiss silk merchant of Bahnhof street?"

Kaufmann threw back his head and laughed.

"My passport recently vised by your State Department is made out to Adolf Kaufmann of Zurich. I have Swiss friends in New York and Chicago who will identify me."

"Naturally," said Trent, "simple precautions of that sort would have to be taken. That's elementary."

"Let us get back to business," said the other, "I want those papers. Will you get them for me? Think it over well. You may say you will not. You may say you prefer to remain here in this delightful place and catch trout. Let us suppose that you say you defy me. What happens? You lose all chance to look at trout for ten, fifteen, twenty years accordingly as the judge regards your offenses. I have mentioned only two crimes to you. Of these I have data and am certain. There are two others in which I can interest myself if necessary. I do not wish to bother myself with you after you do as I command. Get me the papers and you may remain here till you have grand-children of marriageable age. Is it worth defying me, Mr. Trent?"

The younger man groaned as he thought it over. The fabric he had made so carefully was ready to fall apart. Kaufmann went on talking.

"The man you must follow is called Commander Godfrey Heathcote, of the British Navy. On his breast he wears the ribbons of the Victoria

Cross—a blue one for the Navy—and the red ribbon, edged with blue, of the Distinguished Service Order. He is a man much of your build but has straw colored hair and light blue eyes. He walks with a limp owing to a wound received at the Zeebrugge affair. He is supposed to be over here to stay with relatives who have a place on the James River. He leaves for Washington soon where his business is with the Secretary of the Navy. The papers I want are in a pigskin cigarette case, old and worn. You'd better bring the case in its entirety."

Kaufmann rattled off his instructions in a sure and certain manner. Evidently he had no fear of being denied.

"Isn't it unusual for an English naval commander to carry trade secrets about with him?" Trent demanded.

"Why keep up the farce?" Kaufmann exclaimed. "You, too, are a man of the world. You realize you are in my power and must do as you are bid."

"Must I?" Trent answered with a frown. "I am asked to play the traitor to my country and you expect me to accept without hesitation."

"Why not?" Kaufmann returned. "Would you be the first that fear of exposure has led into such ways? If I were to tell you how we—" he paused a moment and then smiled—"how we silk merchants of Switzerland have used our knowledge of the black pages of men's lives or the indiscretions of well known women, you would understand more readily how we obtain what we want."

"I understand," said Anthony Trent gloomily. He was a case in point.

"And you will save yourself?"

"I don't know," said Trent hesitating. But he knew that Kaufmann had made such threats as these to others and had gained his desires. "What's in those papers?"

"Dye formulae," smiled the elder man.

Anthony Trent looked at him angrily. His nerves were on edge. Plainly Kaufmann felt it unwise to stir the smouldering passion in him.

"England," he informed the other, "has recently reorganized the mine fields outside Sheerness at the mouth of the Thames. Commander Heathcote, who is here ostensibly to recuperate from wounds, is chosen to carry the plans to the Navy Department. There you have all I know."

"But that's treachery!" Trent cried.

"What's England to you," Kaufmann answered, "or you to England? I'm not asking you to take American plans."

"It's the same thing now," Trent persisted. "We're allies and what's treachery to one is treachery to the other."

"Admirable!" Kaufmann sneered, "admirable! But I invite you to come down to mother earth. You are not concerned with the affairs of nations. You are concerned only with your own safety which is the nearer task. You get those plans or you go to prison. You realize my power. I need you. You may ask why I have gone to this trouble to take you, a stranger, more or less into my confidence. Very well. I shall tell you. My own men are working like slaves in your accursed internment camps and I am alone who had so many to command."

"Alone," said Anthony Trent in an altered voice and looked at him oddly.

Kaufmann observed the look and laughed.

"I am a mind reader," he said cheerfully, "I will tell you what is passing through your brain. You are wondering whether if those strong hands of yours get a grip of my throat your own troubles, too, would not be at an end. No, my friend, I still have my Bayard with me. And why run the risk, if you should overpower me, of being tried for murder? What I ask of you is very little. Remember, also, that I have but to say the word and you land in prison."

"You'd go with me," Trent exclaimed.

"I think not," smiled Kaufmann. "Jerome Dangerfield and others would vouch for me whereas I fear you would be friendless. And even if I were interned how would that help you? Be sensible and get ready to accompany me to New York on the five o'clock train. I have your reservations."

It was not easy to explain things to Mrs. Kinney. Trent told her that his suspicions of Kaufmann's German sympathies were wrong. He said he was compelled to get the dye formulae and would return within a few days.

"I shall come too," Mrs. Kinney observed. "I left a lot of my things at the flat and I shall need them."

It seemed to Trent that she was not deceived by his words; and while he would have preferred to leave her in Maine he could think of no reason for keeping her there if she wished to leave. All the way he was gloomy. To Kaufmann's sallies he made morose answers. Presently the so-called Swiss left him alone. But Trent could not escape the feeling that his every action was watched. He was to all intents and purposes bond servant to an enemy of his country.

"Just a final word," said Kaufmann as they neared the 125th street station.

"What else?" Trent said impatiently. He was filled with disgust with himself and of hatred for the German.

"Remember that the cigarette case which holds my formulae is a long flat one holding twelve cigarettes. On it is stamped 'G. H. ' He does not secrete it as you think but exposes it carelessly to view. I advise you to go straight to your apartment and await my letter. It is necessary for me to find out particulars which it might be unwise for you to do. I don't want you to fall under suspicion."

"You are very thoughtful," sneered Trent. He knew well enough that he had a value in Kaufmann's eyes which would be destroyed were he to come under police supervision. That this was the only case where he was to be used was unlikely. Having used him once he would be at their command again. But would he? Anthony Trent sat back in his chair deep lines on his drawn white face. This was the reward of the life he had led. And the way to break from Kaufmann's grip was to run the risk of the long prison term, or—the taking of a life. And even were he to come to this Kaufmann might be only one of a gang whose other members might command his services.

"I shall send you a message by telephone if it is still in your flat. It is? Good. That simplifies matters. Wait until you receive it and then act immediately."

Anthony Trent disregarded the outstretched hand and cordial smile, when a minute or so later, the train pulled into the Grand Central. He hailed a taxi and drove to his rooms utterly obsessed with his bitter thoughts. It was not until he pulled up the shades and glanced about the place that he remembered Mrs. Kinney. He had forgotten her. But he relied on her common sense. Sooner or later she would come. Meanwhile he must wait for Kaufmann's telephone message.

The message arrived before the woman. "To-morrow," said Kaufmann, "your friend leaves for Washington. He is staying at the Carlton and goes to his room after dinner. He will be pleased to see you. To-morrow night I shall call upon you soon after dark."

The Carlton was the newest of the hotels, the most superbly decorated, the hotel that always disappointed the *nouveau riche* because so little goldleaf had been used in the process. Anthony Trent had spent a night or two in every big hotel the city boasted. In a little note book there were certain salient features carefully put down, hints which might be useful to him. Turning to the book he read it carefully. He was already acquainted with the general lay-out of the hotel which had been generously explained in the architectural papers.

The hotel detectives were men of whom he liked to learn as much as possible. The house detective, the head of them, was Francis Xavier Glynn who felt himself kin to Gaboriau because of his subtle methods. He would often come to the hotel desk and register talking in a loud tone about his Western business connections. He dressed in what he assumed was the Western manner. To his associates this seemed the height of cunning. As a matter of fact the high class crook who prefers the high class hotel knew of it and was amused. Clarke was Trent's informant. The old editor had pointed him out to the younger man one day when they had met near enough to the hotel's café entrance to go in and have a drink.

As a rule Trent made elaborate plans for the successful carrying out of his work. But here he was suddenly told to engage in a very difficult operation. Disguises must be good indeed to stand the glare of hotel corridors and dining rooms. He decided to go and trust to some plan suggesting itself when the moment arrived.

He registered as Conway Parker of York, Pennsylvania and the grip which the boy carried to his room had on it "C. P. York, Pa." Trent had given a couple of dollars for it at a second hand store. It dulled suspicions which might have been aroused where the bag and initials glaringly new. It was part of Francis Xavier Glynn's plan to have the hotel boys report hourly on any unusual happening.

As Trent had waited to register he noted the name he was looking for, Commander Heathcote, had a room on the 17th floor. Parker was assigned to one on the seventh. Directly the boy had left Anthony Trent started to work. He found just cause of offense so far as the location of his room went. It was an inside room and the heat of the day made it oppressive. Commander Heathcote, as he found by taking a trip to the seventeenth floor, had an outside room. A further investigation proved that immediately over the Commander's room was an unoccupied suite. To effect the exchange was not easy. Trent could not very well dictate the location of the room or betray so exact a knowledge of hotel topography without incurring suspicion. But at last the thing was done. The gentleman from York wanted a sitting room, bedroom and bath and obtained it immediately over those of the naval officer.

He passed Heathcote in the dining room, and looked at him keenly. The two men were of a height. Heathcote was broader. Trent instantly knew him for that fighting type characterized by the short, straight nose, cleft chin and light blue eyes. It was a man to beware of in an encounter. He limped a little and walked with a cane. And while he waited for his *hors d'œuvres* he took out a long pigskin cigarette case. It was within ten feet of the man who had come to steal it. For a wild moment he wondered whether it were possible to lunge for it and make his escape. A moment later he was annoyed that such a puerile thought had visited him. It meant that his nerves were not under their usual control.

After dinner two or three men spoke to the Commander as he limped toward the elevator. One, a British colonel, shook hands heartily and congratulated him on the V. C. Another, a stranger evidently, tried to get him into conversation. Trent noted that the Commander, although courteous to a degree, was not minded to make hotel acquaintances. He declined a drink and refused a cigar by taking out his cigarette case. The stranger looked at it curiously.

"Seen some service, hasn't it?" the affable stranger remarked and took it from the owner's hand.

"A very old pal," said the naval man. Trent had observed the slight hesitation before he had permitted it to leave his hand. "I wouldn't lose it for a lot."

Trent stood ready. It might be that this thick skinned stranger was after the same loot as he. But he handed it back and strolled off to the café where he joined a group of perfectly respectable business men from Columbus, O.

As most travelers in first class hotels know, the eighteenth story of the Carlton looks across a block of fashionable private houses on its north side. There is on that account no possibility of any prying stranger gazing into its rooms from across the way. Towering above these lesser habitations the Carlton looms inaccessible, austere, remote.

In the grip which had once belonged to the unknown "C. P. of York, Pa." Anthony Trent had put the kit necessary for a short stay. There was also certain equipment without which certain nervous travelers rarely stray from home. For example there was a small axe. In a collision at sea many are drowned who might escape did not the impact have the effect of jamming the doors of their state rooms. The axe in the hands of the thoughtful voyager could be used to hack through thin planking to freedom. There was also a small coil of high grade rope, tested to three hundred pounds. In case of fire the careful traveler might slide to earth. Not, of course, from an eighteenth floor.

At half past one that night it was very dark and cloudy. A light rain dropped on dusty streets and there was silence. Tying his line to the firm anchorage of a pipe in the bath room Anthony Trent began his work. He was dressed in a dark blue suit. He wore no collar and on his hands were dark gray gloves. Below him was the green and white striped awning that protected Commander Heathcote's windows. It was almost certain that an Englishman would sleep with windows open.

It was not difficult for a gymnast to slide down the rope head fore-most. When Trent could touch the top of the Heathcote awning he took a safety razor blade from his lips and cut a slit across it sufficiently wide to admit his head and shoulders.

It was not a descent which caused much trouble. There was the chance that the rope might break. He wondered through how many awnings he would plunge before consciousness left him.

Heathcote was asleep. By a table near the bed was an ash tray, matches, Conrad's "Youth" and the cigarette case. And lying near was the stout cane which the man who was wounded in that splendid attack on Zeebrugge used to aid himself in his halting walk.

Trent, with the case in his pocket, walked to the door. It was not his intention to make the more hazardous climb up to his room when so easy a way of getting there presented itself. It was locked and barred.

In his room he sat and looked at what he had taken. It represented, so Kaufmann said, his freedom from arrest. It contained plans of vital importance to the allies. They could only be used by the enemy to bring destruction to those who fought for right. And what punishment would be given the wounded hero for losing what was entrusted to him? For an hour Trent sat there looking at the pigskin case. And gradually what had seemed an impossible sacrifice to make, came to be something desirable and splendid. Anthony Trent had never been able to regard his career as one justified by circumstances. There burned in his breast the spark of patriotism more strongly than he knew. He had fought his fight and won. His eyes were moist as he thought of his father, that old civil war soldier who had been wounded on Gettysburg's bloody field and walked always with a limp like the English sailor beneath.

When he opened the door Heathcote was still slumbering. He replaced the case as nearly in the position he found as he could. In that moment Anthony Trent felt he could look any man in the face.

He was still slumbering when Commander Heathcote awoke. Presently the officer saw that the door was unbarred and as investigation proved, unlocked.

"I'd have sworn," muttered the Commander, "that I locked and barred it."

CHAPTER XXIX

MRS. KINNEY INTERVENES

At his apartment, which he reached by noon, he found a note from Mrs. Kinney advising him that she would not be back until late. A salad would be found in the ice box. But his appetite had deserted him and strong tea and crackers sufficed him. The feeling of exaltation which had carried him along was now dying down leaving in its place a grim, dogged determination. He saw now very clearly that the time was come to pay for his misdeeds. Dimly he had felt that some day there would have to be a reckoning. He had never thought it so near.

It would not have been difficult to make his escape from the man who threatened. With his swift motor he could cross some sparsely peopled border district into Canada. Or he could drop down into South or Central America and there wait until the years brought safety or he had deteriorated in fibre as do most men of his race in tropic sloth.

The thing that kept him was a chivalrous, burning desire to capture Kaufmann. Anthony Trent wondered how many men weaker than he had been forced to betray their country as he had very nearly done. And the knowledge that he had even considered such baseness for a moment awakened a deep smouldering wrath in his mind that needed for its outlet some expression of physical force. Kaufmann was strongly built and rugged but it would hardly be a smiling suave spy that he would drag before the police. At least they would go down to ruin together.

At ten thirty the bell rang. But the feeble steps that made their weary ascent were those of Mrs. Kinney. When first he flung open the door he hardly recognized her. As a rule neat and quietly dressed in black she was to-night wearing the faded gingham dress she used for rough work, a dress he had seldom seen. She wore no hat; instead a handkerchief was on her head. She looked for all the world like some shabby denizen of the city's foreign quarters.

"Are you expecting him?" she demanded.

"Yes," he said dully. It was a shock not to meet him when he was nerved to the task.

She looked at him with a certain triumph in her face that was not unmixed with affection.

"He will never come here again."

"What do you mean?" he cried.

"He's dead." It was curious to note the flash of her usually mild eye as she said it. For a moment he thought the old woman was demented. But her voice was firm.

"I followed him on his way here," she went on. "I found out where he lived. As he crossed Eighth avenue at 34th street I told people he was a German spy. There were a lot of soldiers on their way to the Pennsylvania station and they started to run after him. Then a man tripped him up but he got to his feet and crossed the road in front of a motor truck."

"You are certain he was killed?"

"I waited to make sure," she said simply. "Nobody knew it was I who started calling him a spy."

There was a pause of half a minute. The knowledge of his safety was almost too much for Trent after his hours of suspense.

"I suppose you know," he said huskily, "that you've probably saved my life. I didn't do as he wanted me to. I was prepared to denounce him to the police."

"But they'd have got you, too," she said.

"I know," he returned. "I'd thought of that."

"Oh, Mr. Trent!" she cried, "Oh, Mr. Trent!" Then for the second time in the years he had known her she fell into a fit of weeping.

When she was recovered and had taken a cup of strong tea she explained how it was she had tracked Kaufmann to his home. She had slipped away from Trent at the Grand Central when he was too much worried to notice it. Kaufmann walked the half dozen blocks to his rooms in the house occupied by a physician on Forty-eighth street, just west of Fifth avenue. Applying for work Mrs. Kinney was engaged instantly for two days a week. The need for respectable women was so great that no references were asked. She was thus free of the house and regarded without suspicion.

She worked there the whole day but learned nothing from the cook and waitress of Mr. Kaufmann. He rented the whole of the second floor and had a fad for keeping it in order himself. It saved them trouble. The maids said, vaguely, he was in the importing business and very wealthy.

It was while Kaufmann went down to sign for a registered letter that Mrs. Kinney slipped into the room. There was nothing in the way of papers or documents that she could see.

Because he could not bear investigation, Anthony Trent telephoned to the Department of Justice as he had done in the case of Frederick Williams. He felt certain that Kaufmann was a highly placed official. But there was no newspaper mention of the raid. Trent was not to know that no news was allowed to leak out for the reason that matters of enormous importance were discovered. He was right in assuming Kaufmann to be a personage. The mangled body was buried in the Potters' Field and those lesser men depending on the monetary support and counsel of Kaufmann were thrown into confusion. His superiors in Germany, when later they found the Allies in possession of certain secrets, assumed their agent to be interned. Altogether Mrs. Kinney deserved her country's thanks.

"And now shall we go back to Kennebago?"

"Not yet," he said smiling a little gravely. "Not yet. It may be I shall never see Kennebago again."

She looked at him startled. The affairs of the past week had been a great strain to her.

"I'm going to enlist," he said.

CHAPTER XXX

"PRIVATE TRENT"

Before Trent went to enlist, he had an understanding with Mrs. Kinney as to the Kennebago camp. She was to live there and keep the house and gardens in good order until he returned. He had none of those premonitions of disaster which some who go to war have in abundance. Now that the danger of his arrest was gone and Kaufmann could never again entrap him he felt cheerful and lighthearted.

"I shall come back," he told the old woman, "I feel it in my bones. But if not there will be enough for you to live on. I am seeing my lawyer about it this morning."

On the way to the recruiting station, Trent met Weems.

"What branch are you going in?" he asked upon learning of Trent's plans.

"Where I'm most needed," Trent said cheerfully. "Infantry I guess."

"You can get a commission right away," Weems cried, a sudden thought striking him. "It was in last night's papers. It said that men holding the B. S. degree were wanted and would be commissioned right off the reel. You're a B. S. You wait a bit. Be an officer instead of an enlisted man. I bet the food's better."

He was a little piqued that Anthony Trent betrayed so little pleasure at the news. It so happened that Trent had given a deal of thought to this very thing. And his decision was to allow the chance of a commission to go. There was a strain of quixotism about him and a certain fineness of feeling which went to make this decision final. He loved his country in the quiet intense manner which does not show itself in the waving of flags. To outward appearances and to the unjudging mind, Weems would seem the more loyal of the two. Weems wore a flag in his buttonhole and shouted loudly his protestations and yet had made no sacrifice. Trent was to offer his life quietly, untheatrically. And he wanted to wear no officer's uniform in case his arrest or discovery would bring reproach upon it. In his mind he could see headlines in the paper announcing that an officer of the United States Army was a notorious—he shuddered at the word—thief. And again, there was no certainty in his mind that he would give up his mode of life. In the beginning he had set out to obtain enough money to live in comfort. That, long ago, had been achieved. Then the jewels to adorn his lamp occupied his mind and now the game was in his blood. He wanted his camp for recreation but it would not satisfy wholly. When the war was over there would be Europe's fertile fields to work upon.

There were many things to aid him in his feeling that the turning over of a new leaf would be useless. Nothing could ever undo what he had done. Try as he might he would never face the world an honest man. He would go to war. He would be a good soldier.

It was in the infantry that they needed men and Camp Dix received him with others. So insignificant a thing was one soldier that he presently felt a sense of security that had been denied him for years.

The experiences he went through in Camp were common to all. They were easier to him than most because of his perfection of physical condition. On the whole it was interesting work but he was glad when he marched along the piers of the Army Transport Service, where formerly German lines had docked, and boarded the *Leviathan*. Private Trent was going "over there."

It was common knowledge that the regiments would not yet be sent to France. What they had learned at Camp Dix would be supplemented by a post-graduate course in England.

Curiously enough Trent found himself on the Sussex Downs, those rolling hills of chalk covered with short springy aromatic grasses and flowers. Here were a hundred sights and sounds that stirred his blood. Five generations of Trents had been born in America since that adventurous younger son had set out for the Western world. The present Anthony was coming back to the ancient home of his family under the most favorable circumstances. He was coming back with his mind purged of ancient enmities fostered so long by Britain's foes to further alien causes; coming back to a country knit to his own by bonds that would not easily be broken.

It was curious that he should find himself here on the high downs because it was from this county of Sussex that the Trents sprang. Not far from Lewes was an old house, set among elms, which had been theirs for three hundred years. When he was last in England he had made a pilgrimage to it only to find its owner salmon fishing in Norway. The housekeeper had shown him over it, a big rambling house full of odd corridors and unexpected steps and he had never failed to think of it with pride. On that visit he had been disappointed to find the village church shut; the sexton was at his midday dinner.

Trent had been under canvas only a few days when he obtained leave for a few hours and set out to the church. He counted three Anthony Trents whose deeds were told on mural tablets. One had been an admiral; one a bishop and the third a colonel of Dragoons at Waterloo. He sauntered by the old house and looked at it enviously. "If I bought that," he thought, "I would settle down to the ways of honest men."

He shrugged his shoulders. There were many things yet to be done. It was only since he had been in England and seen her wounded that he realized what none can until it is witnessed, the certainty that there must be much suffering before the end is achieved.

The men in his company were not especially congenial. They were friendly enough but their interests were narrow. Trent was glad when the training period was over and he embarked in the troop train for Dover *en route* to the Western front. He made a good soldier. More than one of his mates said he would wear the chevrons before many weeks but he was anxious for no such distinction.

At the time his regiment arrived in France the American troops were at grips with the enemy. It was the first time that they held as a unit part of the line. The Germans, already making their retreat, left in the rear nests of machine gunners to hamper the pursuers. To clear these nests of hornets, to search abandoned cellars and buildings where men or bombs might be lying in wait was a task far more deadly than participation in a battle. Only iron-nerved men, strong to act and quick to think, were needed. There was a day when volunteers were asked for. Anthony Trent was the first man to offer himself. Under a lieutenant this band of brave men went about its dangerous task. The casualties were many and among them the officer.

He had made such an impression on his men and they had gained such favorable mention for gallant conduct that there was a fear lest the new officer might be of less vigorous and dashing nature. It was work, this nest clearing danger, that Trent liked enormously. He had come to know what traps the Hun was likely to set, the tempting cigar-box, the field glasses, the fountain-pen the touching of which meant maiming at the least. And against some of these trapped men Trent revived his old football tackle and brought them startled to the ground. It was the most stirring game of his life.

But one look at the new officer changed his mood. He looked at his lieutenant and his lieutenant looked at him. And the officer licked his lips hungrily. It was Devlin whom he had laughed at in San Francisco. Instinctively the men who observed this meeting sensed some pre-war hatred and speculated on its origin. Recollecting himself Trent saluted.

"So I've got a thief in my company," Devlin sneered. "I'll have to watch you pretty close. Looting's forbidden."

It was plain to the men who watched Devlin's subsequent plan of action that he was trying to goad the enlisted man into striking him. In France the discipline of the American army was taking on the sterner character of that which distinguished the Allies.

No task had ever been so difficult for Anthony Trent as this continual curb he was compelled to put upon his tongue. Devlin had always disliked him. He was maddened at the thought that Trent had taken the Mount Aubyn ruby from under his nose. It was because of this, Dangerfield had discharged him from a lucrative position. And in the case of the Takowaja emerald it was Anthony Trent who had laughed at him. Many an hour had Devlin spent trying to weave the rope that would hang him. And in these endeavors he had gathered many odds and ends of information over which he chuckled with joy.

But first of all he wanted to break his enemy. There was no opportunity of which he did not take advantage. Ordinarily his superior officers would have witnessed this policy and reprimanded him; but conditions were such that their special duties kept Devlin and his men apart from their comrades. Devlin was a good officer and credit was given him for much that Trent deserved.

It chanced one night that while they waited for a little wood to be cleared of gas, Devlin and Trent sat within a few feet of one another. It was an opportunity Devlin was quick to seize.

"Thought you'd fooled me in 'Frisco, didn't you?"

Trent lighted a cigarette with exasperating slowness.

"I did fool you," he asserted calmly. "It is never hard to fool a man with your mental equipment."

"Huh," Devlin grunted, "you've got the criminal's low cunning, I'll admit that, Mr. Maltby of Chicago."

He made a labored pretence of hunting for his cigarette case.

"Gone!" he said sneering; "some one's lifted it but I guess you know where it is. Oh no, I forgot. You weren't a dip, you were a second story man. Excuse me."

He kept this heavy and malicious humor going until Trent's imperturbability annoyed him.

"What a change!" he commented presently. "Me the officer and you the enlisted man who's got to do as I say. You with your fast auto and your golf and society ways and me who used to be a cop."

Winning no retort from his victim he leaned forward and pushed Trent roughly. He started back at the white wrath which transfigured the other's face.

"Look here, Devlin," Trent cried savagely, "you want me to hit you so you can prefer charges against me for striking an officer and have me disciplined. Listen to this: if you put your filthy hand on me again I won't hit you, I'll kill you."

Towering and threatening he stood over the other. Devlin, who knew men and the ways of violence, looked into Trent's face and recognized it was no idle threat he heard.

"That would be a hell of a fine trick," he said, a little unsteadily, "to empty your gun in my back."

"You know I wouldn't do it that way," Trent retorted. "Why should I let you off so easily as that?"

"Easily?" Devlin repeated.

"When I get ready," Trent said grimly, "I shall want you to realize what's coming to you."

"Is that a threat?" Devlin demanded.

Trent nodded his head.

"It's a threat."

Devlin thought for a moment.

"I'll fix you," he said.

"How?" Trent inquired. "You've tried every way there is to have me killed. If there's a doubtful place where some boches may be hiding with bombs whom do you send to find out? You send Private Trent. I'm not kicking. I volunteered for the job. I came out to do what I could. My one disappointment is that my officer is not also a gentleman."

Devlin's face was now better humored.

"I'll fix you," he said again, "I'll see Pershing pins a medal on you all right."

Trent wondered what he meant. And he wondered why for a day or two Devlin goaded him no more. Instead he looked at him as one who knew another was marked down for death and disgrace. It was inevitable that Anthony Trent could never know how near to discovery he was. The odds are against the best breakers of law. The history of crime told him that the cleverest had been captured by some trifling piece of carelessness. Had Devlin some such clue, he wondered?

CHAPTER XXXI

DEVLIN'S REVENGE

There came a night when Devlin's men were called upon to clean out part of a forest from which many snipers had been firing, and where machine guns and their crews were known to be. It was work for picked men only and Trent admitted Devlin made a courageous leader.

The Americans met unexpectedly strong opposition. It was only when half their little company was lost that they were ordered to retreat. The way was made difficult with barbed wire and shell splintered trees. It was one of a hundred similar sorties taking place all along the Allied lines hardly worthy of mention in the press.

Trent, when he had gained a clearing in the wood, saw Devlin go down like an ox from the clubbed rifle in a Prussian hand. Trent had put a shot through the man's head almost before Devlin's body fell to the soft earth. He had an excellent chance of escape alone but he could not leave the American officer who was his enemy to bleed to death among his country's foes. He was almost spent when he reached his own lines and the Red Cross relieved him of his inert burden. They told him Devlin still lived.

Three days later Trent was called to the hospital in which his officer lay white and bandaged. Although Devlin's voice was weak it did not lack the note of enmity which ever distinguished it when its owner spoke to Anthony Trent.

"What did you do it for?" Devlin demanded.

"Do what?"

"Bring me in after that boche laid me out?"

"Only one reason," Trent informed him. "Alive, you have a certain use to your country. Dead, you would have none."

"That's a lie," Devlin snarled, "I've figured it out lying in this damned cot. You saw I wasn't badly hurt and you knew some of the boys would fetch me in later. You thought you'd do a hero stunt and get a decoration and you reckoned I'd be grateful and let up on you. That was clever but not clever enough for me. I see through it. You've got away with out-guessing the other feller so far but I'm one jump ahead of you in this." He paused for breath, "I've got you fixed, Mister Anthony Trent, and don't you forget it. You think I'm bluffing I suppose."

"I think you're exciting yourself unduly," Trent said quietly. "Take it up when you are well."

"You're afraid to hear what I know," Devlin sneered. "You've got to hear it sometime, so why not now?"

Trent spoke as one does to a child or a querulous invalid.

"Well, what is it?" he demanded.

"Never heard of any one named Austin, did you?"

"It's not an unusual name," Trent admitted. But he was no longer uninterested. Conington Warren's butler was so called. And this Austin had met him face to face on the stairway of his master's house on the night that he had taken Conington Warren's loose cash and jewels.

"He's out here," Devlin said and looked hard at Trent to see what effect the news would have.

"You forget I don't know whom," Trent reminded him. "What Austin?"

"You know," Devlin snapped, "the Warren butler. I was on that case and he recognized me not a week ago and asked me who you were. He's seen you, too. We put two and two together and it spells the pen for you. He was English and although he was over age the British are polite that way. If he said he was forty-one they said they guessed he was forty-one. I went to see him in a hospital before he 'went west' and he told me all about it."

Anthony Trent could not restrain a sigh of relief. Austin was dead.

"That don't help you any," Devlin cried. "Don't you wish you'd left me in the woods now? That was your opportunity. Why didn't you take it?"

"You wouldn't understand," Trent answered. "For one thing you dislike me too much to see anything but bad in what I do. That's your weakness. That's why you have always failed."

"Well, I haven't failed this time," Devlin taunted him. "I've laid information against you where it's going to do most good."

He hoped to see the man he hated exhibit fear, plead for mercy or beg for a respite. He had rehearsed this expected scene during the night watches. Instead he saw the hawk-like face inscrutable as ever.

"I've told the adjutant what I know and what Austin said and he's bound to make an investigation. That means you'll be sent home for trial and I guess you know what that means. I'm going to be invalided home and I'll put in my leave working up the case against you. They ought to give you a stretch of anything from fifteen to twenty years. I guess that'll hold you, Mister Anthony Trent."

The other man made no answer. He thought instead of what such a prison term would do for him. He had seen the gradual debasement of men of even a high type during the long years of internment. Men who had gone through prison gates with the same instincts of refinement as he possessed to come out coarsened, different, never again to be the men they were. He would sidle through the gaping doors a furtive thing with cunning crafty eyes whose very walk stamped him a convict. How could so long a term of years spent among professional criminals fail to besmirch him?

He took a long breath.

"I'm not there yet," he said. "It's a long way to an American jail and a good bit can happen in three thousand miles."

He was turned from these dismal channels of thought by a hospital orderly who summoned him to the adjutant's quarters.

In civil life this officer had been a well known lawyer who had abandoned a large practice to take upon himself the over work and worries that always hurl themselves at an adjutant.

He had heard of the rescue of Lieutenant Devlin by a man of his company and was pleased to learn that it was an alumnus of his old college who had been recommended for a decoration on that account. He looked at Trent a moment in silence.

"When I last saw you," he said, "you won the game for us against Harvard." He sighed, "I never thought to see you in a case of this sort."

"I don't know what you mean, sir," Trent answered him.

"For some reason or another," the adjutant informed him, "Lieutenant Devlin has preferred charges against you which had better been left until this war is over in my opinion as a soldier."

"I am still in the dark," Trent reminded him.

Captain Sutton looked over some papers.

"You are charged," he said, "with being a very remarkable and much sought after criminal. Devlin asserts you purloined a ruby owned by Mr. Dangerfield worth a hundred and seventy-five thousand dollars, and an emerald worth almost as much."

"What a curious delusion," Trent commented with calmness.

"Delusion?" retorted the adjutant.

"What else could it be?" the other inquired.

"It might be the truth," the officer said drily.

"Does he offer proofs?"

"More I'm afraid than you'll care to read," Captain Sutton told him. "You understand, I suppose, that there are certain regulations which govern us in a case like this. I should like to dismiss it as something entirely irrelevant to military duties. You were a damned good football player, Trent, and they tell me you're just as good a soldier, but an officer has preferred charges against you and they must be given attention. Sit down there for a few minutes."

Devlin, feeling the hour of triumph approaching, lay back in his bed gloating. The hatred that he bore Anthony Trent was legitimate enough in its way. By some accident or another Devlin was enlisted on the side of the law and his opponent against it. One was the hunter; the other the hunted. And the hunter was soon to witness the disgrace of the man who had laughed at him, beaten him, cheated him of a coveted position. Naturally of a brave and pugnacious disposition, Devlin saw no lack of chivalry in hounding a man over whom he had military authority. If Trent had been his friend he would have fought for him. But since he was his foe he must taste the bitterness of the vanquished.

So engrossed was he over his pleasurable thoughts that he did not see the distress which came over the face of the nurse who took his temperature and recorded his pulse beat. Nor did he see the hastily summoned physician reading the recently marked chart over the bed. Instead he was filled with a strange and satisfying exaltation of spirit. Catches of old forgotten songs came back to him. He felt himself growing stronger. He was Devlin the superman, the captor of Anthony Trent who had beaten the best of them. It was almost with irritation that he opened his eyes to speak with the doctor, a middle-aged, gray man with kindly eyes.

"Lieutenant," the doctor said gently, "things aren't going as well with you as we hoped. You should not have exhausted yourself talking. It should not have been allowed."

Devlin saw the doctor put his hand under the coverlet; then he felt a prick in his arm. Dully he knew that it was the sting of a hypodermic. Then he saw coming toward him a priest of his race and faith and knew he came in that dread hour to administer the last rites of the church.

"Doc," he gasped, "am I going?"

It was no moment to utter lying comfort.

"I'm afraid so."

Then he saw an orderly bringing the screen that was placed about the beds of those about to die.

When Captain Sutton and Anthony Trent came into the ward the priest had finished his solemn work and was gone to console another dying man and the physicians to make one of those quick operations unthinkable in the leisurely days of peace.

Trent had no knowledge of what had taken place during his absence. He saw that his enemy was more exhausted. And as he looked he noticed that the eyes of Devlin lacked something of their hate. But it was no time for speculation. Trent saw in the sick man only his nemesis, the instrument which fate was using to rob him of his liberty. He was not to know that here was a man so close to death that hate seemed idle and vengeance a burden.

"Lieutenant," Captain Sutton began, "I have here a copy of your statements and the evidence given by Sergeant Austin of the British army. I will read it to you. Then I shall need witnesses to your signature."

"Let me see it," Devlin commanded and drew the typewritten sheets to him. Then, with what strength was left him, he tore the document across and across again.

Captain Sutton looked at him in amazement.

"What did you do that for?" he asked.

But Devlin paid no heed to him. He gazed into the face of Anthony Trent, the man he had hated.

"I made a mistake," said Devlin faintly. "This isn't the man."

And with this splendid and generous lie upon his lips he came to his life's end.

www.ingramcontent.com/pod-product-compliance
Lightning Source LLC
Chambersburg PA
CBHW031430250626
47155CB00004B/1690